MOVIN' ON UP

The Queen

ISBN-13: 978-1-7336442-3-5

For information regarding special ordering for bulk purchases, contact:
Queendom Dreams Publishing - www.queendomdreamspublishing.com

Queendom Dreams Publishing

ACKNOWLEDGEMENTS

As always, I give all honor and thanks unto Jehovah God. For without His grace, no talent that I have been blessed with would come to fruition. I thank Him for the past, present, and the blessings to come.

Thank you to all along my path who have supported me in this journey. Anyone that's anyone knows who they are and don't need acknowledgment in a book to know how priceless they are in my life because I continually let you know personally.

My readers and fans of The Queen, words will never express the level of gratitude I have for you. Without you, I am just another person writing books. Prayerfully, you will stick with me along my journey and inspire me to want to give you more.

The Queen

MOVIN' ON UP

The Queen

Queendom Dreams Publishing

www.QueendomDreamsPublishing.com

1

ow! That was amazing!"

Desiree Flowers forced a smile as she stood to her feet, fixing her breast back into her bra and buttoning up her top.

"What's more amazing is how you swallowed every drop with ease. That had to be the best blowjob I have ever had. I wish I could take you home and let you teach my wife a thing or two. Twenty-five years of marriage and three boob jobs, you'd think she'd learn something new by now."

"Well, Mr. Daniels, I'm glad I was able to do something nice for you for a change. You're a very generous boss, and I am so appreciative of your confidence in promoting me," she responded, sounding as professional as she would on any other day.

"I'll admit I've had my eye on you for quite some time. Honestly, it's hard not to look. You're very attractive and the outfits you wear are distracting to say the least."

Desiree frowned as she looked at Mr. Daniels smiling and taking inventory of her physical assets as he fixed his clothes. "Oh, I'm sorry. I didn't mean to wear distracting or inappropriate clothing to work. I only graduated from college a few months ago, and finances have been kind of tough for me. Especially while trying to raise a three-year-old. I hadn't had an opportunity to purchase business suits and stuff."

"Desiree . . . Desiree, it's okay." Mr. Daniels laughed. "Actually, now that you've been promoted from an admin assistant to an account rep, I'm pretty certain you'll find that you can close more accounts than some of the others. I think you'll do well and make both of us gobs of money in the process."

That made her smile brightly. Those were just the words she needed to hear. "I promise I won't let you down. And if there's anything else I can do for you, please don't hesitate to ask," she said with a hint of seduction.

He looked her body up and down. "Hmmm, I believe I most certainly will."

Desiree headed to the door. "Well, I'm about to head on out. Have a great weekend. I've already emailed you your calendar with your appointments for next week."

"Thank you. However, I do need for you to add one more appointment for next week, but you don't have to do it now. Do it when you get in on Monday."

"Oh, sure. What should I add?"

"I want to take you to lunch next week. Whenever I have a free time slot. I know you have to get your child in the evenings, so dinner is probably out of the question. We have to celebrate your new promotion."

Desiree was beaming. "Absolutely!"

"And, uh, Desiree, you can wear something kind of nice—no pants," he said uncomfortably.

She nodded once she figured out what he was implying. "I'll look in my closet for the perfect dress."

"Great! Great!" he said with a grand smile.

"Goodnight, Mr. Daniels."

"Goodnight, Desiree."

After Desiree stepped out of his office, she wanted to scream from the excitement of her new promotion that she earned after being on the job a mere six weeks. She grabbed her purse from her drawer and her coat and then headed for the elevators. She thought of heading to the ladies' room to fix her makeup and rinse her mouth, but she was too excited to get home. She decided she could do it when she got to her car, where she kept a small bottle of mouthwash.

While standing, waiting at the elevator, and fixing her coat on, she heard two of her coworkers approaching. They didn't make it a secret that they were talking about her.

"I'm pretty certain I read in our employee handbook that women weren't allowed to dress like hoes in here. We're supposed to dress professional," one woman said.

"I guess some people are professional strippers and don't know there's a difference between how you dress professional for the gentlemen's club, versus how you dress professional for corporate," the second woman said as if she were trying to sound empathetic.

"You're probably right. Then again, these kids nowadays don't have a clue. When my younger daughter went on her first job interview, she was about to wear some hoochie dress. I had to make her ass take that mess off and put on some real clothes. I guess if you don't have anyone to teach you any better, then you just go through life looking stupid."

Desiree wanted to turn around and curse them both out but decided to remain quiet as the elevator door opened. Instead of getting on the elevator with the two messy, middle-aged women, she detoured to the ladies' room after all to avoid them. The last thing she needed was to get into an unnecessary confrontation and end up losing her job. She figured she'd have the last laugh when they all would learn of her promotion during the Monday-morning team meeting.

2

Heyyy, Malcolm!"

"Hey, Sharquita!" Malcolm chuckled.

"Why you laughing?"

"I'm laughing because I know your ass got to be cold. You looking sexy as hell, but it's cold as shit out here."

Sharquita smiled. "You think I look sexy?"

"Hell yeah. If I didn't have my little man with me, I'd probably be trying to get up in that."

"Uhm! Well, what you doing later? You wanna come over my house?"

"Nah, you know I ain't going up in those projects. They be acting a fool. Besides, my girl will be home from work. I'll probably run by Smitty's Bar later on tonight. Maybe I'll see you there," he said, looking at Sharquita in a suggestive manner.

"Fuck that bitch! You need you a new girl. One that'll treat you right," Sharquita snapped. "She ain't got nothing going for her but that long, wavy hair."

Malcolm looked at Sharquita as if she was crazy. "Yo! What you talking about? My girl got it going on. She went to college, got a good job, and we got that nice crib."

"Oh. Well, I guess I won't be meeting you at Smitty's Bar then. Let your girl entertain you." Sharquita rolled her eyes and pretended to start walking away.

"Girl, stop being like that." Malcolm laughed as he playfully pulled her back. "You better be at that bar around eleven tonight. If I don't see you there, then don't be saying shit to me when you see me on the street."

His words pleased Sharquita, but she tried to play as if they didn't. "Uhm-hmm. If you say so. I bet that insecure bitch won't even let you out the door. I be seeing how she's always clinging all over you like somebody's trying to take you from her ass."

"She's cool. She don't be tripping. As long as I treat her well and make sure she's taken care of, she's good."

"See, that's what I'm talking about. If you and I got together, I'd make sure you were taken care of, and you wouldn't have to be worried about making sure I was taken care of."

"Hmm, I like that. Sexy, short, and sassy."

"Daddy, can we go? I'm cold," three-year-old, Tayshon asked, looking miserable as he always did when his father stopped to have conversations with different women.

"Okay, Little Man. We're going home to get you some dinner. Daddy's just trying to find a new babysitter for you—someone to come over and help Daddy out when I'm tired. 'Cause you know you be getting into shit."

Tayshon stomped his foot and pouted, while Sharquita came to life.

"You need me to come help you babysit some time? I can do that. I'd love to babysit. I can make sure Daddy is taken care of too."

"I'm counting on it." Malcolm gave a devious smile and then repeated, "I'm counting on it."

"Well, I'll see you later on tonight."

"Can't wait. I'm hard already, just thinking about that fat ass of yours."

"Boy, you so crazy." Sharquita giggled as she walked off.

Malcolm picked up his son to carry him.

"Little Man, one day I'm gonna teach you everything you need to know about the pimping game. And you got that good hair with them light eyes, so them hoes are really gonna be going stupid over you." Malcolm laughed.

"What's pimping?" Tayshon asked his father.

"That's when the hoes make sure the man is taken care of, and you don't have to want for nothing."

"What's hoes?"

Malcolm laughed before kissing his son. "You ask a lot of questions, but that's good. That's real good. You'll learn everything in time. Your big brother used to ask a lot of questions too. Malcolm Junior's mom didn't like me trying to teach him, so now she got him over there acting like a damn sissy. A fuckin' nerd."

"Daddy, don't say that word." Tayshon put his hand over Malcolm's mouth.

"I'm sorry, Little Man. I forgot. You want some Mickey D's?"

"Yeah!"

"Cool. We'll go in there and see what them bitches will give you for free. They be loving when you come up in there, so be nice to them and you can get anything you want."

"Okay," Tayshon innocently replied as they walked on.

3

Malcolm! Malcolm!" Desiree yelled as she came in the house.

"What the hell? What's going on?" he asked, frantically running from the kitchen toward her.

"I got a promotion. My boss just told me I've been promoted to account rep."

"Yo! Damn! That's great! I told you! I told you to stick with the plan, and you'll be moving up that ladder so fast, it'll make all them bitches' heads spin. Didn't I tell you?"

"Yes. Yes, you did," she said hugging him.

Malcolm wrapped his arms around her waist and took her in for a deep kiss.

"You was trying to wear all them stupid, grandma-looking suits. I told you that wouldn't get you noticed. Bet you glad I picked out those outfits for you, aren't you?"

Desiree pulled away and looked down as if feeling defeated.

"What's wrong?" he asked, pulling her arm to keep her from walking away from him.

Her eyes had filled with tears. "You have no idea how mean those bitches at my job are. They say all kind of cruel shit to me."

"Curse them bitches out!"

"I can't. I might lose my job."

"Well, then you better step your game up with your boss and get them bitches fired. I bet if you let that motherfucker suck on a tittie or feel on some pussy, he'll do whatever you say. And if you tell him them bitches are giving you a hard way to go, they'll be out the door. I bet they're ugly, aren't they?"

Desiree rolled her eyes in disgust. "Yeah, and old. One of them is fat and has hairs growing all over her face."

Malcolm cracked up laughing. "That's why they hating on my baby."

She laughed. "Yep!" Her expression turned serious. "Guess what?"

"What?"

"He asked to take me to lunch next week to celebrate my new promotion."

"And you better wear something sexy," he instructed.

She just smiled, afraid to tell Malcolm what she'd already done to show her appreciation.

"You listen to what I tell you, and you'll be the boss to all them hatin'-ass bitches by the time you hit your twenty-third birthday, six months from now."

"I'll be twenty-three in two months, not six months." She playfully pouted. "You can't even remember your own fiancée's birthday. That's a damn shame."

"Four baby-mommas. You know I be getting y'all confused."

"I'm not your baby-momma. I'm your fiancée. Big difference."

"You my son's mother, so that makes you a baby-momma too."

Sadness overcame Desiree's face. She couldn't mask her hurt. She'd been his fiancée since she was pregnant with Tayshon and was no closer to setting a wedding date. Even worse, she had yet to receive a ring, as his second child's mother received. As such, Malcolm would always say that a ring means nothing, and the fact that he's not with his second child's mother should be proof.

Desiree often wondered if she should even consider marrying and planning a future with Malcolm. Since she'd known him, he had yet to get a real job. He would often have sex with his other children's mothers to get them to back off of their child support cases. He was almost forty and still hung in the bars more than a twenty-one-year-old. Worst of all, he separated her from her family.

She hadn't seen her own mother and father since her son was born, when they questioned Malcolm about how he would provide while Desiree continued to pursue her marketing degree. Malcolm would challenge the validity of her love for him if she chose to have a relationship with anyone who didn't want to see them happy together. He would say that he and little Tayshon were all the family that she needed. She also decided she didn't want either of her two sisters around her man, because she was convinced that Malcolm would try to get with them if they hung around. He'd often make lewd comments in regards to them.

After dinner while relaxing on the sofa, Desiree said, "My boss said I could make a lot of money in this new position, and I was thinking maybe we could find a nicer home in a nicer neighborhood."

"What's wrong with this home? This place is nice. We got two bedrooms, with two and a half bathrooms. How much more space do we need?" Malcolm asked.

"We live a block away from the projects. We might as well live *in* the projects. I hate going to the stores around here. I don't want to stay out here with all these ghetto bitches. Then I'm always stressed every time you go out that something might happen to you. There's a lot of gangs around."

"I don't know about all that. You're starting to sound all uppity and you haven't even started the new position yet."

"I'm not trying to be uppity. I'm just tired of all these girls disrespecting me because they want you. Then they are always asking if my hair is real or a weave like theirs."

"Let them hoes know you're half Puerto Rican."

"Why? I shouldn't have to tell them anything. I just want to move from around here."

"I don't know. I'll have to think about it."

Desiree wanted to argue the point, but she decided not to. It was getting close to the time when Malcolm would hit the streets, and she hated when he was gone until the following afternoon or night to teach her a lesson for saying stupid stuff to him. Instead, she smiled and said, "Thank you, baby."

That made him smile.

"Go get Little Man to sleep so I can take you in the room to celebrate your promotion. We're gonna be celebrating all night tonight."

She smiled, but she wanted to laugh. Malcolm didn't have an "all night" clue. With oral sex included, he wouldn't last longer than twenty minutes.

4

The banging on the door was startling to Desiree. Whoever it was, they were both pounding on the door and ringing the doorbell. Although no more was said on the subject of moving, she couldn't wait to get paid more and move from the neighborhood.

Malcolm got up at the crack of dawn to run out to find Desiree some new outfits for work. He took joy in picking out her clothes, and he felt he knew best about what appealed to men. Desiree learned to stop fighting with him on the matter, because he would often remind her of the many times he helped her get through college and how she would have never graduated had it not been for him. That was partially true. Desiree had missed so many days from some of her classes that she was sure to fail. She'd be so stressed out, stressing him out, and causing strife in their home life. She remembered as if it were yesterday how her man—her fiancé—told her to seduce her professors to get a better grade so she could graduate and get a good job. He told her to do whatever it took. Anything. When it worked that first time, she learned there was no end to the boundaries of his suggestions. The most hurtful part was how he treated one of his own daughters, who was only four years younger than Desiree. He'd have a fit if she dared to wear anything revealing. His daughter was so perfect in his eyes that he refused to believe she was sexually active.

Altogether, Malcolm had seven children by four different women, with the first five being born interchangeably between the first two mothers. Through all that, he had pretty much avoided paying child support for any child. Although he refused to get an on-the-books job to avoid child support, he mysteriously kept a steady flow of income. Desiree made the mistake of questioning how he gets his money, and that caused him to become physical with her. She never questioned him again. Since Tayshon was born, Malcolm was always there to care for the child while Desiree continued with her education and worked a part-time job babysitting Malcolm's daughter from his third baby-momma. Once upon a time, Desiree had a good relationship with the woman. The woman was happy and supportive that Desiree was focused on getting a college degree and had big plans for her future. That was until she became pregnant with Malcolm's child in the woman's home.

When the woman put Malcolm out of her home and he went to get his own place, he was all too happy to bring the youthful Desiree to come live with him, taking her away from her sister's home. He used a ring-less proposal to convince her to move with him. And from there, no one could tell Desiree anything.

Desiree loved watching Malcolm interact with their son, and despite knowing how Malcolm made sure that little Tayshon was always stylishly dressed in the best. Malcolm took care of them the entire time Desiree worked her way through college, and he let her keep her income from her part-time job as her pocket-change. So, when she finished school and got a real job, she had no problems turning over her paycheck to him to manage the household.

The advertising company where she currently worked happened to be her third job in the six months since she'd graduated. Her first job let her go because of her inappropriate attire in the workplace. Malcolm chalked that up to her having too many women bosses who were all hating on her.

Malcolm wanted her to find a company with a male boss. She found a small advertising company, with a male boss who was very appreciative of Desiree's attire. He appreciated it so much he blackmailed her for sex in order to keep her job. When she gave him what he wanted, he still terminated her, saying her work was not up to the company's standards. That sent Malcolm over the edge—not the sex part, but the fact that the man dismissed Desiree *after* she gave him what he wanted. Shortly thereafter, the man was severely brutalized, and had yet to make a full recovery. Unfortunately for him, no one was ever caught. Without discussion, Desiree knew Malcolm had something to do with the vicious beating of the man, which also caused his small company to have to shut its doors due to his inability to work.

With this new company, Desiree decided to be a bit more cautious. She decided to be a bit more subtle in her seduction. She knew that getting her foot in the door as an administrative assistant would eventually open up bigger doors for her. At least, that's what Malcolm told her. Her boss, Mr. Daniels, had slipped up and told her that she was a very sexy woman on more than one occasion. He was the senior vice president of marketing and knew he had a lot to lose with his comments. When she found out that he went to bat for her with the other executives to get her promotion approved, she felt he deserved to be rewarded for his dedication to her. Thus, the blowjob. She didn't want Malcolm to know about the blowjob, because although he seemed to encourage her to do whatever it took, he always emotionally and sexually distanced himself from her when he knew she did. And if he knew, he most certainly wouldn't have provided her with such a romantic Friday night to celebrate. He would have been in the streets as every other Friday night, and she wouldn't be having the relaxing Saturday morning that she was having, since he took their son out with him.

Desiree threw on some sweat pants and a t-shirt to go answer the door. She often feared that the police would one day come searching for Malcolm. Though she had no idea how he earned his income, she knew it had to be something illegal. The last thing she was going to do was go to the door half dressed, not knowing if that would be the day.

"Sharquita!" Desiree said when opening the door.

"Hey girl! What you doing? You still in the bed? I ain't see your man's car outside," she said extra friendly, letting herself in.

"I was trying to relax a bit. Malcolm took Tay with him to the mall. He loves to shop," Desiree answered. "You eat yet? I'm about to fix me some breakfast," she said, heading to the kitchen with Sharquita on her heels.

"Girl, you ain't had breakfast yet? How you let your man leave out without breakfast? You better take care of that man."

"Honey, I ain't worried about my man going anywhere. Especially not after last night." Desiree closed her eyes with a warm smile as she reminisced.

"Damn, girl! It was that good?"

"It was that good!"

"I thought he be down at the bar or club on the weekends. How you get your man to stay at home on a Friday night?"

"My man knows there's nothing but junk in the streets—a bunch of thirsty hoes trying to replace me." Desiree laughed.

Sharquita gave a fake smile. "I'm sure."

"So, what brings you by so early in the morning, dressed like you're about to go to the club? Bitch, I know your coochie is cold out there. It's like thirty degrees today, and they're calling for snow tonight."

"I been out all night, and you know I can't go home. My momma will kick my ass. I figured I'd tell her I stayed over here with you and little Tay."

"She's not going to know once she sees that little dress you have on? Didn't she see you leave last night?"

"Hell no. I didn't leave until after she went to work. I meant to beat her home this morning, but since she's doing a double and going in at three today, I'll just hang out here until she's gone."

"Shar, you are not even eighteen yet. Where do you be hanging out at all night? You're not even old enough to get in a club."

"Girl, please! You think them horny-ass bouncers be checking my ID after getting a look at this body? Hell no! Besides, I stole my older sister's ID about a year ago, so I have my back-up plan." Sharquita laughed. "Not only that, who said I was hanging in the club last night?"

Desiree stopped rustling through the pots and pans long enough to ask, "You met another dude and gave it up to him, right? Don't you feel you're worth more than a drink?"

"Dude took me out to eat, and then we went to a hotel. A nice one. He's part of J-Tron's crew."

"J-Tron, the rapper?"

"Yeah, girl." Sharquita giggled. "So next time J-Tron performs in town, you know we're in there. We can get backstage passes and all."

"I don't wanna go see no damn J-Tron. He's whack as hell. Half the shit he's saying, I don't even understand. Not only that, I'm sure them dudes be going through a different bitch every night, and your boy probably won't even remember you by then."

Sharquita rolled her eyes. "Whatever! I'm sure he'll never forget what I put on him last night. Or should I say this morning?"

Desiree laughed. "Girl, you're a mess. You should only be worrying about getting your education right now."

"You had a baby when you were my age, and you turned out all right, so why can't I have me a little fun too?"

"First of all, I was almost 19 when I had my son. I was in college and had already graduated from high school when I was your age. And I wasn't giving it up to a bunch of guys. Malcolm was my second boyfriend. My parents weren't having that shit, and I didn't get to be out in the clubs and stuff until I turned twenty-one."

"You always be acting like you so much better than everybody."

"I don't think I'm better than anybody. All I'm trying to do is help you. I want to see you do well. You're a smart young lady when you put your mind to stuff. Didn't you say you wanted to open up an organization for victims of sexual abuse one day? You'll need to get you a degree to help people."

"I changed my mind about that. Them girls will eventually be okay. Hell, I turned out just fine, and I had all kinds of dicks up in me before I even turned twelve. Bitches need to just get over it."

"Get over it?" Desiree was shocked by Sharquita's senseless words. "I can't believe you would say something like that. And I don't believe you are over it yet. You can say you are all day long, but there are old women who still suffer from abuse they suffered as little girls."

Sharquita tried to hide her hurt as she got up from the table and turned to walk away from Desiree's intense stare. "Well, I ain't Jesus, and I can't save the world. That ain't my responsibility. My mother is a CNA and comes home all stressed out all the time, carrying everyone else's burdens. I don't want to do that to my life. I'm just gonna find me a good job and make a lot of money just for me and my man. I ain't gonna be worried with everyone."

Realizing she was making Sharquita uncomfortable, Desiree went back to preparing her breakfast instead of staring.

"So, what kind of good job will you get without a degree?"

"I was talking to J-Tron's boy last night, and he told me, with an ass like this, I could be in all kinds of videos and making lots of coins."

Desiree turned to see Sharquita back in a happy place, patting her own behind. "You're planning on being a video ho? That's your career choice now? Did the guy say they were going to give you a job?"

"For your information, he told me if I was willing to fly out to Cali, I could be in their next video," Sharquita snapped, rolling her eyes at Desiree.

"And he gave you a plane ticket?"

"Why would he give me a plane ticket? It's not like I can go. My momma ain't going for that. Soon, I'll be eighteen and she can't say anything anymore. I mean, she really don't have room to say shit now, since it was all of her different men fucking me. Don't act all concerned now."

Desiree was frustrated with Sharquita. Talking to her seemed to be worse than trying to talk to her three-year-old. She turned away from Sharquita to keep her from seeing her roll her eyes at the foolishness, then turned back to say, "She's still the one taking care of you."

"My mom don't do shit for me. Yes, I live in her house, but dudes be buying me stuff, not my mother. My mom spends all her money getting her hair and nails done. She's always shopping for herself. I do more for my little sister than she does."

"How old is she now? I haven't seen her in a minute."

"She's fifteen. She's talking about being a doctor or nurse. She gets good grades in school."

"That is wonderful." Desiree placed a plate of eggs, bacon, and potatoes on the table for Sharquita. "Here, eat this, and go get you some rest before you head home. You can rest on the futon in Tay's room. If you weren't so short, I could let you have a pair of my sweats."

"I'll be good in this. I just need a cover. I get cold when I sleep."

"There should be one on the shelf in the closet. I'm going to eat up in my room. I'm still exhausted, and I need to get my rest before Malcolm gets home."

"What time is he coming back?" Sharquita realized she might have sounded a bit desperate, so she added, "I need to know how long I have to get some good sleep. It'll be my luck that little Tay will come busting in his room as soon as I doze off." She laughed to be convincing.

Desiree laughed also, putting Sharquita at ease. "Yeah, that's what I'm afraid of also. The weather is calling for snow, so I doubt they'll be out too long, but with Malcolm, you just never know." She carried her plate out the kitchen and up the stairs as she yelled out, "See you when I wake up."

Sharquita was still fuming over being stood up by Malcolm the night before, and she couldn't wait for Desiree to let him know that another man got what he could have had. She'd had a crush on Malcolm since she was fifteen, and Malcolm would always call her a kid. Only recently did he seem to take notice of her womanly body and act as if he would be interested in being with her. She knew that Desiree would be crushed once she found out, but the truth was, she didn't like Desiree—never had. Sharquita had only befriended Desiree and her son to get closer to her intended target: Malcolm.

She trashed the plate of food Desiree had cooked for her. She didn't want anything from Desiree but her man. She wanted him so much, she decided to take off the thong she was wearing and put into her purse. She would make sure Malcolm got to see what he was missing out on when he arrived home.

However, when she awoke from her deep sleep, she realized it was dark outside. She hadn't heard anyone, but she smelled fish being fried. She got up to see where everyone was at. She wondered if Malcolm had already come in and seen her goodies but left the room. That thought depressed her.

"Girl, that dude must have really put it on you last night. You were out. I could hear you snoring all the way from down the hall. Malcolm was cracking up."

"Huh?" was all Sharquita could say. She was totally pissed about missing Malcolm, who was now nowhere to be found.

"Malcolm was about to go in there to pack a bag to take Tayshon to his daughter's mother's house to spend the night. He heard you snoring and asked if a bear was in the room sleeping. I told him you were in there, so he didn't want to bother you. He just found another bag."

Sharquita was having a difficult time masking her anger. She was furious that Desiree intercepted Malcolm's opportunity to see what he'd been missing.

"Damn! You look like you're about to kick my ass. I didn't mean to laugh at your snoring. That's not right. I'm sorry. If you heard Malcolm cracking jokes, you'd understand. I'm sorry for both of us laughing," Desiree said with outreached arms.

Sharquita waved her hand, dismissing Desiree's attempt to hug. "Y'all can kiss my ass. I'm going home. It looks like the flurries already started."

"It has, and the temp is now down to 26 degrees. Your ass is really going to be cold walking home. Maybe I should have woken you up and let Malcolm drop you off. But then again, you said you had to wait till your mother was gone, so she didn't see your half naked ass in that little dress."

"Your dresses be smaller than mine. What you talking about?"

"I'm an adult. Big difference."

"Barely."

"Okay, whatever. I'm not going to get into it with you. You want a plate of food to take for you and your sister? I fried some fish, plantains, and made some rice and beans. Gotta stay true to my Puerto Rican heritage."

"How are you Puerto Rican and just as black as I am?"

"Uhm, because my mother is Puerto Rican and my father is a black Puerto Rican. His complexion is very dark, but he's from Puerto Rico just like my mother."

"Yeah, okay. Everybody's always trying to be everything but black. Your ass is black just like I am."

Desiree felt herself getting annoyed by the immature girl's comments about her heritage. "Alrighty now, I guess that's your cue to hobo your way on home now. Now you want to disrespect me, in my home, no less? I'm not having that. Bye bye."

"Fine! I'm out. Thanks for letting me crash."

"Sure thing," Desiree said before slamming the door once Sharquita was out of it.

That exchange aggravated Sharquita even more, making her more determined to find a way to take Malcolm from Desiree.

Desiree was already on edge, assuming that Malcolm was going to go have sex with his daughter's mother, Tia. Although Tia despised Desiree for her betrayal, she seemed to love little Tayshon, and he was fond of her too. She often volunteered to keep Tayshon on the weekends. She was so pleasant, it pained Desiree that she'd betrayed her the way she had. She too was successful in her career, and Desiree often wondered if the woman had paid the same dues to get ahead. Despite having a successful career, a huge home, and being attractive, Tia hadn't had a man in her life since Malcolm. It made Desiree wonder if Malcolm was still the man in her life. Supposedly, the woman didn't want a bunch of men around her seven-year-old daughter, which made sense to Desiree.

5

Oh great, Desiree, you're here. I didn't think you'd make it in with the snow. We got hit pretty hard for the past two days. They still haven't cleaned up the streets in most areas," Mr. Daniels said when he arrived to see Desiree at her desk, pecking on the keys of her computer.

She stood and greeted him with a huge smile. "I am so happy that I would have plowed the roads myself to make it here this morning."

"And that's just the type of people we need on our team. Most make excuses. Some of the account reps have already begun emailing me with their excuses of why they can't go meet with some of their clients. That's money going out the window. I can see now, that when you start your new position next week, you will kick down doors to get your accounts."

"I most certainly will. But we do have one small problem. The temp that was supposed to start today said she won't be able to make it in because of the snow. I was hoping to have her trained before I abandon you next week."

"I'm sure everything will work out perfectly fine," Mr. Daniels said, going into his office with Desiree following behind him. "Did you get me an updated calendar for this week?"

"Yes, I was actually just sending it to your email, and I also placed a printed copy on your desk." Desiree handed him the tall Starbucks cup and said, "And here's your latte, just how you like it."

"Wow! You made it to Starbucks before coming in?"

She shrugged. "Absolutely! They were open, so I stopped in."

"Damn, I'm going to miss you when you're gone. If I wasn't so certain of all the money you'll make for the company, I'd keep you in your position with a raise."

Desiree smiled. "Thank you, sir. That means a lot coming from you."

Mr. Daniels then decided to whisper, just in case the walls had ears, "Oh, and I could not get you out of my mind all weekend. You deserve a raise for that alone. And by the way, you look as gorgeous as ever. Did you come in like that?"

"Thank you. No, I actually changed when I got here. I wore jeans, a heavy sweater, and snow boots in."

"Well, I definitely prefer this look. Much more appealing."

"Thanks again. I better let you get settled in. You have a conference call with California in about an hour. If you need anything, I'll be at my desk."

"Great! Thanks."

Mr. Daniels watched intensely as Desiree headed toward the door, where the pen he intentionally dropped laid in wait for her to bend over to pick up. Watching her bend over in her short skirts and dresses were more jolting than his latte. It was as exciting as going to a gentlemen's club and watching the dancers bend over. He often had thoughts of bending her over and pushing his cock up inside of her, but he thought there was no chance of ever coming close. However, after the sensational blowjob, he knew he was closer than he could have ever imagined, especially when he had once been accused of on-the-job sexual harassment several years prior. Without fail, Desiree dropped to the ground, swooped up the pen and then brought her ass upwards before raising the rest of her body, conjuring up an instant hard-on for Mr. Daniels. She turned to bring him his pen.

"I have to admit—I couldn't before the other day—but I love when you do that. It is so sexy, and it really turns me on."

Desiree smiled, walked back toward the door, and bent her hips to touch her toes without bending her knees. She arose slowly, looked back at Mr. Daniels, and then silently walked out of his office and back to her desk.

Although many people had called out that day due to the weather, as suspected, there were several unhappy people when Mr. Daniels announced Desiree's promotion. Some blatantly challenged him, asking if she got the promotion because of her skimpy outfits. The accusation angered him. He let them know that Desiree possessed a degree in marketing, and she had come to the company with the intent of becoming an account representative.

Some people seemed surprised by the revelation and were satisfied with that. Still, some were not so convinced. One of the persistent women asked if the rest of the company were able to violate the dress policy, as written in the employee handbook. Mr. Daniels shut the comment down by informing the woman that their big boss, Ted Dinkins, had no problems with Desiree's attire. Mr. Daniels told the woman she should concern herself with her own poor job performance instead of worrying about Desiree's fashion choices.

Desiree was extremely impressed by Mr. Daniels's support for her. Although she scheduled their luncheon for that coming Friday, she figured she'd have to find another way to let him know how much she appreciated him. Later that afternoon, she took her phone with her into the bathroom, lifted a foot on the toilet, and recorded a video of her lady parts, occasionally using her fingers to massage. She then sent the recording to Mr. Daniels as she walked back to her desk. When she got back to her desk, she could hear him yelling on an aggravating call. She was hoping it wasn't her video that caused him to become so irate. But in the midst of his yelling, she received a text back from him, saying:

OMG!!! Friday is too far away for me. Now, I can't wait that long. Thank you for helping to brighten up my gloomy day.

That made her feel better. She smiled endlessly—that is, until one of the marketing directors summoned her to his office.

"Good afternoon, Miss Flowers. Thanks for coming to see me. I don't think we've been formerly introduced."

Desiree apprehensively shook her head and took the seat his hand gesture was offering. "I've seen you around, but that's it."

He smiled. "You look nervous. Don't be. I've heard great things about you. I'm Alex Krammer. I'll be your new boss, and you and I will be working together a lot when you start your new position next week. I wanted to meet with you and maybe get a better feel of how you can best be utilized. I understand you have a young son, but does that mean you will not be open to travel? Some of our clients are on the other side of the country, and you'll be expected to go wherever they are, go to ball games, skiing, dinners—whatever—to keep the clients happy. And a happy client means a happy paycheck, which I'm sure will help create a nice college fund for your son. Wouldn't you agree?"

"Absolutely!" Desiree smiled, but inside, she was nervous about how Malcolm would feel about the news of her traveling all over to please her clients. "I'm definitely looking forward to learning all that I can and being a team player."

Alex slammed his fist on his desk in excitement. "That's what I like to hear. That's just what we need: a team player. So many times, people get into these positions and think this is all about a competition and don't concern themselves with the team. They fail to see that when one of us wins, we all win."

"I agree. I know I am young, but I come with a wealth of fresh ideas, and I also come willing to learn all that I can. I think this is a wonderful opportunity to be able to work in the field of my degree."

Alex smiled, his eyes focused on her full, perky breasts while she spoke. "Well, if you're willing to learn, I'm willing to teach you. If you don't mind my asking, how young are you? I think I saw you already graduated from college with an MBA and a very impressive GPA at that."

"I'm twenty-two. I was very focused on succeeding. I had a son, and all I could think about was providing him with the best life possible. He was my motivation."

"I'm impressed, and that's not easy to do. I don't know if Mr. Daniels made you aware, but there'll be times when you'll have to work late when we are strategizing on dealing with our clients and their over inflated egos."

"That'll be fine. I pretty much assumed that going into this career. No pain, no gain."

"Yes! I like that. I also like that you are comfortable with yourself. I've heard that there are some in this office who might be giving you a hard time because of your attire. Just know, we will not tolerate bullying or employees making others feel uncomfortable, especially when the bullies are non-essential employees who can easily be replaced."

Those words made Desiree want to jump up and down and scream, "Hallelujah." However, she contained her excitement as he continued.

"I'd just like you to know that I have absolutely no problem with your attire, but it was brought to our attention that you may be having financial difficulty trying to purchase business suits."

Desiree was stunned and embarrassed.

"Don't feel bad, but I spoke with Ted Dinkins, the owner, and he authorized me to provide you with the normal $5,000 signing bonus that we offer most of our newly hired account reps."

Desiree's hand flung over her opened mouth to keep from screaming out loud.

"I think that will help you to get a couple of business suits, because there will be times when you'll absolutely need it. I hate to put it like this, but there will be times when you will encounter some women who are not attractive or are insecure with themselves, and they will try to penalize you in some way, causing you to lose accounts. We wouldn't want that to happen. But just know, that will be a rare occasion, and most times, how you are dressed now will be perfectly fine."

"Oh my goodness! Thank you so much, Mr. Krammer."

"Alex. Please call me Alex. Mr. Krammer makes me feel so old."

"Thank you, Alex."

"Thank you, Desiree, for joining our winning team. We're looking forward to you earning six and seven figures with us."

"Six and seven figures?"

"Absolutely! Some of our star players earn seven figures. That's why a lot of them don't want to leave their position to take management roles. In a management role, such as mine, you only get a salary and a bonus based on your team's overall performance. Definitely no seven figures. Just about everyone else earns six figures. I can tell you now, if you're not a six-figure performer, Ted won't be keeping you around. I wouldn't want to keep you around, because that ultimately impacts my quarterly bonus, so we expect strong performance from all of our players."

"I can definitely appreciate that, and I promise, I won't let you, Mr. Daniels, or Mr. Dinkins down. Thank you all for believing in me and taking a chance on me."

"A master's degree at the age of twenty-two, with a child, demonstrates that you have a 'kick doors down' personality, and don't let a 'no' stop you from excelling. I know you will do well."

"Thank you so much. Thank you. And it was great getting to meet you."

While his eyes left her eyes to survey her bosom, he said, "Likewise, and I look forward to getting to know you better and seeing you in action."

In Desiree's mind, she wondered if he was speaking of the job or sexually, but at that point, she couldn't care less.

"I sent a memo to HR to process your bonus. It should be included with your pay this Friday. But in the meantime, I guess I better let you get on out of here before the roads ice up again, and you'll have a rough time getting home. You'll be reporting to me next Monday morning. Mr. Daniels will still be your boss, but instead of reporting directly to him, you'll be reporting to me, since he's also my boss."

Desiree smiled as she stood to leave. "Thank you again."

Alex bit down on his finger as he watched Desiree walk out of his office. He was definitely looking forward to spending more time with her.

When Desiree returned to her desk, she saw Mr. Daniels in his coat, ready to leave.

"Oh, I'm sorry I wasn't here. Mr. Krammer called me to his office. He said he's going to be my new boss."

"I'll still be your boss, but I'm his boss as well. The chain of command will be a little different, but if you ever need to come to me directly about anything, feel free to do so."

Desiree smiled. She was feeling special. "Thank you. I see you're about to leave."

"Yeah, I wanted to get on the road before it gets too bad. I couldn't leave without personally thanking you for making my day brighter."

"I'm glad I could help. You've done so much for me. If there's anything else I can do, just let me know."

Mr. Daniels got serious and then closed his office door. "Desiree, I promise you I have never done anything inappropriate with any employee. I've been accused of *saying* inappropriate things before, but that was someone who took a comment out of context. I'll admit I find you very attractive. I'll even admit that half those pens you keep picking up, I dropped on purpose, just to see you bend over. I don't want you to feel like you have to do anything you're not comfortable doing, but I'd really like to see more of you if that's possible. I don't know if our age difference makes you uncomfortable. As you know, I have a wife of twenty-five years. I was hoping during our lunch, that maybe we could explore further possibilities, but when I received your video today, I know I have to have you. I want to be with you. I want to see your entire naked body, and I was hoping that maybe tonight you'd send me a picture to help me have sweet dreams. But if I'm asking too much, please don't feel obligated. It won't affect your promotion. After all, you've already done more than I expected."

Desiree turned to leave, but then looked back at Mr. Daniels and said, "I better hurry up and shut my computer down and head home. I have a nice bubble bath to fix and plenty of pictures to take."

A huge grin grew on Mr. Daniels's face. "Good night, Desiree."

She opened the door and went back to her desk, and Mr. Daniels headed out to leave.

Desiree found herself smiling the entire hectic ride home. She thought that perhaps she was developing feelings for Mr. Daniels. If Malcolm ever found that out, he'd hit the roof. Desiree was allowed plenty of latitude to get things done to benefit them, but getting feelings involved was a major no-no.

Also, for the entire time that Desire had been on her job, she had been afraid to let Malcolm know that Mr. Daniels was an attractive, fifty-four-year-old, African-American man. Somehow, Malcolm was more at ease having knowledge that his fiancée was intimately involved with white men. The one African-American professor she slept with to get a better grade caused Malcolm the most grief and caused their relationship the most tension. He accused her for the longest of enjoying being with the professor, and as a result, he punished her for weeks by letting her know when he was going out to have sex with other women.

That was such an emotionally torturous time in her life that she felt the need to hide Mr. Daniels's ethnicity from Malcolm. Malcolm trained Desiree to always say that she was a single mother raising her son alone and that she had no contact with the child's father, nor did she have any boyfriends or date because of her son, and she'd been sure to stick to the script.

6

You need to get your ass up and go. My girl is on the way home, and she won't be finding you here," Malcolm said to one of his side women, Asia.

"That's fine. You fucked me so good, my legs feel like rubber." She laughed. "You always fuck me good."

"That's what you pay me to do, right?"

"Yeah, but I don't understand—why can't I get to have you for a night?"

"Aren't you married? What you want, for me to come crawl up in the bed with that lame-ass husband of yours to fuck you?" Malcolm laughed.

"He drives trucks across the country. You know how much I hate being alone, especially when I know he's out there fucking a bunch of hookers at those truck stops? I get lonely. I'd rather have you at night than him. He's good for nothing."

"Why'd you marry him?"

"Stupidity," she answered as she took her time getting dressed. "He told me he was going to start a trucking business and buy a fleet of trucks and hire a bunch of drivers. I was attracted to him wanting to be a business owner like myself. Instead, his sad ass ended up just being a truck driver, and he doesn't even have a staff. I keep asking why he won't hire a staff, but he claims they'll be more of a liability than an asset. I think his ass just got used to having different pussy in every state. You can't tell me he doesn't have a bunch of bitches everywhere he goes. So, if he wanna fuck other people, then so can I. I just wish the man I'm paying to fuck could at least get a hotel with me for a night and fuck me all night."

"We'll see, but don't hold your breath. My girl be keeping close tabs on me." Malcolm quickly used a wet washcloth to wipe himself down and then threw his clothes back on before changing the bed linens. In all that time, Asia still wasn't fully dressed to leave. "Asia, stop fucking around! Hurry up and get out of here! She already texted me saying she left work early."

"Fine! I'm going." She smirked as she rolled her eyes. "Can't blame a girl for trying."

When Asia got downstairs to the door, she turned back to Malcolm and said, "Well, can I at least get a kiss goodbye?"

He looked back to see if his son was looking and quickly pecked Asia on the lips.

"Damn, I was hoping to get some tongue at least."

"Yo, fuck that! My son is sitting right there watching TV. Don't try to disrespect my son like that. Otherwise I'll cut your silly ass off."

"Fine! I'm sorry. I'll call you tomorrow and see if you thought about my proposal."

As Asia was stepping out of the house, Sharquita was approaching.

"Damn, man! You couldn't call me? You stand me up and then I don't see you for days," she yelled out as she looked Asia up and down.

Asia turned back and yelled to Malcolm, "Oh, now you're doing little girls? Isn't that jail bait? Statutory rape?"

"Bitch, you better get the fuck up out of my business. Who the fuck are you, and what are you doing at my friend's house? For your information, his woman is my best friend," Sharquita lied.

"Yeah, I bet," Asia said as she was getting into her car. "I bet his woman need to check the bitches she calls her best friends."

Sharquita was about to turn to charge after the woman, who was about to pull off. Malcolm ran out to get Sharquita, making her day as he grabbed her from behind and pressed up against her backside—as she longed for. She was even more thrilled to look down and see his hand cupping one of her breasts.

"Girl, you better chill with that silly shit. Go home. What you doing here?"

"What happened to you Friday? I was at Smitty's Bar waiting for you, out in the cold. They wouldn't even let me come in because they said I was too young and they'd lose their license. I waited over an hour for you. And then you don't even have the decency to call me and say anything."

"I decided to stay in with my girl and chill. But since you're supposed to be friends, I'm sure you already knew that. And why you trying to be hanging around my girl and you can't stand her? Stay the fuck away from Desiree. You all up in my house sleeping and shit, then talking about how you hate her."

"I only came to see you. Then you came in and dipped right back out the door trying to avoid me."

"Trying to avoid you? Wrong! But I do know this much: my girl is on her way home, and you better get ghost before she gets here."

"Or what? What you gonna do?"

Malcolm walked back inside of his home and closed the door. Sharquita started banging on the door, demanding that he open it. As she stood banging, Desiree pulled up.

"Girl, why you banging on my door like you don't have any sense?"

"I was trying to get Malcolm to let me in. I lost my earring, and think it's in Tayshon's room," Sharquita quickly lied.

Desiree wasn't quite buying the line but allowed her into the house. "Go look in the room and see if your earring is in there, and then you're gonna have to go. I need to talk to my fiancé."

"Fiancé? You don't even have a ring."

That angered Malcolm as he was coming down the steps. "Bitch, get the fuck out of here disrespecting my woman. You damn right she's my fiancée. She don't need no fucking ring. She knows her status. She's where everyone else want to be—with me!"

Sharquita brushed past Malcolm, quickly running up the stairs to pretend to look for the invisible earring, and came right back down.

"You find it?" Desiree asked.

"No. I don't know where it is."

"That bitch ain't lose shit. She just wanted to come in here and see what we're doing. Nosy ass," Malcolm yelled before laughing.

Desiree also laughed, as Sharquita left out feeling angered and played by Malcolm. She was even angrier that Desiree was laughing with Malcolm.

Once alone, Desiree was excited to tell her man about her bonus check and how she met her new boss and he couldn't keep his eyes off her breasts while he spoke to her. Then she nervously told him about her being required to travel for her job but added the part about earning six and seven figures and being able to provide their son with everything, and even private schools.

Malcolm took a deep sigh. "Yo, I ain't all that happy about my lady being gone days at a time, but I guess I have to get on board. This is what we've been working toward. It's all about you moving on up. Hell, maybe now we can get that deluxe apartment in the sky," he laughed, emulating the theme song from *The Jeffersons*.

"So, you're okay with us moving out of here and finding a nicer neighborhood?"

"Well, I don't know now. I mean, if you're gonna be gone, I need to be close to where I know people. What if I have things to do and need someone to keep Little Man? You know we can't count on BM-3," he said, referring to baby-momma number-three, as he called her. "That bitch be acting funny. Then if we move to the white neighborhoods, they'll be all up in our business, worrying about our comings and goings and how much traffic comes in or out."

Desiree was disappointed, and Malcolm could tell.

"I'll tell you what, you stick with this job for at least six months, and if we see things are going well, then we will go find a new home. You can't be just starting out and then banking on that. You remember what happened with the first two jobs."

Desiree went to hug Malcolm. "Thank you, baby. You're right. You're always right. I just get so frustrated with the people around here sometimes. I feel like I don't even have any friends."

"You ain't gonna have any friends while you're trying to get yours. Even if you moved to one of them uppity neighborhoods, you really think those people are going to be your friend, or are they just wanting to be all up in your business, just like they do here in the hood? Look at all those reality shows. Those uppity bitches be backstabbing each other, gossiping, and always trying to tear the other one down."

"That is so true. That's why I love you so much. You are the smartest man I know."

"And as long as you be good to me, there will be no end to how far we will get, together. Don't you forget that."

Desiree smiled but wondered what exactly he meant by being good to him, when it was him encouraging her to sleep her way to the top. Thoughts of Mr. Daniels crept into her mind. Guilt. And then she wondered if situations like the one she was faced with could possibly be what he meant.

7

Friday couldn't come fast enough for Desiree. She was longing to be with Mr. Daniels. She hated having to delete the work of art that he texted to her on Wednesday. It was a picture of his erect penis. Typically, she could let Malcolm know about these things, but she didn't think he'd be too accepting of seeing a thick, black, ten-inch penis. She quickly deleted it, along with the photos, videos, and texts she had sent to Mr. Daniels, since Malcolm often went through her phone.

The day was heavily scheduled, and she was still in the process of training her replacement. Some of the staff had actually gotten together to plan an office party to celebrate her promotion. She overheard two women saying they didn't care about celebrating her, but they were happy for the opportunity to get out of doing work for the remainder of their Friday afternoon.

Mr. Daniels had spent much of his morning in meetings with the owner and other senior leaders within the company. She started worrying that they wouldn't get to have their lunch together.

Desiree was doing some filing when she heard her replacement admin, Kelly, say, "Good morning. How can I help you?"

At first Desiree thought she was on the phone and got annoyed because the woman didn't announce the company name when answering the call. However, another voice caused Desiree to peep her head out of the filing room.

"Good morning. I'm here to see Mr. Daniels."

"Oh, I'm sorry, he's been in meetings all morning and has a pretty full schedule today. Was he expecting you?" the Kelly asked.

Desiree's heart sank. She recognized the tall, "capital p-shaped" woman with the dark brown complexion and exaggerated blonde weave, wearing a seemingly signature orange lipstick, from the pictures throughout Mr. Daniels's office. The woman had an abundance of boobs, but totally lacked hips or butt, causing Desiree to wonder why she wouldn't just spend the few extra dollars on surgery for her bottom.

"I'm his wife. I'm trying to take him to lunch."

"Oh, I believe he's already scheduled for a lunch appointment out of the building today."

"Trust me; he won't be keeping that appointment. His schedule just cleared up for that time slot," Mrs. Daniels rudely informed the woman. Just then, Mrs. Daniels caught a glimpse of Desiree peeking from the filing room. "Is that Desiree in there? You're just the young lady I wanted to chat with."

Desiree didn't know what to do. She felt her heart thumping extra hard. She emerged from the filing room with a smile on her face as Mrs. Daniels looked her up and down in a disapproving manner.

"Come, I take it my husband's office is empty right now. We can go in there to talk in private."

Desiree tried to keep a pleasant expression to avoid tipping Kelly off that there was any problem. She followed Mrs. Daniels into the office. Once inside, Mrs. Daniels closed the door and went to take a seat in her husband's chair. Desiree took a seat on the other side of the desk.

"First, I'd like you to know your lunch date with my husband has been canceled. Second, my husband probably neglected to tell you that I own a computer security company, and cloning his phone is like child's play for me." Mrs. Daniels pursed her lips.

Desiree's eyes widened as she thought of the woman seeing the exchanges between her and Mr. Daniels.

Mrs. Daniels continued. "Third, from all the pictures throughout this office, I'm sure you knew you were messing with a married man. Fourth, I have zero appreciation for the skimpy outfits you have been wearing to entice my husband. Fifth, I have even less appreciation for the disgusting photo exchange that has been going on between the two of you. And finally, if I ever hear any mention of you dealing with my husband in any manner other than a professional one, I promise you, I will expose you to the world and see to it that you're never able to work again, other than on a street corner, which is where you belong with that half of a dress you wore to go fuck my husband in."

Mrs. Daniels paused for effect. She clasped her hands together like she was making a deal.

"Now, I heard you got a promotion, so you won't need to interact with my husband anymore. And since you actually have impressive qualifications and received your promotion before you got down on your knees to suck my husband's dick, I'll have to genuinely congratulate you for your hard work and earning that promotion on your own merit." She then smiled for the first time. "Congratulations."

Desiree tried to force a smile. Her disappointment was beyond measure. "Thank you."

"So, I just want to know, are we clear on the messing with my husband thing? 'Cause I didn't get to keep my husband for over twenty-five years by looking the other way. I kept him by intercepting these types of disasters. I absolutely won't sit back and allow this mischief. Our children are older than you. All too often, women come along and think they can steal another woman's husband or boyfriend. And to that I say, the way you got him is exactly how you'll lose him. If you think he'll want you, just wait until the next young, hot body comes along. You'll be treated like yesterday's garbage. And I'm giving you the same advice I gave to my three children."

Desiree felt like she was stuck to the chair.

"Now I'm not going to keep you from your work any longer. I just wanted to approach you like a woman. Next time, I won't be so nice, provided you decide not to take heed to my warning."

Mr. Daniels walked into his office and saw his wife sitting at his desk as if she owned it with Desiree on the opposite side.

"What's going on in here? Evelyn, what are you doing here and sitting behind my desk?" he asked, obviously annoyed by the unplanned intrusion.

"Me and Desiree were just getting better acquainted. I stopped in to take my darling husband out for lunch. I was asking Desiree if she wanted to join us to celebrate her promotion, but she said she had so much work to finish up since today's her last day working for you."

Desiree's eyes met with Mr. Daniels's eyes, and he could see the distress in them.

"Well, I have meetings scheduled all day, so no, I won't be able to do lunch with you today. I'll see you at home for dinner."

"Why Roger, I took time out of my busy schedule to have lunch with you. You can't take at least thirty minutes? Perhaps we can order in and have lunch in your office if you can't get out."

"Nope! Can't do that either. I was just coming back to have Desiree order lunch for all the execs."

"Well, that's what your new assistant is for. You can't keep having Desiree do these menial tasks."

"Goodbye, Evelyn. Go back to your office and let me do my job how I see fit."

Desiree took note of the fact that his wife hadn't let on that she had knowledge of his indiscretions. Actually, the more she listened, it sounded as if their marriage might have been over many years ago, and his wife was clawing for dear life, probably to save face with the women at a country club she's a member of.

"Roger! Why are you being so short with me? I'm your wife. I only wanted to take you out for lunch."

"Don't *Roger* me!" he snapped. "Since when have you popped up for lunch without checking with my schedule?" Roger Daniels looked at Desiree and said, "I'm sorry, Desiree. Can you step out and let me have a quick word with my wife in private? Also, I need for you to order a veggie platter and those sandwiches you ordered the other week. Have the order sent to Ted's conference room on the 30th floor, and put it on my account."

"Sure thing," Desiree said with a forced smile as she hurried on out of the office, closing the door behind her.

It took no time before Desiree heard Roger Daniels yelling at his wife and not allowing her a word in. Not even thirty seconds later, Evelyn waltzed out, looking as if she was trying to maintain her dignity.

Mr. Daniels followed her out of his office, stopping to apologize to both Desiree and Kelly for any problems his wife may have given them. Kelly was brown-nosing, talking about how beautiful and pleasant Mrs. Daniels was.

Desiree's eyes said what her mouth wouldn't say. He could see her hurt, particularly since he hadn't had the opportunity to let her know he'd have to cancel their lunch. Somehow, he thought she pretty much figured that out already, based on her look of disappointment. Additionally, he could just imagine what his wife might have said. He was pretty certain that it wasn't to celebrate Desiree.

After the office party, just as Desiree was packing up to leave for the day, Alex summoned her to his office to provide her with some reading material to go through over the weekend, to help her get a fresh start on the coming Monday when she began her new position. By the time she returned to collect her belongings, most of the office had already cleared out. When she had gone to see Alex, Mr. Daniels was back up in his meetings with the seniors. He was back in his office when she returned.

"Desiree, you have a minute? I know you have to hurry to get your son, but I was hoping to catch you before you left."

Her face wore a troubled smile as she entered his office.

"I know you are very disappointed about our lunch. I promise you, I will find a way to make it up to you. I had no idea that Ted was going to keep us tied up all day. I would have never stood you up. I hope you know that."

"Mr. Daniels, I understand. I'm okay with that."

"Then why the sad face? Did my wife say something to you to upset you?"

Desiree thought for a long pause about whether or not to tell him about the conversation. Then it angered her how she noticed that the woman didn't say a word to him about her having knowledge of the infidelity. So Desiree decided to spill it all. Funny thing was, he seemed more upset about Desiree being upset than he was about his wife cloning his phone.

He took a deep breath and said, "Look, the truth is, my marriage was over ages ago. Unfortunately, in this business, they look for family men. They look for people with stability. That's why I stay. She knows our marriage has long been over, but she doesn't want her family to find out that her marriage failed. Our children are all grown, and she's realizing that she pretty much has nothing left to use to hold onto me. She keeps having all these cosmetic surgeries, thinking that will fix everything, but she fails to see that she's the problem. Her over-the-top behavior—stuff like cloning my phone—that widens the distance between us. Not any other person. Our love life has pretty much been over for three years. We lay together out of convenience and not out of love or romance. She's an attractive woman, but her personality is so dark and ugly.

"Believe it or not, even before you came along, she threatened to cause me to lose my job here and said I'd be forced to depend on her financially and wouldn't want to ever leave her. It's that kind of behavior that opens the door for someone else to walk into."

"Why do you stay with her? If you're so unhappy, why not leave her?"

"In my eleven years with this company, I have witnessed three executive staff members go through a messy divorce, and they are all gone. Each of them lost their jobs because of the negative publicity the company frowns upon. Evelyn is not going to just let me walk away from her without a messy fight. She's made that clear at least a hundred times."

"Oh. I'm so sorry," Desiree said, feeling bad for the trapped man.

He smiled. "First, stop calling me Mr. Daniels. All of the other account reps call me Roger or Mr. D. If the owner of the company allows all of his employees to call him Ted, surely there would be no problem with you calling me Roger."

Desiree smiled. "Okay, Roger. I think that might take some getting used to." She laughed.

"And I was going to say, you have no reason to be sorry about my marriage. It is what it is."

"Do you really think she'll do something with my pictures like she said she would?"

"I think if we keep things hidden, she won't have any reason to bother you again. She already knows you won't be working directly with me anymore. Perhaps that'll make her back off. She hasn't mentioned anything about the pictures to me, so I'm going to keep them and enjoy them for as long as I can—if that's all right with you."

She shrugged her shoulders. "I guess."

"So, how did you enjoy the picture I sent to you? I hope it didn't upset you or anything."

"For the record, I was quite pleased. I spent a great deal of time looking at it—reminiscing on last Friday . . ."

"But?"

"Unfortunately, I had to get all the photos out of my phone. My son plays games in my phone all the time, and the last thing I need is for him to open those pictures. I even have a passcode on my phone, and he still knows how to get in. Don't ask me how." She laughed.

"I understand. Yeah, that would be horrible if he saw that. He'd be traumatized for life."

There was an awkward silence between them. She wanted to be with him and couldn't see how she'd have the opportunity once she moved into her new office and new position.

"It's awful quiet out there. Is everyone gone already?" he asked, causing her to go look outside of his office.

She turned her desk lamp off and grabbed her bag, bringing it with her back into Mr. Daniels's office.

"Are you getting ready to head out now?" he asked, looking at her in a way that begged her to stay.

"If you want me to," she replied, putting the ball in his court.

"It's late. Will your son be all right?"

"He'll be fine. After all, he's going to have to get used to his momma being away from him for days at a time when I start this new job."

"That's probably true. The first year is the hardest. After you start seeing all the dollars coming in, it gets so much easier, especially when you get to put your kids in good schools as a result of your hard work and dedication."

"Yeah, I guess."

"You hungry?" he asked, making awkward small talk.

"A little bit. I'm sure I can wait until I get home.

"That was probably a stupid question, since I don't have any food to offer you. That is, unless you want to go out to get something."

Desiree took a deep breath. She dropped her bags on the floor, turned to lock his office door, and then began peeling off all of her clothes as he watched in pure amazement, as if seeing her body for the first time. She kept her heels on as she walked to where he was seated behind his desk and began removing his already loosened tie and unbuttoning his shirt. He kept his eyes locked onto hers as she worked to get his shirt unbuttoned and his belt buckle unfastened. She was hoping he helped a little bit, but he allowed her full control as she undressed him. He didn't touch her body until she placed a nipple to his lips as she bent to kiss his earlobe. He opened up to take her nipple into his mouth, then lifted his hands to rub her silky thighs. The more intense she became with his ear, the more intense his actions became, causing her to moan softly.

He stopped her briefly to ask her, "Are you sure you want to do this?"

"Yes. Yes, I want to feel you inside of me," she seductively replied.

That caused him to stand up from his seat. He already had an erection.

He grabbed Desiree and gave her the most passionate kiss she had ever had. As they kissed, their bodies attempted to become familiar with one another. She could feel the heat emanating from his body, and he could feel every hair on her body standing to attention.

His fingers went on an exploration between her legs, in search of a hot wetness. He released her lips to glide down below her shoulders, as he planted tender kisses while making his way to each nipple. His fingers found their intended target while smothering her breasts with kisses. She could feel a fire shooting through her body. As his fingers explored the wetness a bit deeper, his tongue slid down her torso to meet up with the treasures found by his fingers.

Desiree was already going crazy. She didn't know what to do with herself as she stood vulnerable. He spread her standing legs to allow him enough space as he crawled in between. Her clit was throbbing before his lips could find their way. The sensation was so overwhelming, she wanted to scream, but had to keep reminding herself of where she was. She would occasionally look around her immediate vicinity for something that she could eventually grab hold of to muffle her screams of pleasure that she was already anticipating. When his tongue connected with her clitoris and his fingers pressed their way deeper inside of her, her knees began to buckle, making it more difficult to stand. She grabbed hold of his strong shoulders and the back of his head for support. As the excessive wetness escaped past his fingers and started making its way outside of her cave, he then moved his tongue to expertly capture her flow. The gush was so great, Desiree started to wonder if she was peeing or cumming. Whatever it was, Mr. Daniels didn't come up for air until every drop was cleared up.

When he worked his way back up to her lips, he kissed her passionately as he backed her onto his desk, while spreading her legs to make his grand entrance. She pulled away long enough to let him know that she had a condom in her bag. They both looked at the great distance to her bag near the sofa across the room.

Inside Desiree's mind, she was screaming for a condom. Although she used birth control, she hadn't been unprotected since her son was conceived. At the same time, she longed to feel him inside of her naturally. Inside Roger's mind, he too wanted to feel her naturally, but he hadn't been inside of another woman since the day he made his vows to his wife, over twenty-five years ago. Common sense told him that the girl was very young and could be promiscuous, and he probably needed to protect himself.

Thankfully, common sense prevailed. He lifted her body up, and she wrapped her legs around his waist as he made their way to the sofa. While she searched her bag for a condom, he planted more kisses all over her body and even turned her over to plant some on her back and ass. She was happy when she found that condom. He wasted no time slipping it on, flipping her on her back and sliding up inside of her.

Tears formed in Desiree's eyes. His love making skills were majestic—magical. As much as she loved Malcolm, she could never remember him making her feel the way she was feeling with Mr. Daniels. She didn't know what happened, but somehow the feeling became even better. They both noticed. The condom was helping him to maintain his rhythm, but whatever had just happened was providing a much more powerful sensation and made it too difficult for him to keep going. The strong contractions of her vaginal muscles let him know that she had a mighty orgasm. That, along with her repeatedly whispering, "Oh my god! Oh my god!"

He collapsed on top of her as she continued to gently bite into his shoulder. They stayed in that position as their bodies enjoyed the aftershocks. They lay still and in silence, as if any movement would ruin the moment. Again Desiree wanted to cry, because in that very moment, she wondered if she was in love with Roger Daniels, and even if she was, there was no way they could ever be together.

By that point, Malcolm would have selfishly rolled off of her, but Roger continued to hang on, as their bodies experienced every single after-tremor together. Before then, Desiree hadn't known such a thing existed. With Roger, she just knew she never wanted to let go.

After what seemed like an eternity, they finally decided to separate their bodies. As Roger pulled out, they quickly discovered why the sensation improved. The condom was broken. Panic caused Roger to then question Desiree about birth control. He told her he couldn't dare entertain the thought of a baby. He then decided to ruin the moment by reminding her that he had no intention of leaving his wife for any woman. Although she told herself that sex with Roger was supposed to be part of a mission, his comments suddenly made her feel cheap and worthless. What felt like love just minutes prior, quickly turned into "a fuck."

"I use birth control and I'm not trying to fuck up my career by having another baby," she snapped. Her feelings were hurt. "And I'm not trying to take you from your wife. Just like she said, I'd lose you the same way I got you."

Desiree tried to dress quickly to leave, as she fought her tears.

Roger realized she was hurt and debated on whether or not to console her. Finally, he gave in and went to wrap his arms around her, causing her to sob into his chest.

"I'm sorry, Desiree. I didn't mean to hurt you. I didn't mean to lead you on or give you false hopes about you and me. This is the first time I have ever been with a woman other than my wife. I don't know what to think or feel right now. I don't know how I have managed to control myself all of these years, and to now lose control. I don't know what it is about you that made me cross a line that could have cost me my whole life. But whatever it is, I know I didn't mean to hurt you. I should have known better than to let this happen. I should have stopped you last Friday, but I already wanted to be with you. The way you just made me feel, I will never have any regrets. I never knew I could feel this good. But like I said, I do regret causing you any pain or hurting you in any way."

Desiree pulled her emotions into check and put on her game face. "Hey, it is what it is. At least we don't have to wonder anymore. Soon I'll be on the road, and we'll be over it."

Roger felt offended. He then thought of Desiree just callously moving onto the next man. He let go of her and went to retrieve his clothes to put on. "Well, if you need anything, I'll still be here for you. That won't change," he said, forcing a smile.

She picked up her bags and walked over to Roger, reached up to kiss his lips, and then turned to leave. He watched as she left.

To both their surprise, Alex Krammer was heading to Roger's closed door office, and witnessed a frazzled Desiree leaving after 7pm.

"Oh, you're here late. I thought for sure you'd left hours ago," Alex said to Desiree.

She nervously answered, "Uh, I just wanted to make sure everything was set up for next week. We had some things to go over, and I didn't want to have to count on the new girl, because then I'd have to split my time between positions while I'm training."

Alex clapped his hands and looked as if he was not buying the bullshit she was selling. "Wow! That's why I can't wait to work with you. I know with your level of dedication; you'll definitely get the job done."

Both Desiree and Roger smiled, seeming comfortable with Alex's response.

"I tell you, I'm half tempted to renege on her promotion, because I don't know how I'm going to make it without her. I'm trying to figure out how I got along before she came."

"I bet," Alex said, walking away to go back to his office.

"Alex, did you need something?" Roger asked when noticing that Alex didn't state his reason for coming to his office that time of night.

"It's nothing. It can wait until Monday. It's already late," he said as he continued to walk away.

Desiree and Roger exchanged a concerned look. It almost seemed as if Alex was angry. They watched as Alex disappeared, and then Roger blew Desiree a kiss as she headed toward the elevator.

8

"Damn! Why you so late? I was about to call someone to watch Little Man. You couldn't let me know you got caught up?" Malcolm scolded the minute Desiree walked through the door.

Tayshon ran from his seat in front of the television in the living room to greet his mother. After Desiree hugged and kissed on her son, Malcolm sent him back to his spot in the living room to finish watching television, while Desiree led Malcolm up the stairs to speak out of her son's earshot.

"If I didn't call or text you, then that meant I couldn't. This has been a very hectic day for me," she said, trying to quickly get out of her shoes and dress.

"Well, so what, you been fucking this dude since lunch?"

"No, Malcolm! We didn't even go to lunch. His clown-looking wife showed up and threatened to destroy me, and he was in meetings with the company president all day."

Malcolm looked at Desiree as he tried to make sense of her statement. "Why would his wife come after you? Was there something else going on that you haven't told me about?"

Desiree was about to panic but rebounded quickly, thankful she was rummaging in her closet for something casual to change into as she thought of her response. "One day he sent me a text saying he was looking forward to our lunch together on Friday. That's why his wife showed up. She said she works or owns a computer security company, and she saw his message talking about us having lunch together because she tapped in his phone. She saw the dress I had on and was convinced I was setting out to sleep with her husband, so she threatened to destroy me."

"I wish you would have let me know. I would have dealt with that bitch. So, where have you been all this time if you didn't have lunch with dude?"

"I was at the office, and now I think I might have an even bigger problem," she said as she plopped down on the bed when changed into her shorts and tee.

"Why?"

"Right when I was about to leave for the day, my new boss called me down to his office to give me a bunch of books to read over the weekend. When I went to his office, my previous boss wasn't in his office. But when I returned, he was there and was waiting to talk to me and apologize for his wife threatening me, as well as not being able to take me to lunch because of his meetings with the company president. At this point, pretty much everyone was gone. Things got kind of hot."

"Kind of hot? You fucked him in the office after his wife threatened you?"

"It didn't go all the way," she lied, deflecting her eyes.

"I'm not saying anything is wrong with it. You handling your business. I'm cool with that. You don't have to lie or sugarcoat it, but what you mean there was a bigger problem?"

"As I was leaving out of his office, my new boss was heading there and he seemed like he got really pissed when I told him I was just trying to make sure things were in order for the following week, since I would no longer be working there. I don't think he believed me. He seemed like he was gonna spit fire. He didn't even say why he came. He just left—went back to his office. Now I don't know how to act with him next week. How's he gonna treat me if he thinks I was just fucking his boss? He can make things really rough for me."

"I wouldn't stress it. As long as you're in good with his boss, what the fuck can he do but be mad? If he come at you sideways, you let the other dude know."

"Yeah, but what if other dude gets flaky because of his wife finding out?"

"Look, you do what you gotta do, and let me handle all the other bullshit. I'm gonna take Little Man to BM3 so you can get your work done this weekend. You need to go in there on top of your game Monday, especially if you're thinking that motherfucker might try to fuck with you."

Malcolm walked into Tayshon's room to get his an overnight bag, as Desiree followed.

"I agree. I don't have any room for mistakes right now."

"Shit like this is why I try to tell you to hold your horses with trying to move into some new home. Now we gotta make sure this motherfucker don't try to fuck with our dough."

Desiree smiled. She appreciated having Malcolm to keep her from stressing, but she had a feeling he was about to cause her stress since he knew she fucked another man. She certainly didn't expect the question he threw at her after he dressed and collected Tayshon and was walking out the door.

"So was it good?"

"Huh?" she asked to buy herself a moment to think. She fully understood what he was asking. She just didn't know how to answer it.

"Huh? I know when you say that, you're trying to think of a good answer. This dude must have fucked you good—got you lying to me and all."

He walked out of the door with his son in tow, letting it slam behind him, to make it obvious he was angry.

Desiree ran to open the door, calling out to him, but he just ignored her as he placed their son in the car seat.

"Close the door and get in the house. You have work to do, remember?" he said before pulling off.

The day was overwhelming. At that point, all she wanted to do was take a nice hot bath and go to bed. She figured she'd read her manuals until she fell asleep.

She should have known that her actions wouldn't come without a consequence. Shortly after four in the morning, she was awakened by faint screaming. She lay still to figure out if the noise was coming from a neighbor's house, but she eventually realized the sound was coming from within her own home. She could feel her blood boiling. She knew the sound. It was people having sex, and the noise was coming from her son's room. Malcolm was punishing her for enjoying the sex with Roger. If he knew Roger was a black man, it would really send him over the edge.

Desiree thought about busting into the room and telling them to get out, but she knew that wouldn't end well for her. For a quick minute, she cried. She hated Malcolm right then. She decided to go to the room, open the door, and nicely call Malcolm out to speak with her. When she opened the door to the dark room, she was hoping to catch a peek at who the woman was. She figured it must have been some random chick he found in the bar or club.

"Malcolm, can you come out here? I need to speak with you."

"Close that door! I'm taking care of business. Go back to bed," he ordered.

At first, Desiree did as told. She cried even harder that time. There were days when she was absolutely convinced that Malcolm loved her and only her. However, times such as this caused her to wonder if he even liked her, let alone loved her.

After a while, she left her bedroom and decided to camp out downstairs on the sofa, so she could torture herself and see the woman her fiancé felt the need to bring into her home as a punishment. She was determined to stay awake, but she eventually dozed off. It was morning when she finally heard Malcolm calling out for her. She let him know she was downstairs.

He came down wearing only his boxers. She wondered where the woman was and why the bitch hadn't left yet.

Malcolm sat next to Desiree, taking her into his arms. "What you doing down here? You need to be getting your rest. And don't forget, we gotta go get you some new work clothes today."

He spoke like he was so loving and concerned, yet he had a woman hiding out in their home.

"Where is she? Who is she? Why is she in our home?" Desiree asked calmly, hoping not to incite Malcolm's anger.

"That's what I wanted to talk to you about. I came in the bedroom, but I didn't see you. I don't want you to get all angry and crazy. I need you to think about the big picture. I need you to think about you climbing this corporate ladder, and not let bullshit get in the way."

"What does my job have to do with who you are in my home fucking? You do all your dirt outside. You even stay gone for days at a time when you get mad at me, but now this?"

"Baby, I'm not mad at you. I don't want you to think this is me trying to get back at you. You know we keep everything on the one-hundred. We don't lie or hide anything from each other. I know you lied to me last night about dude, but I understand why. I understand that you were just trying to protect my feelings. I love you for that. Last night you got in real late, and you didn't even start the new position yet. I am thinking ahead. I know you're going to be gone a lot, and we're going to need help with Little Man."

Desiree could feel the air escaping her as Malcolm talked and she anticipated where he was going with the conversation.

"You brought in a babysitter for our son, but you have the nerve to be fucking her first? Are you serious, Malcolm?"

"Baby, you need to stop tripping. This is business. All this bitch wants for babysitting is some dick. Even better, she wants to help out around the house and help pay some bills."

"No! Absolutely not!" Desiree said as her voice grew louder.

"Don't be like that. Plus, she needs a place to stay for a while until she finds a new place. I think you need to give it a chance and see how things work out."

"So while you're fucking this bitch, who's supposed to be watching our son? Huh? Answer that."

"You know what? I'm trying real hard to be nice. You out here fucking and sucking on all these different motherfuckers, and I still stay with you. I left all them other bitches to be with you. All of them are jealous because I'm with you. The reason I'm with you is because we got a great thing going. You don't be questioning me. I help you when you gotta deal with these jokers who be trying to fuck you over. Hell, you wouldn't even have a fucking degree if it wasn't for me telling you how to deal with those horny motherfuckers. I'm not trying to replace you. All I'm trying to do is make sure we'll be good with everything when you're gone out of town. I didn't want to just find any random bitch who'll be treating our son all fucked up."

That really confused Desiree, and it made her think that she must know the woman. And as Desiree wondered, she heard the familiar voice call out, "Malcolm! Where you at?"

"Sharquita? Shar-fucking-quita! Malcolm, please tell me you don't have that bitch in my house and she already made it clear that she doesn't like me. Wait! Hold up! I just realized that bitch is not even legal. You're willing to go to jail for her ass? Her mother finds out she's here and she'll have your ass locked the hell up."

"Her mother don't gotta know all that. She knows y'all are cool—"

"No, we are not!"

Sharquita decided to come down the stairs with only a sheet wrapped around her naked body. "Is everything cool?" she asked.

"Is everything cool?" Desiree repeated. "Girl, you must have lost your fucking mind. You better go get your clothes on and hurry up and get the fuck up out of my house before somebody goes to jail this morning." Desiree stood up with a deranged look on her face and started short pacing.

Malcolm tried to hold her.

"Let me go Malcolm. I'm trying to stay calm right now. Just leave me be, and get that ho up out my house."

"Yo Shar, you need to go get dressed before my girl lets loose. We need to talk."

"We don't need to talk about shit. There is nothing I want to hear, and there is nothing I have to say. I want her ass out of my motherfucking house—NOW!"

Sharquita rolled her eyes. "How you be fucking all these other dudes and wanna have a problem when your man wants to fuck other women?"

Desiree looked at Malcolm in disbelief. The only way Sharquita would say such a thing, is from what Malcolm may have told her. She calmly walked to the kitchen without saying another word.

Malcolm yelled to Sharquita to run. Sharquita stood in the middle of the steps still not understanding, but then she noticed Malcolm trying to wrestle a huge knife from Desiree. That caused Sharquita to run back to the bedroom and lock the door.

"So you're willing to throw away your whole life, your career, your son, and everything because you're threatened by a piece of ass? Now you're being stupid. Not only that, how about if you're going to be this stupid, I'll just leave your dumb ass alone and you'll be by your fucking self. Now put that fucking knife down!"

Through pouring tears, Desiree yelled out, "Why? Why her? Why would you do this to me?"

"Ain't nobody trying to do anything to you. That's what's wrong with you. You know why I left my other baby momma to be with you? Because she started acting stupid, just how you're acting now. When you were all up in the bed with me at her house, that was okay, but now you talking about you don't want anyone up in your home. I guess you forgot this is actually my place, and I brought you here for the baby. I don't know what's in your fucked-up head right now, but I just know you better chill with the bullshit."

"Please get her out of here, Malcolm. I can deal with anyone else but her. You know she can't stand me and is disrespectful to me. No! I'll leave you before I sit up in my own home with this bitch," she pleaded, on the verge of hyperventilating.

"Baby, she has no place to go. She got into a fight with her moms and got put out. I thought you'd at least feel some compassion."

"Not for that trick. Tell the groupie ho to go back and fuck that dude that wore her ass out last week."

Malcolm looked annoyed. "Wait, what? What dude? Why you didn't tell me about some other dude?"

"She was fucking one of the guys from J-Tron's entourage. She even talked about trying to fly out to Cali to be in one of their videos. That ho knows she's been passed around the whole entourage."

"Why wouldn't you tell me something like that?" Malcolm asked again.

"Why did I need to tell you? I never thought you'd fuck with her. Hell, I just saw you cussing the bitch out a few days ago. Why would I think you needed to know who she's fucking?"

"Yo, Shar!" Malcolm called out. "Bring your ass down here."

Sharquita came down dressed in a pair of nylon leggings with holes down each side, showing no sign of panty lines, and a halter top, despite the frigid temperatures. Oh, but she did wear a pair of boots and had a thin, waist-length leather jacket in her hands.

"My girl said you fucking with J-Tron's crew. Is that true?" Malcolm asked, looking like he'd beat the life out of Sharquita.

"That was a long time ago," she answered.

"Last week. Last Friday night and Saturday morning to be specific," Desiree told.

"Oh, that was just that one dude last week. I didn't fuck with the crew last week."

Malcolm and Desiree both looked at each other, unbelieving of the level of Sharquita's ignorance.

"Malcolm, I'm not even going to blame her ignorant ass for being so stupid. That's your fault. You're almost forty years old. You should know better than to be fucking with a child."

"I ain't no child, and surely your man can tell you that," Sharquita challenged.

"And you think I'm gonna let her disrespectful ass stay up under my roof?"

"Yo, you need to bounce up out of here. Your lying ass just swore to me that you ain't been with no motherfuckers in a minute, and now I hear your ass got all kinds of niggas running trains all up in you. Get the fuck out of here!"

"Malcolm, I didn't lie. That train thing was almost a year ago. It was right at the end of winter. I haven't done that ever again. I swear."

Desiree laughed as she shook her head. "I hope your ass wore three condoms on that ho."

Those words caused Malcolm to take a seat and cover his face in frustration.

"No condom!" Sharquita laughed. "And when we did it the other day, we didn't use a condom."

"Wait! What? The other day? What other day?"

Sharquita got quiet and decided to look at Malcolm to let him tell Desiree.

"Get the fuck out of my house and don't you bring your dirty ass back around here again."

Malcolm stood up, went and opened the front door, and as soon as Sharquita was on the other side of it, he slammed it closed.

"Don't say a word. We're going to just forget all this shit happened and move forward. Understood?" Malcolm ordered.

"The sooner we forget this shit, the better. But I can't believe that you'd fuck that nasty ho raw," Desiree said turning up her nose from the foul thought.

"I just said don't say nothing else, and you gotta say something."

"Fine, I won't say anything else, but you definitely better go to the clinic and get some shots and some antibiotics."

"First thing Monday morning."

9

Desiree knew from the moment that Alex caught her leaving out of Mr. Daniels's office that night, there were going to be problems. However, she greatly underestimated the magnitude of her problems.

By the middle of her second week, Alex let Desiree know that she'd be flying out to New Orleans with another account rep to work on an account together, while Desiree would be there to learn. Then he let her know that she'd be flying out to Colorado in two weeks for a ski event. He seemed to be quickly filling up her schedule to keep her away from the office.

However, although troubling, none of those things worried her as much as the invitation Alex gave her to come to his home that night, to go over some work. His invitation sounded more like a threat, which was what troubled her most. She had already informed Malcolm and let him know she was worried. He reminded her of her mission and the fact that she wanted to move from their neighborhood. There was something very dark and untrusting about Alex that concerned her. She desperately wanted to send a text to Mr. Daniels to make him aware of this meeting, but she had to worry about his wife seeing the text and causing further problems.

That evening, she drove the 30 minutes to get to Alex's secluded home. The home was impressive and definitely one she'd love to have some day. When he opened the door, he seemed pleasant. He offered her a glass of wine or beer. She opted for the wine. He then took her on a grand tour of his massive home. Desiree was on edge the entire time. After the tour, they returned to the kitchen to eat the pasta dish he cooked for her. Then they settled on a large sofa with a big television. He actually put on a work related video and spoke while Desiree took notes. She also took note that he was on his fifth beer and beginning to slur as he spoke.

"Can I feel your pussy?" he asked out of nowhere.

"What?" Desiree asked, shocked by his candid request. "I think it's time I get going."

"I think it's time you do as I say if you want to stay with this company."

"I'm sorry, Alex. I can't do what you're asking, and I don't appreciate you threatening my job if I don't allow you to violate me."

"I remember that Friday I went to Roger's office to speak with him about you. Imagine my surprise when I heard the sounds of two people having sex. I listened for a long time. And the more I listened, the angrier I became. Since I first saw you, I wanted to fuck you. I wanted to put my hard cock down your throat. Those thick lips scream to have a dick, and I thought it would be wonderful to have your lips on my dick. But now in these times, we can't say things like that to employees or coworkers without losing our jobs. Everything is sexual harassment these days. Everything is so politically correct. But while I worried myself about being politically correct, then I see you coming out of Roger's office, right after listening to the two of you in there fucking. Then you wanted to lie and tell me some bullshit about you finishing up some work for the following week. Insulting my intelligence. Very insulting. I left after that because I didn't know what to say or do. My first instinct was to expose both of your asses. However, I then thought about how much I wanted to fuck you myself and thought, why not just invite her over and fuck her? It's not like you have any position to negotiate or turn me down."

"Alex, I really do have to get home to my son."

"Fuck your son! We don't want to hear any bullshit excuses in this business. You knew that when you took this job."

Desiree stood to leave. "I'm sorry, but I have to go now."

"You leave, and I promise you, there will be an interoffice memo sent to everyone in the company about you and Roger—a married man. Both of you will lose your jobs. Hell, he's only in that position because they needed a token black man. I know more than he does, so I would love to have this opportunity to knock his smug ass off of his pedestal."

"Alex, we can't do this," she said with tears in her eyes. "How do you think we're supposed to have a working relationship if you're going to be threatening and blackmailing me?"

"We're going to have a working relationship where you will give me some pussy anytime I want it. You will suck my dick anytime I say so. When I tell you to jump, you will ask me how high. And as you already know, if you fall below on your earnings, then Ted will get rid of your ass anyway. So, that's how we will have a working relationship. Have I made myself clear?"

Desiree hated the position she found herself in. She reluctantly answered, "Yes."

"Well, if you understand, then why are you still in those clothes? Get 'em off! I want everything off."

She was hesitant in undressing as she tried to weigh out her consequences of refusing him. The crazy thing was, she seemed more concerned with Roger losing his job than herself.

When she was fully uncovered, Alex's grin reminded her of the Grinch. She tried to stare him directly the eye, but it was like looking the devil in the eye.

Desiree cried on the entire ride home. She had never felt so violated before. She couldn't imagine keeping her job and being continually being subjected to the humiliation Alex put her through. To add insult to injury, she spotted Sharquita walking away from her home while she assumed that Malcolm was completely done with the girl. Even more insulting, the following day when she was going by Mr. Daniels's office to let him know her dilemma, she noticed the admin that she helped trained was no longer there, but a Desiree 2.0 now sat at the desk. In that moment, Desiree couldn't wait to start traveling and putting distance between herself and everything and everyone. She even contemplated suicide for a brief moment.

10

Damn, girl! This pussy is so damn good. I keep saying I ain't fucking with you no more, and that shit is like a drug. I can get locked up for fucking with you."

"I told you. I told you before we did it. You said you could just hit it once and leave it alone. It's been almost every day for the past two weeks, and you still ain't had enough," Sharquita said with a giggle.

"I ain't gonna lie, you got me all fucked up. I don't care where I'm at, my dick'll get hard just thinking about this shit," Malcolm said as his hand continued to gently rub Sharquita's hot spot.

Malcolm's words made Sharquita happy. She was hoping to replace Desiree, and with her new job, it was only a matter of time. Sharquita was even hoping she'd hurry up and get pregnant since they weren't using any condoms or protection. She figured that would guarantee a place in Malcolm's life. With Desiree off to New Orleans, Sharquita was able to peacefully go to bed at night with Malcolm and wake up with him in the morning. But even before Desiree left, Sharquita was happy about the two times that she knew Desiree saw her leaving the home after sexing Malcolm. When Sharquita asked Malcolm if Desiree said anything, Malcolm told her nothing was said, and that she was probably starting to come around. He just figured it would be best that the two weren't in the house at the same time. Sharquita agreed to avoid Desiree as long as Malcolm was giving it to her each day.

What Malcolm loved most about Sharquita was that there were no limits to what she'd do. There was no orifice on her that was off limits. After the night she allowed him and two of his friends to rotate her for hours on end, he knew then she was a keeper. The one time he tried to run a train on Desiree, she cried the whole time, blowing the entire mood. When he asked her why she agreed to do it in the first place, she said it was because she loved him and wanted to make him happy. What would make Malcolm the happiest of all was if he and his friends could rotate both Sharquita and Desiree together. He knew it would be just a matter of time before he'd get to move Sharquita into their home, and he hoped one day he could wake up with both of them in the same bed. He didn't want his women having sex with each other. He wanted them to only focus on him. Desiree was due home that night, and he decided to press his luck and see if he could wake up with the pair the following morning.

Desiree sat outside in her car for the longest. She dreaded going in. While she was away, Malcolm informed her that Sharquita was staying with them and he wasn't going to have any drama in his house.

As Desiree sat and thought back to the day she met Mrs. Daniels, she remembered the woman saying, "How you get them is how you'll lose them." Desiree didn't set out to take her friend's boyfriend, but somehow she ended up doing just that. She remembered that Malcolm would have still been there, along with Desiree, if the woman hadn't put them both out of her home. Looking back, Desiree couldn't believe she'd stoop so low and sleep with a man who shared a bed with her friend under the same roof. In reality, Desiree had almost the same type of friendship with BM3 that she had with Sharquita. The big difference was, with BM3, Desiree was the young girl that BM3 was trying to help. With Sharquita, Desiree was trying to help her. And in both cases, the "helpee" ended up being a man-stealing backstabber.

Desiree was so ready to quit her job already. While in New Orleans, she must have had at least ten sets of Japanese hands inside of her pussy. Thankfully, that was all she had to do. This trip she took with another female account rep, Karyn. Sadly, it was Karyn that was asking the pack of drunk Japanese men if they had ever touched black pussy before. She made up a blindfolded pussy-feeling contest, to see which felt better. She wasn't so happy when only two said hers felt the best. The entire trip, Karyn would continually let Desiree know that she would have to use her assets to close almost every deal, because it's a man's world, and they were already at a disadvantage. She told Desiree to expect to have plenty of sex when she got to Aspen for the ski event.

As Desiree sat in the car outside of her home, she thought about what career she could switch into without sex being the criteria. She also wondered if it was too late to get her position back with Mr. Daniels. She regretted leaving the comfortable position. Also, her new position seemed to somehow open a door for Sharquita to take up residency in their lives.

Finally, she climbed out of her car and entered her "House of Dread." She could hear the television blaring from her bedroom the minute she stepped into the house. She left her bag at the door as she climbed the stairs to assess her hell. Before she could reach the top of the stairs, she could already hear Sharquita and Malcolm laughing at the rerun of a *Martin* episode. Desiree stood outside the door, out of their view, as she tried to listen to their conversation. Desiree was so exhausted and just wanted to be able to come home and relax in her own bed, only to find the new mistress had moved in and taken over.

"You laying up there watching this TV. You know you better be getting all the pussy you can before she gets in and want to start some shit tonight. And you better not be letting her put me out again. I'm getting sick of that shit. Next time you do that, I'm not fucking with you no more."

"Calm down! I already let her know you're here. She's cool with it."

Desiree wondered how Malcolm decided that she was cool with Sharquita's presence.

"But still, why we laying here watching this bullshit when I'm horny as hell?" She laughed.

"You always horny. I don't know why you're asking. You know what you gotta do to get it up."

Not even a minute later, Desiree listened to Malcolm's moans, as she also heard Sharquita's slobbering on Malcolm's dick.

"Damn, that shit feels good. Turn that ass around here so I can see up in that pussy while you do that," he instructed her.

Desiree covered her mouth as the tears poured from her eyes. Maybe three minutes after that, she listened as Malcolm was then penetrating Sharquita, and then listened how each told the other that they were the best sex ever. After the tears dried up and the anger started setting in, Desiree decided to stand in the doorway and watch the pair until they discovered her there. Eventually, she got her wish, and they looked at her watching, but it didn't disrupt any of the motion going on.

"Really? Really, Malcolm? You're just gonna keep fucking that dirty ho like I'm not standing here?"

"Come on now, don't start with the bullshit. Just let me finish getting my nut, at least."

"Sharquita, if you don't get the fuck up out of my bed, fucking my fiancé, I swear I will stab your ass to your death on this night."

At first they were going to ignore Desiree's creepy calm tone, but then Sharquita noticed the light hit off of the blade Desiree was holding. That made her jump away from the doggy-style position Malcolm had her in.

"Oh, and if you think you're sleeping in this house tonight, you better think again. You will die if you try to."

"Malcolm, you said you wouldn't let her do this shit to me again."

"Desiree, I already told you I'm not having the stupid shit."

"Stupid shit? Stupid shit? You ain't having the stupid shit, but got this bitch up in my motherfucking bed, and I can't even come home and get comfortable in my own bed after a long, miserable fucking trip," she started yelling. "Oh, and I can't even talk to my fiancé about the hell that I've had to endure these past few days, because this motherfucker decided he ain't gonna have my stupid shit? But peep this stupid shit, I don't give a fuck where you go, both of you are getting the fuck up out of here, and if you try me, see won't I call the police and let them know you're up in my motherfucking house, fucking a minor. You are a motherfucking child molester. A forty-year-old child molester. You wanna leave me? Leave! But this bitch right here is getting the fuck out of here right now."

Sharquita started toward the master bathroom.

"Where the fuck do you think you're going?"

"I'm going to get my clothes so I can leave. And Malcolm, you better be leaving with me."

"You ain't getting no fucking clothes on. You have two fucking seconds to get down those stairs and out my motherfucking house. You're leaving butt-ass-naked and with empty hands. I don't give a damn that it's only ten degrees outside, 'cause your hot ass should have thought about that before you tried to fuck with me yet again," Desiree yelled.

Malcolm sat calmly on the bed and said to Sharquita, "You need to just chill. She ain't trying to stab anybody." He turned to Desiree. "I know one thing, you better put that fucking knife down before someone gets hurt."

Desiree calmly dropped the knife. "You're right. I'm not trying to stab anyone, but I will blow somebody's motherfucking brains out if I have to say, 'get the fuck out' again." That time Desiree pulled a Glock from behind her back that was tucked in her waistband. That time Malcolm jumped up from the bed, and Sharquita ran down the stairs for the front door without any clothes on.

"You pulling motherfucking guns on people now? It's gonna be like that now? Is this how you want it?"

"I have been traumatized for the past three days. I have been traumatized last week by that ignorant, racist, bastard, and I told you about it and all you can do is get your tool greased by some dirty, underage ho? Yeah, I'm about done with your ass too. I've had enough. You can leave me. I don't give a fuck. As I was coming home, I realized that you were never mine in the first place. You have seven fucking kids, and trying to make an eighth child with that dirty bird, thinking you're just gonna cram her down my motherfucking throat. I used to think you were a good father, but then you're fucking all these different bitches right in my son's face. Did you think he can't see and talk? He'll be four soon, and he's very smart."

"Do you really want me to go? You think you don't need me anymore just because you got that new job?"

"I want you to go because right now I feel like I don't have anything else to live for. To keep my job, I have to be some glorified hooker and let all kinds of people do whatever they want to me, and *hope* that they'll be gracious enough to give me their account after so I can one day get paid for the deed. To keep my man, I have to watch him in my motherfucking bed, fucking some skank. To keep a father for my son, I have to sit back and let my child be trained on pimping. And the more I think about it, the more I realize that I was the hooker the entire time, and you were pimping me.

"And if you're wondering why I have this gun, it's because of the motherfucker who told me that he was going to sodomize and rape me as often as he felt like it. See, my so-called pimp should have handled that shit when I told him I didn't feel comfortable going out to the motherfucker's house late that night. Then he set me up to be further raped in New Orleans by a bunch of Japanese men, and then again in Colorado, where I'm expected to have endless sex with an endless line of men."

"What do you want me to do? You're the one who decided to fuck someone in the office and not be careful. What was I supposed to do? You want me to go kill dude?"

"I don't want you to do shit but get the fuck out of here."

"This is my place. How you gonna put me out?"

"Well fine, then stay. I dare you to fall asleep in this house again."

Malcolm looked at Desiree as if she might actually be crazy. "You know what? I'm gonna leave tonight, but I will be back tomorrow or the next day. I think you just need a minute to think about shit. I don't believe you don't want to be with me anymore."

"Knowing you put a lip, finger, dick or even a fucking leg inside of that nasty ho after everything you know about her, that's all the reason I don't want to be with you anymore. I'm tired of being engaged to you. We've been engaged for four years now, and you won't even get me a ring, based on what someone else did to you, that had nothing to do with me." Desiree stopped to scream. "Oh my god! I can't do this anymore. I just can't. I feel so stupid. Just go."

"You're going to regret it," Malcolm said as he squeezed past Desiree after he was fully dressed.

"I regret meeting you."

"Damn! It's like that now?"

"Just like that! Now go! Get the fuck out of here!"

As Malcolm walked out the door, he turned and said, "And for the record, I really do love you and wanted you to be my wife."

"Shut the fuck up before I shoot you in the back of your head, you fucking liar."

Malcolm hurried out the door with a sinister laugh, shaking his head.

The entire time they were upstairs, it hadn't occurred to Desiree to look in the room for her son. As she looked around, she realized her son was not even in the house. She then started calling Malcolm's phone, but he wouldn't answer.

After Malcolm was gone, the silence was deafening to Desiree. She didn't know what to do with herself. She considered ending her life with the gun she sat looking at for over an hour. She assumed that her son was safely tucked away with BM3, but didn't want to contact the woman and let her know that karma had made its rounds, just as predicted. As she thought of all the humiliation that Malcolm had subjected her to over the years, she debated whether she could actually survive without him giving her step-by-step directions to get through life. She wanted to call her parents or sisters but had long ago lost their numbers, causing her even greater distress, thinking about how Malcolm kept her away from her family.

Desiree began to laugh hysterically as her mind switched to the look of fear in Sharquita's face when she saw the gun. The fact that she was able to run the tramp out into the cold night with no clothes on made her laugh even harder. However, when she finished laughing, she thought of her so-called fiancé running out to be with that girl, the same way he did after BM3 ran him out. That made her angry again. That made her want to fight for her man, but the damage was too great, and the thought of him having sexual relations with a minor made her wonder just how young he'd be willing to go.

The chime from a text coming through on her phone interrupted Desiree's sporadic thoughts. She immediately assumed it would be Malcolm finally responding about the whereabouts of their son. To her surprise, it was a text from Roger Daniels. Without reading the content, she smiled at the fact that he was obviously thinking of her and not caring about his wife knowing he was texting her.

I'm hoping you made it home safely by now and are just about settled in. I wanted to let you know before you made it into the office tomorrow that I am no longer with the company. You made me realize that life is too short to be lived in a box. As such, I have decided to leave the company and my wife and to stop living in fear of how I must fit into someone else's criteria of happiness. You have shown me that I would never be happy without you, and I know I can never have you as long as I am there. I will be starting my own company and would love for you to join me on my new adventure once I get it all set up. Starting off, the salary won't be the same, but I think the long-term rewards will far outweigh the dollars. No pressure. Just something for you to think about. If it's not too much of a problem, I'd greatly appreciate if you could send me a little something to think about. Hope to hear from you soon. ~RD~

Desiree couldn't stop grinning. She had no idea that Roger thought so much of her that he'd walk away from his wife and his job just to be with her.

Actually, she wasn't sure if she wanted him to. She was especially surprised after having seen "Desiree 2.0" and knowing that Roger would have been drooling all over her. She also wasn't certain of what role she'd have with Malcolm going forward, being they shared a son.

Desiree tried to call Malcolm one more time before turning in for the night, hoping that maybe they could talk things out.

"Hello!"

Desiree was put off by the female voice answering Malcolm's phone. At first she thought she must have dialed the wrong number, but she looked at her phone and saw it was indeed Malcolm's number that she'd dialed.

"Who is this?" Desiree asked.

"Bitch, don't be calling my man's phone asking me who I am. Who the fuck are you?"

"Huh? Wait, what? *Your* man?"

"Yes, *my* man."

"Since when did my fiancé and child's father become your man, and he only left here a few hours ago?"

"Bitch, please! You wish he was your fiancé." The woman laughed. "Funny, I've never called his phone and you answered."

"Just like I've never called and you answered, until we seemed to have a little spat this evening."

Just then, Desiree could hear Malcolm in the background, "Who you on the phone with?"

"Some bitch calling your phone. She seems to be under the impression she's your fiancée."

"Oh, that's just my crazy ex. I told you a long time ago that the bitch was crazy."

Desiree could feel herself suffocating while listening to Malcolm deny her existence to whoever this woman was.

"And what is she talking about you're her child's father? Is there something I should know?" the woman asked him while Desiree listened.

"Bae, why you letting that silly broad get to you? Just hang up the phone."

"So, just to be clear, you do not have any child with this crazy bitch and you are not engaged to her?"

"No and hell no! You know how many different guys that bitch was sleeping with? That's why I couldn't be fucking with her."

"Okay, because you know I'll be down at the abortion clinic tomorrow if I find out you're lying to me," she warned him.

"Stop talking about trying to kill my baby. As a matter of fact, come here and let me talk to my baby. I'm gonna whisper something in his ear," he said seductively.

The woman giggled. "You are so nasty."

The woman started moaning, obviously having tossed the phone to the side for Desiree to listen. And Desiree tortured herself as she listened the entire 43 minutes.

Abruptly, as Desiree continued to listen, she heard the woman yell into the phone, "Damn, you desperate, bitch! You still sitting there listening? I hope you caught a good earful of what you will never have again."

"Tell Malcolm to bring my son home and both of you can go kill yourselves for all I give a shit. I just want my fucking son. Oh, and while you're thinking you're all that, I just ran the child molester out of my house when I caught him in my bed with a little girl. I just want my son back home, that's all. And you can let him know that if he doesn't get my son back to me tonight, I will not only call the police about my son, but I will call them about catching him with a little fucking ho."

"Malcolm! Malcolm, wake up!" the woman yelled for Malcolm. "Why is this bitch talking about you were fucking a little girl earlier this evening and you have her son somewhere? This bitch said she's calling the police. Do you need to tell me something?"

"Carol, I told you the bitch is crazy, now would you hang up the fucking phone? Why you still sitting there talking to the dumb bitch? Let her call whoever the fuck she wanna call. You know damn well I was at my mother's house earlier. Didn't my mother tell you that I was there?"

"Yeah."

"So why are you listening to this bitch and upsetting my baby?"

"You're right. I'm sorry."

Then the call ended.

Desiree could not believe the woman's stupidity. But then she thought of her own stupidity, as she realized that this woman must have been around for quite some time. And how could she not know about their son? She didn't know how, but Desiree was determined that she'd find a way to learn the woman's identity and expose Malcolm. She also wondered about this mother that Malcolm was claiming to be spending time with, because as far as she knew, Malcolm's mother was living in Alabama and had suffered some kind of brain injury from a car accident long before Desiree knew of Malcolm. It was in that very moment that Desiree realized that she and her son had never met Malcolm's mother, because he never took them to Alabama when he did go. She then wondered if his father was actually deceased as Malcolm said he was.

Desiree couldn't imagine her night getting any worse, but then her doorbell rang.

It was Sharquita's mother, LaToya, holding her son.

Desiree didn't know what to expect from the woman, based on what she'd done to Sharquita.

"You know, I had half of mind to do your son like you did my motherfucking daughter, but you can bet your last fucking dollar that you will be going to jail," LaToya said, handing Desiree her son.

"Huh? What *I* did?"

"My daughter came home with no fucking clothes on and said that you made her strip at gunpoint and walk home butt-fucking-naked. And then you have the nerve to have my other daughter babysitting your fucking child? Are you fucking stupid or what?"

"Miss LaToya, I *just* returned home from a business trip. I returned and found my son missing, while your daughter and my son's father were busy fucking in my bed, preventing me from being able to come home and relax. Do you see what I'm wearing? This is the same suit that I flew all the way back from New Orleans in. I have been frantically searching for my son, because his father took off with your daughter and wouldn't tell me where my child was."

"My daughter is only seventeen years old. Why would she be in here having sex with that man and he is almost my age?"

"You'd have to ask them that. I'm just as appalled by it. If you don't believe me, you can go take a look upstairs in the bedroom, because I haven't touched a thing in there. You'll see all their nasty underwear and sex stains all in my fucking bed. I think I even saw a bag of her clothes up there. I believe she was here the whole time I was away."

"I know you are lying to me. My minor daughter would not have been up here having sex with your old-ass man. She told me that you accused her of having sex with him and made her strip and go out in the cold."

"Miss LaToya, that doesn't even make sense. Ask yourself, why was my son at your house with your fifteen-year-old daughter while they were here alone? What do you think they were doing that my son couldn't be here? Also, they have had sex in front of my son. This wasn't the first time I caught the them."

LaToya grabbed the rail and took a seat on the cold concrete step outside. "Why would my daughter lie to me like that?"

"I hate to be the one to tell you, but you don't know the half about your daughter. A few weeks back, she asked to hang out here because she didn't want you to know she was out all night with some rapper and his crew. I have tried to help her and guide her as best as I could, even though I knew she didn't really like me, but her messing with my son's father in my home—probably trying to get pregnant, since she said they don't use any protection—is the ultimate."

LaToya stood back up, defiant. "I don't believe you. I don't believe any of this. Just give me my daughter's belongings and stay the fuck away from her, and don't think you're in the clear, because I'm still going to file a police report."

"You want to file a police report against me? You know what? You can go up into my bedroom and retrieve all of your daughter's belongings out of my house. And take those nasty fucking sheets, and have them examined for your daughter's nasty DNA while you're at it. See, I have a plane ticket showing I was out of town when all of this was going on."

Desiree stepped aside to allow LaToya into the home and watched from downstairs as she went to the bedroom to witness all of her daughter's deceit.

LaToya came back down empty-handed and crying. "I can't. I'm sorry. I can't. Burn that shit. I don't care anymore. I try to be the best mother possible, working extra hard, trying to find them a way out of the ghetto, and—I just can't."

"I'm sorry, Miss LaToya. I didn't mean to hurt you, but I have been getting slammed from the moment I walked into my door, and all I wanted to do was come home, hug my son, and take a nice hot bubble bath and relax. It's almost ten o'clock and I am just numb right now. When your daughter left, so did the father to my son, and my fiancé who didn't even have the decency to let me know where I could find my son. I didn't know who to call, and I knew I couldn't call the police, because they'll say he's the father."

"Where is he right now? I'm going to press charges against him. He had no business touching my minor daughter."

"I agree. Unfortunately, I don't know where he is at. I haven't spoken with him since he left," Desiree told her, not wanting to reveal the new revelation of yet another woman.

LaToya went and stood on the outside of the door and turned back around to face Desiree. "I guess I should tell you now before it comes out later when I press charges against him . . ."

Desiree could almost anticipate what was about to be said and didn't know if she could handle it.

LaToya continued, "It was a few years ago, and I didn't know anything about you, so it wasn't like I was trying to hurt you. I didn't find out about you until much later. It wasn't like we had a real relationship or anything. It was just two grown, consenting adults trying to fill a temporary need. What's worse is Sharquita knew about him being in my home, which is why I really don't understand why she'd do what she did."

Desiree could feel the vessels about to blow inside of her head. "You slept with my son's father?"

"Desiree, I swear, I didn't know anything about you or your relationship."

"Sharquita knew all this time?"

"You can't blame this all on Sharquita. Malcolm knew just as well. Your son was already a year old at the time, so he knew good and well that he had a woman and a child. I didn't know, because he'd spend several nights at my place, so I didn't think he had anyone special."

"So how did it end? Did it end when you found out about me?" Desiree asked as the tears streamed down her face.

"It ended when I realized that I was nothing more than a source of income for him. I wish I could say I came to my own senses. It was my older daughter that told me he's known as a pimp out in the streets. I didn't dare tell how much money I had already given him, but that was the end. I was literally taking food from my own children's mouths to hand over to him."

Desiree could not stand to hear anymore. She felt like such a fool. All the while she thought Malcolm was the one taking care of her, in that moment she realized that it was she that was providing for him. "I'm sorry. I can't hear anymore. I have to go," she said before slamming the door closed. She went to sit on the sofa and sobbed as she held her son who tried his best to console his mother.

11

Thanks again for meeting me here."

"Desiree, it's my pleasure. I can't tell you the last time I've been inside of a Chuck E. Cheese." Roger chuckled. "I might even try to play a few games before we leave."

Desiree also chuckled. "Yeah, this is one of my son's favorite places. I like to take him whenever I can."

"Your son is absolutely adorable. I can see he gets his great looks from his mother, for certain."

"Thank you." She smiled.

"Okay, but I'm sure there's a reason you asked me to meet you here. I hadn't heard from you in quite some time, so I figured you forgot about little ol' me."

"It's not that I didn't want to contact you, but your wife did say she monitors all of your communications. I really didn't want any trouble. It's just that I've reached a point that I don't know what to do anymore, and I don't know how much more I can take. You might be the only one I can talk to."

Roger took hold of Desiree's hand that rested on the table they were sitting in view of Tayshon playing. He could see the tears forming in her eyes. "What's going on?"

"I can't keep working for Alex. I can't keep doing the things they expect me to do to bring in accounts. I have a master's degree, yet, I'm like a prostitute. But with Alex, it's worse. He makes me feel like a slave woman being summoned by her master. He's been forcing me to have sex—not just sex, but demeaning things—because he knows about you and I being together. And he plans to keep punishing me for as long as I work there. I need this job. I need the money. I have a son to take care of."

"Why didn't you tell me this before?" Roger asked, quite disturbed by the revelation.

"I couldn't call you because of your wife, and then when I stopped by your office to see you, your new admin—I don't know. I just didn't know what else to do. I was happy to go to New Orleans just to get away from Alex, but then . . ." The tears poured as Desiree buried her face into her hands.

Roger moved near her to hold her tightly, grabbing a few napkins to help her wipe her tears. "Oh, Desiree. I am so sorry. I'm trying to hurry up and work on some things so we can go forward and start a new company. It's not going to be a quick fix, but I think if you go and talk to Ted Dinkins, he'll definitely have your back. He really frowns on sexual harassment in the workplace, and what Alex is doing goes way beyond. That's like rape. You have no desire to be with Alex, is that what you're telling me?"

"Absolutely not! He's a fucking nasty, disgusting pig. The things he does to me are to intentionally inflict pain on me. He says if I were to tell anyone, I'd be out of a job, because Ted hates troublemakers."

"I say go speak with Ted. I doubt if you lose your job. If that doesn't work, then that should tell you it's not the ideal company for you to work for. I understand you are concerned about caring for your son. I will try to help as much as I can and try to get this new company going as quickly as I can."

While Tayshon was preoccupied, Roger lifted Desiree's chin and kissed her on the lips. Desiree was nervous about the kiss in public, and where her son might witness, but she didn't reject it because she didn't want to alienate Roger as well. She then told him she needed to get going, but he wanted her to hang around longer so Tayshon could enjoy himself. Ignoring her request, he decided to talk about his ideas for his new business venture. Every now and again, he'd kiss her.

The following day, Desiree went to meet with the company CEO, Ted Dinkins. She had never had a conversation with him, other than small talk in passing. Employees made it sound as if Ted was the next best thing to God himself.

"Good morning, Desiree. How can I help you? Are you enjoying your new position here?" he asked as he directed her to take the seat on the opposite side of his desk.

When she was seated, she said, "Thank you for taking the time to speak with me this morning. I didn't realize it would be so easy to get an appointment with you."

"Ah, yes, I like to have an open-door policy for our employees. I don't want anyone to have the impression that they have an unapproachable boss sitting high up on his horse. I don't get too many requests from employees, so when I do get one, I absolutely do my best to accommodate."

Desire smiled. "I appreciate it."

"So, what can I do for you? How are you and Alex getting along? I guess soon you'll have a new direct report, since I'm considering putting Alex into Roger's position. It's a shame he left us."

"Well, that's kind of what I wanted to speak with you about. I spoke with Mr. Daniels and he suggested I speak with you regarding my treatment from Alex."

"Treatment from Alex?" Ted asked as if he was insulted.

"Yes. From the time that I have been in my new position, I have been summoned to his house and forced to do things I don't want to do to keep my job. I want to keep my job and I need the money, but I don't want to have to keep doing those things with Alex to keep it."

Ted was turning red. "When you say, 'do things,' like what, sex acts?"

"Yes. Demeaning sex acts. I have been totally violated by him. He has used objects on me. He's had me crawl around naked with a leash on my neck." Her eyes welled up with tears. She took a deep swallow and continued. "The things . . . the things he's been doing, and says he will continue to do in order for me to keep my job, are things I don't even want to speak of. Also, he's saying I must have sex with all of my clients to close deals, or else I will fall below quota and lose my job."

Ted sat silent for the longest. If looks could kill, Desiree was feeling as if she'd already be dead.

"Desiree, I have to say, I didn't expect to hear what I just heard. Honestly, I'm quite disappointed. Roger had nothing but wonderful things to say about you, and yet here you are, speaking so ill of Alex. I've known Alex for quite some time. He has dinner with my family often. And now you're here telling these lies on a man that I personally know would never do such despicable things."

Desiree was shocked. She couldn't believe Ted was sitting there accusing her of lying. She wanted to cuss him out, but in the back of her mind, she was unsure of how she'd manage without Malcolm until she found a new job.

Ted continued. "You know what? I think you're a very beautiful and intelligent young lady. I will give you the option of leaving this office and this building, or leaving this office to return to yours and act like we didn't have this conversation. I'll keep it between you and me. I won't even tell Alex about it. As a matter of fact, I'll even tell him that I heard you were such an outstanding employee I wanted to speak with you personally. And I'll also tell you this: if you choose to stay, do understand that we haven't reached this level of success by keeping people who stir up mess. Also keep this in mind: you can't keep going to someone's house and say they are forcing you to do things you don't want to. I wouldn't use my gas to drive somewhere that makes me uncomfortable. You are two grown, consenting adults, and what you do outside of this office is none of my business, and I don't want your relationship drama back in my office. Now, if you have something to discuss about the job or better ways of doing things around here, then feel free to come see me anytime. Just leave me out of the personal relationships."

"This is not a personal relationship. I am being threatened with losing my job if I don't participate," Desiree pleaded with tears.

"Have a good day, Miss Flowers. I'll know your decision by the end of the day, depending on if I still see you."

Ted sat back in his chair with his hands folded across his large belly, as Desiree still sat stunned by his dismissal. Eventually, she got up, wiped her tears away, and left his office. She went to the ladies' room to unleash all of her tears. When she was done, she pulled herself together and went to her office. She tried to call Roger but didn't get an answer. She wanted to quit right then, but she needed to know if Roger could at least help her until something else happened.

"Hey, Desiree," Alex called out for all the other account reps to hear, "I need you to come see me in my office when you can. We need to discuss the Aspen trip you have coming up."

Everything in her screamed, "WALK OUT," but the fear of not being able to manage financially terrified her.

As quickly as she made it to Alex's office, he said, "Come in and close the door."

She wondered if Ted had a discussion with Alex about their meeting. She did as told then took the seat he offered.

"I'd like for you to stop by my house later tonight so we can talk about Aspen."

"I won't be able to. My regular babysitter quit, and I don't have anyone to keep my son right now. I'm trying to find a new babysitter before I have to take the trip to Aspen."

"Bring your son with you then," he said callously with a smile. "I'm sure he'll fall asleep."

"I can't do that."

"You can't or you won't?"

"I will not bring my son from his own home to sleep in a strange place. He has a set bedtime and a set routine. So, no—I can't and I won't."

"I don't like being kept waiting. You have exactly three days to get it worked out, or don't come back. Have I made myself clear?"

"Why can't we discuss the Aspen trip here in your office right now? Do the others have to see you in your home to discuss the trips they take for their accounts?"

Alex looked at Desiree as if he'd spit fire. "You have three days. Now get out of my office."

Desiree got up and left. She immediately attempted to reach Roger again. Still, no response.

12

addy!" Tayshon screamed while Desiree was in the kitchen fixing his dinner.

She ran out to find Malcolm there hugging a jovial Tayshon. Her son was so happy and she was so confused. She was angry. She was hurt.

"Hey, Little Man, let me have a few minutes with your mommy. We got some things to talk about," Malcolm said, putting their son back down to watch television.

"Okay!" Tayshon innocently replied.

Malcolm followed Desiree back into the kitchen.

"We don't have shit to talk about. I'm crazy and you don't have any son with me, remember?"

He hugged her from behind and kissed on her neck. "Stop being like that. Nobody thinks you're crazy, and I would never deny my Little Man. That's my heart right there. Both of you."

"Please! I heard you, Malcolm. I heard you tell that bitch—what was her name, Carol?—I heard you say I was crazy and we don't have any child. I heard y'all talking about the baby she's having."

"Baby, that was probably somebody playing games with you. You didn't hear me say no shit like that. I'm here with you just about every night, so you know that's bullshit."

"I called your fucking phone, and heard your fucking voice, and I also heard you fucking the bitch. And then after all that, I learn that you have been fucking Sharquita's mother? That's some really sick shit."

"Who fucked LaToya? Me?"

"Yes you! She told me you fucked her."

"Please, she's just saying that shit to upset you. You know all these project bitches around here don't like you. I had lost my phone and just got it back the other day. That's probably what you were hearing when you called. Somebody was just fucking with you."

Desiree pushed away from Malcolm as he continued to grope her.

"Get the fuck off of me. You think I'm so stupid. Why are you here now anyway? Where's your little bitch, you fucking child molester? Go be with her—them—I don't care anymore."

The tears poured from Desiree and Malcolm grabbed hold of her to console her. He dug into his jacket pocket and pulled out a little box. He got down on his knee as Desiree's eyes widened and she covered her mouth.

"I want you to be my wife, for real. I want us to get married. I know I said it before, but here's the ring to prove it this time. I can't live without you, Desiree. You and Little Man are everything."

"And what about all those other bitches?"

"They don't mean shit to me. Just like you have to do what you have to do, I have to do what I have to do, but we in this together. Bonnie and Clyde. Forever. Don't be stupid like BM3 was, just throwing me away. She threw me away, and I've been rocking with you ever since. I ain't trying to make no fucking Sharquita, or any other bitch, my woman." Malcolm tried to slide the ring onto Desiree's ring finger, but it was way too big. "We're going to have to get this sized right."

"This ring is not even new," Desiree said upon examination of the ring.

"You ain't ever satisfied, are you? You said you wanted a ring. I'm trying to give you a fucking ring and you want to be an ungrateful bitch. I don't know why I keep fucking with you. You're selfish as fuck."

"I'm sorry. Malcolm, wait!" she called as he was about to leave. "Wait, I'm sorry. I appreciate the ring. I'm just hurt and confused right now."

He turned back and hugged her before kissing her.

"What's going on? You still having problems with your job? They fucking with your coins?" he asked, seeming concerned.

"That dirty bastard hasn't let up. He told me I have three days to be at his house or else I can't return to work. He wanted me there the other night, and when I told him I didn't have a babysitter, his grimy ass is going to tell me to bring my son with me. I refused, so he gave me three days to find an arrangement. I was thinking of just quitting, because I can't deal with that shit, and I definitely won't be having him doing disgusting shit to me in front of my son. I got my paycheck today. It was a lot. Way more than I expected, so now I don't know what the fuck to do. I want to get out of here."

"Well, it sounds like you know what you gotta do. How you gonna talk about you wanna get out of here, but quit your job?"

"So you think I should be taking my son to let some racist bastard degrade and fuck me in front of?" Desiree asked, fuming.

"Hell no, my son ain't gonna be sitting up there with that shit. I'm back. You go handle your business."

"But who said I want you back in here?"

"Well, it sounds like you want to take Little Man with you and let him watch you getting fucked. Is that what you're saying?"

"No! Hell no! I don't want to go let that bastard touch me, is what I'm saying."

"If you quit your job, what will you have then? How you gonna provide for your son?"

"So, you wouldn't help me until I find something else?"

"I've been helping us, but when are *you* going to try to help us? This is the first time you're really trying to help us, and now you want to quit that. You think I like doing half the shit I have to do to provide for us? And don't forget, I have other kids I have to provide for as well, and you knew this when you got with me. I'm just saying, do this little bit until you find something else. You're the one talking about moving on up like *The Jeffersons*. Well, this is called paying dues to live like *The Jeffersons*."

"Malcolm, that bastard does things to hurt me. He tries to inflict pain on me. I tried to go tell the CEO and he wouldn't even believe me. Accused me of lying."

"Now that was some stupid shit. Why would you do something so stupid?"

"I wanted to stop being raped, that's why."

"That shit ain't rape. No wonder dude didn't believe you. You running around talking that bullshit. No, you are voluntarily fucking to keep your job. That is not rape. Nobody is making you fuck to keep your job. That's your choice."

"And if I don't do what I must to keep my job, then I'll be in the streets with my son."

"Man! You must forget who you are talking to. So, you just had to fuck the other dude to keep your job after you already got a promotion?"

Desiree got quiet. Things had become so blurred; she didn't even know what the purpose of her having sex with these men was all about.

"What is it about this guy that makes it so bad? Is it because he busted you with other dude? I don't see what's the big difference. Just go in there and act like you want to fuck him instead of making him feel like he has power over you. You take the initiative. That'll confuse his ass. I bet you might enjoy it better. A lot of these hookers, they start off hating that shit. Later, them bitches be so horny, always wanting a dick up inside of them."

"He sticks things inside of me, and they hurt. He made me walk around like a dog, while he called me his bitch."

"Turn that shit around on the mother fucker. You take the items and stick it in your own pussy, so it won't hurt."

"Ahhhghh!" Desiree screamed. "I don't even know why I'm talking to your ass. Why would I expect you to understand or have an ounce of compassion?"

"I know you think I don't care and think I don't understand. Trust me, I do. I listen to you. I hear everything you say. I want what you want. I believe in you. I also know you have to get some experience on that resume of yours in order to get to the next company and walk in there with a good position. If you don't pay dues now, you'll pay them later or else you'll always stay on the bottom, mad and hating on other bitches, just like the ones hating on you now."

"So, how long are you suggesting I do this shit?"

"If you do things like how I say do things, after while, dude ain't even gonna want you to come over, because he'll realize he can't control you anymore. If he sees you being a freak and running things—please—his ass will quickly find the next bitch to bully."

"You're saying I should go there and act like I want to have sex with him?"

"Yep, and take you a bag of toys and whatever else you think you might want to help you get off. Don't wanna taste nasty, sweaty balls? Then take you something to sweeten that shit up with. Take some chocolate. Some whipped cream. Whatever. Turn the tables on his bitch ass."

As the wheels twirled in Desiree's mind, she was actually glad to have Malcolm there to help her through her crisis. In that moment, she didn't care about all of his other dirt. She also decided that she would not just hand him over to Sharquita nor the potentially pregnant Carol, as BM3 did to her when she got pregnant with Tayshon.

"When are we going to get my ring fixed?" she asked with a smile.

"We can go right after dinner," he replied, as he embraced and kissed her.

The following night, Desiree did as Malcolm advised her. She went and turned the tables on Alex. At first, he was annoyed, but she was determined to control the situation. He ultimately enjoyed it, and for the first time, she felt less violated by the arrangement. In actuality, she enjoyed showing Alex how to please her. She actually smiled all the way on her ride home, because she was so impressed with her performance. As usual, Malcolm wouldn't have sex with her that night, nor did she let on that she was satisfied by Alex, but Malcolm did have a nice hot, candlelit bubble bath waiting for her when she arrived home.

13

Things seemed to be going well in Desiree's mind. Well, at least it was becoming more tolerable. Although Alex was being less of a jerk toward her, he was still dictating when he wanted her to come see him, and each time, she had to play the willing role.

Malcolm suggested she stick with her job for at least six months. However, the trip to Aspen, Colorado had her questioning how much more she'd be able to tolerate. She realized that her sole purpose for being on that trip was to perform sex acts to any and all who wanted, while one of the male account reps handled all of the business dealings. In those five days, she had sex with five different men. On her first night there, she was asked to do a striptease for the men, as her coworker also watched. Although the touching began that night, the sex didn't begin until the following day. She was sure to make the most out of her last encounter, since she already knew that Malcolm wouldn't be touching her when she got home that night. She was at least glad to have him to talk to about everything when she got home.

The house was super clean when she arrived home, and she was certain Malcolm wasn't the one who cleaned it. There was even a plate of food waiting for her to eat, which she also was certain that he didn't cook. Despite starving, she told Malcolm she wasn't hungry and had already eaten. After he ate the food, she went on and fixed herself something else. She chose not to get into any arguments about the food or who cleaned the house. Instead, she just pretended to suddenly be hungry after the mysterious plate of food was no longer a factor. Their son was already cleaned up and in bed by the time she arrived home, which also was unusual. It even surprised her that Malcolm didn't bolt for the door to avoid sex with her, as he normally would. He didn't touch her, but he didn't leave either. He wasn't horny, which let her know that he had just gotten his fill of sex right before she arrived. She fought hard not to bring that issue up as well.

At 4:10 in the morning, there was a loud banging at the door. Desiree turned over and saw Malcolm was still in the bed with her. Although they were upstairs, the banging sounded like it was inside the house. Eventually, she could see flashlights inside the home, which terrified her. The gun she had was hidden in the ceiling of the hallway closet, and there was no way she'd be able to get to it.

However, as the light approached, so did the word, "POLICE!"

Then she became terrified for her son across the hall. He could get up and startle the police, and end up getting shot.

"I'm in here," Desiree yelled out. "Please don't hurt my son. He's in the other room. He's only three."

"Be quiet!" Malcolm whispered.

Just then, a bunch of police swarmed their bedroom.

"Malcolm Waters! We have a warrant for your arrest."

"What the fuck? What warrant?" he yelled as the police officers wrestled him to the floor and cuffed him. "Damn! Can I put some fucking clothes on?"

"Oh my god! What the hell is going on? Malcolm, what did you do?" Desiree cried as another police officer held her at bay.

Tayshon started making his way to the room. One of the police officers grabbed him and took him back inside of his room.

"Please let me go get my son. He's scared. Please let me get him. I don't know what's going on. What is this all about? Please, someone tell me something."

"We have a warrant for Mr. Waters for the statutory rape of a minor who is pregnant with his child."

"Sharquita ain't no fucking minor. That bitch be with all kinds of niggas," Malcolm yelled.

"In the state of Delaware, she's a minor and her mother wants you behind bars."

"Pregnant? Sharquita's pregnant? And you knew she was pregnant?" Desiree asked Malcolm, getting angrier by the second. It was one thing to assume it would happen, but to actually hear it, and to hear that Malcolm didn't seem surprised about the pregnancy was most disturbing. "Malcolm, how long have you known Sharquita was pregnant? Did you know she was pregnant when you came up in here with this bullshit ring?"

"Would you shut the fuck up with the crazy shit? Damn! These motherfuckers got me in handcuffs and no clothes, and you worrying about some damn Sharquita. First of all, she ain't no damn minor, and second of all, she's a ho and ain't no telling whose baby she carrying. I told her to go find her baby daddy. I ain't it."

"The legal age of consent is eighteen. She's not yet eighteen, and her mother has a right to press charges."

"Her stupid fucking mother is just mad that I won't fuck with her no more, grimy bitch."

The police officers all laughed at Malcolm's stupidity. Rather than allow him to put clothes on, they threw a blanket over him and escorted him out into the cold.

"Can you at least take some clothes for him to put on? That's not right to do him like that, and it's only an accusation," Desiree foolishly yelled out to the police as they were escorting Malcolm out. She also noticed in that moment, that her front door lock was broken out. "What the fuck? Look what y'all did to my fucking door! I have a child in here."

"Ma'am, please step back before we take you in for obstruction," an officer said to her.

Desiree went and sat on the sofa and cried. Her son ran into her arms.

"Mommy, I'm scared. Where they taking Daddy?"

"I don't know, baby. I have to find out so we can get Daddy back home."

A more compassionate officer watching the interaction came back to provide Desiree the information of what would happen next and about the nature of the charges brought up against him.

"I know it sounds like I'm trying to defend him, but I swear to you, that girl sleeps with everybody. She even told me she's been sleeping with all of her mother's boyfriends since she was like eleven or twelve years old. I'm not saying it's okay for my fiancé to be with her, but I do know there ain't no way in hell she'd know who the father is. She used to come over here bragging to me about all the different guys she had sex with. Sharquita is a straight up ho."

"Mommy, Miss Sharquita cooked me dinner last night. She let me help her clean up the bathroom."

Desiree could feel her blood boiling. "Sharquita was here yesterday?"

"Yes." Tayshon innocently nodded. "She and Daddy babysit me when you go to work. She was mad Daddy told her she had to go home because you would be mad."

Desiree looked up from her son and saw the police officer writing in a little notebook. She didn't want Tayshon to say anything else, since she figured the police officer was taking note of everything the child was saying.

"Okay, go back up to your room now. Mommy will come up and check on you in a few."

"I'm scared. Where they taking Daddy?"

"I'm sure Daddy will be home soon. Maybe in a couple of days. I don't know."

"Ma'am, I don't mean to be all in your business like this, but you can do much better than this. You have a little boy to think of. He's being exposed to your boyfriend's inappropriate behaviors, and that can't be good for him. I'm sure you both deserve better."

"That's my son's father!" Desiree snapped.

The officer held up both hands. "Forgive me. I was just trying to be helpful. I apologize. You might want to find something to secure that door. I'm going to get going now. I was just hanging around to try to help you." The officer headed to the door.

"I'm sorry. I didn't mean to yell at you. I'm just so upset right now."

"Understood," the officer turned to say before leaving.

Desiree was on the phone calling around for twenty-four-hour locksmiths. She wouldn't be able to rest with her door as it was, especially with a crowd of people still hanging out front in the cold still gossiping. She was thankful to have someone there within an hour, although it was costing a small fortune.

It was difficult for her to sleep after that, because she was angered by her son's words. She was angered about Malcolm having knowledge of Sharquita's pregnancy, yet he said nothing. She was angered that Malcolm would put a ring on her finger, yet expect her to continue sharing him with Sharquita. She was angered that she had to be the one to find a way to get her son's father out of jail and back home. And she was angered that if and when she found a way, he'd still find a way to be with Sharquita.

14

It took almost a week for Malcolm to get a bond, and Desiree was determined to do whatever it took to get him out of jail. Although it wasn't the first time Malcolm was missing from the home, it was the first time that Tayshon cried nonstop for his father.

She even went to Alex for an advance on her pay, since she still hadn't been able to reach Roger. Alex sent her to the home of one of his friends, and then he authorized her request for an advance. Never before had Desiree considered herself a prostitute, but after sexing the 400-plus-pound man with one leg, she definitely considered herself one on that day. He was a pure slob. His body odor was repulsive. He was adamant about having sex without any condoms, because he hadn't had any sex in several years and wanted to savor the moment, since he knew it would never happen again. He warned that he'd let Alex know that she didn't make him happy if she refused. The only thing she was happy about was that his penis was so short and stout that he didn't even realize that he wasn't inside of her as she rode on top of him. She especially couldn't stand him trying to eat her pussy, treating it like it was a Twinkie that he was trying to cram down his throat. Nonetheless, she did her part, and Alex was kind enough to keep up his end of the bargain.

Desiree paid the bondsman $7,500 for Malcolm to be released. She was certain that they said he'd be out by that evening or the next morning. Almost two days had gone by, and she had yet to see or hear from Malcolm. She called the bond company to see if they had her money and decided not to bond him out.

"Hi, my name is Desiree Flowers, and I came in and paid you guys $7,500 for my fiancé's bond, two days ago. I was told that he should have been out that night or the next morning. I haven't heard back from anyone."

"What is the inmate's name?" a woman asked.

"His name is Malcolm Waters."

"Give me a minute. Let me check and see what's his status."

"Thank you," Desiree said before the woman place her on hold.

The woman returned to the phone after a few minutes. "Hi, Miss Flowers?"

"Yes."

"I checked our records and then called over to the jail. Mr. Waters was released that same night, day before yesterday."

"I'm sorry, but I'm confused. He hasn't been home at all."

"Well, I'm not sure what else to tell you. I will say this, woman-to-woman, we see this happen all too often. Men use women to get them out of jail, and then the woman never hears from him again."

"That's my fiancé. We share a son together. We've lived together for the past four years. He was in the bed with me when the police came to pick him up, with our child watching," Desiree said, getting desperate as she began to choke up. She couldn't—she refused to believe Malcolm would do something like that to her. "Well, maybe he just didn't want to be back in the house after being traumatized like he was that night. I could understand that."

"But he didn't even call you to let you know he was out, and you're the one who put up all that money for his release? It's one thing to not come by the house, but it's another thing that he wouldn't even pick up a phone to say thank you or let you know he was out. That's not cool at all."

Desiree didn't want to hear another word. She hung up on the woman and immediately began trying to call Malcolm.

"Hello," the familiar voice answered.

"Where's Malcolm?" Desiree asked, remembering the voice as the one she heard called Carol, that Malcolm swore was someone pranking her.

"He's sleep. Who's this?"

"I'm his fiancée. I'm the one who bailed him out of jail."

"Fiancée? Jail? I don't know what kind of game somebody has been running on you, but there is no way in hell that *my husband* is your fiancé. Second, my husband was not in any damn jail. He was away on business, like he normally is. Come to think of it, you sound like that same crazy bitch calling here before talking about your baby daddy bullshit."

"What do you mean, your husband? Are we talking about Malcolm Waters?" Desiree asked, feeling the air escape her.

"And that would make me Mrs. Waters, so I suggest you stop bothering him before we file a restraining order against your dumb ass. It's like this: If you have to keep calling here and have me keep telling you the same thing over and over, then obviously that should be your clue that regardless of whatever fling you had, he just wasn't that into you."

"How long have you been married to Malcolm? We've lived together for the past four years," Desiree said, still refusing to believe the woman.

"I really don't need to answer any of your fucking questions, but it seems you're going to be on some bullshit if I don't prove it to you. Also, you need to really stop with that shit about y'all living together for some four years," Carol laughed. "You know what? I'm going to send you a text message from this number in a few minutes, so you can see who the fool is. Hopefully, you'll leave us alone, because if you don't, like I said, we will get a restraining order against you." Then she hung up.

Desiree was on the verge of hyperventilating, but she was still holding on to the idea that the woman was lying and that somehow she got hold of Malcolm's phone and was saying those things to hurt Desiree. However, minutes later, multiple text messages started coming through on her phone. They were all from Malcolm's number. There were several photos. One was a marriage certificate for Malcolm and Carol from three years prior. The next photo was Malcolm holding a little girl that looked around five or six years old, who was obviously his daughter. The next photo was Malcolm and the woman together, kissing for a selfie. Another photo was of Malcolm sleeping in a large, beautiful bedroom. There was a photo of her hand with an expensive looking wedding ring. Finally, there was a photo of her pregnant stomach with a piece of paper showing the date, letting Desiree know the woman JUST took the photo to send to her. Finally, she got a text reading:

You satisfied now? STAY THE FUCK AWAY FROM MY HUSBAND!!!

In that moment, Desiree realized she was in a huge financial hole. That $7,500 she got was an advance on pay she hadn't earned yet, and it would be deducted from her next paycheck. She sat for the longest, trying to wrap her mind around how Malcolm could have pulled off the game he had. She couldn't believe that Malcolm married the woman while they were actually together. Despite the photos, Desiree still was not willing to believe it. She would need Malcolm himself to tell her. She decided that the marriage certificate was a fraud or something made up on a computer. She figured the photo of Malcolm sleeping could have been taken any day. However, when she checked the photo details, it showed the current date, and the time was only minutes earlier.

Desiree was at her wits' end. She wanted to end her life. Tayshon was still crying for his father to return. As if matters couldn't get any worse, Sharquita was at the door. Feeling completely defeated, Desiree just let her in.

"Where's Malcolm?"

"I don't give a fuck anymore. Didn't you have him locked up?"

"I didn't do that. My mother did that. I would never go to the police about anything. My mother gonna act all brand new because I'm with Malcolm now. She didn't seem to give a fuck when her grown, old-ass men were fucking her little daughters. She's only mad because I'm pregnant by the man she wants to be with. She talking about she can take him anytime she feels like it, but she just don't want him anymore."

Tayshon came running down the stairs and was excited to see Sharquita. Desiree went upstairs and left them alone. A while passed and Desiree hadn't returned. Sharquita called for Desiree to come back down because Tayshon was hungry and wanted Sharquita to fix him something to eat. Desiree stumbled down the stairs and then went and plopped down on the sofa.

"You okay?" Sharquita asked. "I wanted to know if it's okay for me to cook for Little Man. He said he's hungry. I'm pregnant now and ain't trying to have any drama or be fighting, so I'm asking you if it's okay. If not, I'll just leave and you can do whatever."

Desiree wasn't really answering. She was just waving her hand as if she were speaking.

Sharquita looked at her and asked again, "Are you okay? Are you high?"

Desiree started slurring and then rested her head back on the armrest of the sofa and closed her eyes.

"Desiree! Did you take something? Are you high?"

Desiree continued to slur incoherently.

Sharquita pulled out her phone and frantically called 9-1-1.

"Oh my god! I'm here with this girl and I think she's trying to kill herself or something. I don't know if she's high. She was fine a little while ago, but then she came downstairs and now it looks like she's high or something. I can't make out anything she's saying. I'm here with her son. He's like four years old—or he's getting ready to have a birthday like next week," Sharquita screamed into the phone. "Desiree! Desiree!" she yelled, trying to wake Desiree. "She's not waking up. I'm pregnant. I can't pick her up. I'm way short, and she's much taller than me. I'm not trying to hurt my baby. Y'all just need to hurry up and get here."

"My mommy sleeping?" Tayshon asked Sharquita.

"Why would this selfish bitch do this in front of her son? Now he's over here looking at her, asking if she's sleeping, telling her to wake up," Sharquita cried into the phone.

Within minutes, paramedics, police, and firemen were at the door and went to work to try to resuscitate Desiree from her overdose of pain pills. She was then rushed to the hospital, while Sharquita kept Tayshon.

15

i, Desiree. I'm Dr. Churchill. I'm a psychiatrist here to talk to you about what happened yesterday."

Desiree had been sleeping comfortably and was startled by the voice. The sleep was so good she hadn't even realized she was in a hospital bed.

"Desiree, wake up. I came to talk to you about your suicide attempt."

It took a minute for Desiree to get her bearings. She had to think back herself. "Suicide?" she asked.

"Yes. You don't remember trying to kill yourself? You overdosed on pain pills yesterday. You're in the hospital. You're very lucky to be alive right now. Do you want to tell me what brought you to that point?"

As Desiree started remembering everything that led up to that moment of her deciding to end it all, she broke down and cried from realizing she didn't succeed in ending her horrible life.

Dr. Churchill seemed patient and kind. "It's okay. You can let it all out. I'm here to help you. I'm sure things can't be that bad. I know sometimes when we get overwhelmed, it kind of feels like the end of the world for us, but it's just a hurdle, and when we get over it, life gets better. So, take a minute, and when you're ready, you can tell me what brought you to this point."

"I couldn't take it anymore. I just couldn't take it anymore. It was getting harder and harder and harder," Desiree answered when she was composed.

"What's been happening? Did it just start or has it been building up?"

"I think it's been building up. So many times I hated coming home, and I just wanted to die. Sometimes coming home was just as bad as being out."

"Why is that?"

"I had to go to work and be raped time and time and fucking time again, only to come home to a lying, cheating, asshole who I just realized must have been my pimp. We share a son together. I thought we were engaged to be married, even though he would cheat on me or stay gone half the time."

"I'm sorry, when you say you were raped, do you mean that literally?"

"Being forced to have sex and do sex acts against your will. That's rape, right?"

"Yes, but who? You say you had to go to work? Did you report it?"

Desiree gave a hollow laugh. "Report it to who? I told the CEO and he called me a liar. Told me if I wanted to keep my job, then I pretty much needed to shut up and go do my job or leave. I have a son to take care of, so I had to deal with that nasty bastard and everything they'd tell me to do. If they said to go fuck clients and let them do whatever they wanted to me, I had to do that. If he said to be at his house and let him stick shit inside of me and walk me around his fucking house on my hands and knees while he calls me his bitch, I had to do that too. And he even wanted me to bring my son while he raped me. I had broken up with my so-called fiancé, but when he came back begging, he had the nerve to give me a ring, I let him back in, just to keep from losing my job and exposing my son to his mother being raped. That motherfucker didn't give a damn about me. If anything, he would try to intentionally inflict physical pain on me. So you think I think he'd give a damn about shielding my son? No! And then when my so-called fiancé got locked up for statutory rape, like a jackass, I ran to his rescue to get him out. I went to my job to get an advance of $7,500. They made me fuck some one-legged man who is so fucking fat he can't even wipe his own ass. Then the man says if I don't let him do it to me raw, he'll tell my boss that I didn't make him happy."

Desiree screamed into her hands from the overwhelming thoughts and sobbed again. Dr. Churchill tried to console her.

When Desiree pulled herself together, she stoically continued. "Then to make matters worse, I'm waiting for my so-called fiancé to come back home to his crying son, who watched the police take him out of our home in the middle of the night, only to learn he had a wife he decided to go home to. Would you believe that? A fucking wife. We've been living together over four years, and some bitch sends me a copy of their marriage certificate, saying they were married two or three years ago. I'm in the hole for $7,500, that I had to—whatever—to get his ass out of jail to help me take care of my son so I can go to work and keep my job, but then he decides to dip. And to add insult to injury, the underage bitch he got pregnant comes to my house and can console my own son better than I can. My son was miserable as hell until that bitch showed up. That's how much time my so-called fiancé would have that ho around my son while I was out there doing stupid shit to keep my job and a roof over our heads."

Desiree was bitter and angry more than sad in that moment.

"Did you have to give this fiancé your paycheck?"

"Yes. He was the one who was taking care of everything. As far as I know, he didn't have any jobs, but he always had a lot of money. At one point, he would take care of me, so I didn't think it was a big deal for me to give him my money to let him manage the household. He would buy my clothes, pay the bills. I didn't think it was a big deal. I thought we were in this together. When I called his phone yesterday, because I couldn't understand why he hadn't come home yet, and I had already paid the $7,500 for his bond, some woman answered his phone saying he was sleeping. I called him before when we broke up, and the woman answered and said she didn't know anything about me or our son. I heard him talking in the background. Then weeks later, he wants to come back to me with a ring—a used ring—saying he wants us to get married. He swore to me it wasn't him on the phone and someone was playing a trick on me because they hate me. That is true. I hate where we live because I know most of the girls around there can't stand me because they be wanting him."

"You took a $7,500 advance to pay his bond and he never contacted you after that?"

"I didn't even know he was out. I called the bond office and they told me he was released two days prior. That's when I called his phone and the lady answered it. She sent me a whole bunch of photos to prove that they were really married, as well as a picture of her pregnant stomach."

"So, when you went to your job and asked for an advance, how did it come about that you slept with the heavyset man?"

"I went to my immediate supervisor, Alex Krammer, who is the same fucker that forces me to come to fuck him in his home at least once a week, and he told me since this was a special circumstance, I'd have to do something special for it. I didn't know what that meant. He gave me this address and told me I had to go take care of his good friend, and his friend had to report back that he was happy. Otherwise, he would not approve the advance and I'd lose my job for making his friend unhappy. And that was that. I was so stressed, because I wasn't sure if Alex would keep up his end of the bargain once I did what he told me to.

"Not only that, every business trip, they make me be the sex slave for whoever and whatever. In New Orleans, I had to let ten Japanese businessmen dig their hands inside of me, just so they could get the account. In Aspen, they made me do a striptease for five businessmen and my male coworker, and then I had to have sex with those five men during the five days we were there. If I didn't, I wouldn't have a job to return to. And after all of that, Malcolm got to take my money, to supposedly take care of the household. He wasn't even around before I got my paycheck. He just so happened to come that same day I got paid with a ring, talking about let's get married. Stupid me told him about my huge paycheck, and then I turned it over to him to manage everything."

"Did he know your pay dates?"

Desiree seemed to think about it for a moment. "Now that I think about it, he did. That's probably why he decided to come back when he did."

Dr. Churchill nodded her head, indicating she agreed. "Yeah, I definitely think he was playing with you. Did he know about all the things you had to do to keep your job?"

"Yes. He was the one telling me to hold on for at least six months, so I could have the experience on my resume and be able to get a better job somewhere else. I told him I wanted to quit and that I hated what Alex was doing to me and how he was hurting me. Malcolm told me to just deal with it, and eventually Alex would get bored with me and move on to someone else."

"Did he also know about the other men from your business trips?"

"I had just come back from that first trip to New Orleans. I was exhausted and wanted to just get in my bed and relax. I was traumatized from the whole experience. I wanted Malcolm to hold me and tell me everything would be all right. Before I could leave New Orleans, he told me he was moving the little young girl—the minor that he got locked up for—into our home because she didn't have anyplace to go. I get home from my trip that night, and they're in my bed, having sex as if they were waiting for me to come home to see. He knew I was on the way home. I even listened to them say they were getting in another round before I came home. I won't lie; I was ready to kill them that night. All I wanted to do was cry in his arms, in our bed, but I couldn't, because they were too busy fucking in our bed. I got a knife and that's when they ran out the house." Desiree intentionally left the part about the gun out. "I didn't see him again until when I got paid and he came with that bullshit ring.

"That night when I ran him out, I realized my son was missing. I tried calling him and he wouldn't answer the phone. Eventually, the woman who said she's his wife answered, and I actually listened to them having sex. I heard him tell her he didn't have a son with me and I was some crazy ex. Not long after that, the other young girl who he got pregnant, her mother comes to my door with my son, saying she too was having sex with my fiancé. The little young girl, Sharquita, she claims all of her mother's men would have sex with her since she was like eleven or twelve years old."

Dr. Churchill's eyes stretched. "Wow! Sharquita? Isn't she the one who called 9-1-1 yesterday? I believe that was the name I saw on your papers. How did that come about?"

"I don't know. I think I was just at my wits' end by that point. She's the reason Malcolm was locked up, but then she going to come to my house looking for her baby's father. That was right after I learned that he supposedly has a five or six-year-old daughter with that woman who says she's his wife—and a baby on the way with her as well. My son wouldn't stop crying for his father, but the minute Sharquita shows up, he gets happy. I even heard him ask if she's going to stay with him because he loves when she stay with him. I just wanted all the pain to stop, so I found a bottle of pain pills in the medicine cabinet. At first I was going to just take two to rest, but then I figured all of the pain would still be there when I woke up. That's when I decided I didn't want to wake up anymore. I don't really remember much after that. I kind of remember talking to Sharquita, but I don't know what about. I don't remember anything after that."

"That is definitely a lot to deal with. Do you feel in danger with Malcolm? Do you think he'll hurt you?"

"Please, after what he did to me, I'd be afraid of hurting him. I think he's a coward. He couldn't even face me to tell me the truth about his wife and daughter—if that is the truth."

"Why do you think that is not the truth?" Dr. Churchill asked.

"I don't know. It makes absolutely no sense how he could have hidden a whole family for all these years while we're living together, even though he would frequently disappear. That marriage certificate could have been some mess she made up on the computer just to upset me. I'm telling you, there are so many hateful girls where we live. There's project about a block away, and I would tell Malcolm all the time that I wanted to move from over there because those girls hated me."

"Why do they hate you?"

"Because they all want to be with him. And they all say that I think I'm all that. They call me an ugly bitch with good hair, and say that's all I have going for myself."

"Wow! That is mean. I hope you do know, you are a very beautiful young lady, and you have plenty of happy life waiting in front of you. I know it might seem very dark right now, but I want to give you something that will help take the edge off of that depression. I want to keep you here for a couple of more days until I'm comfortable that you are no longer a threat to yourself or anyone else. I also need to contact a police officer to talk to you about the rape situation. I am legally obligated to report it. I don't know what, if anything, they might do, since it wasn't like you reported it when it happened, but at least you can explore your options."

"So basically, I am now out of a job and no longer have a way to care for my son?" Desiree asked as the tears returned.

"Do you really want to have to go back to endure that?"

"No! Hell no! I have a fucking master's degree and I just want to be able to use that and what's in my mind to do my job."

"Okay, well, it's time for you to let go of all that abuse and move forward to a place where you no longer have to do those things."

"How will I take care of my son?"

"Desiree, were you really concerned with your son while you were trying to end your life? You left your son with a pregnant seventeen-year-old, that you just told me shares men with her own mother. Child Protective Services is now involved, but you need to focus on getting yourself better before you think about how you're going to take care of your son."

"Oh my god! They're going to take my son from me?" she cried.

"Should they leave your son in a position to find his mother dead? That's what would have happened had Sharquita not helped you. What if that girl left your house and your son would have been all alone? You didn't think of any of that, and you have to admit, that was pretty selfish of you. Now, for now, let's just focus on you. Do you have any family members that could care for your son while you get yourself together?"

"My family lives up in the Bronx in New York. In the projects. I don't want my son there. My son has been in Delaware his entire life. I was living and going to school in Philly before he was born. After I got pregnant, Malcolm found us the place in Delaware. I hate it, but it's not as bad as living up in the projects in New York. Plus, we live in a townhome, which is much better for my son."

"Like I said, you'll need to get yourself together first. Hopefully, he'll get to go stay with family."

"They've never seen my son!"

Dr. Churchill was stunned. "And why is that?"

Desiree covered her face and took a long pause before answering. "Malcolm didn't feel it was in my best interest to be around my family, because they didn't really give a damn about me. I had to pay my own way through college. My family never helped me, but they always had their hands out. That's why Malcolm didn't want them around."

"Four years? You did say your son is four years old, or did I see that in a report somewhere?"

"My son will be four next week. No, my family has never seen him."

"So basically, he kept you isolated from your family."

"I can't blame it all on him. He is just going by what I told him."

"Desiree, Desiree, Desiree. You are going to need an awful lot of counseling. Right now, I'm just here to do a quick assessment to evaluate you on how you ended up here and how long I think you need to be here. I feel you could use some intense psychotherapy. And you're sure you don't feel threatened by Malcolm?"

"No. Not at all."

"Okay. Well, anyway, you get some rest, and I'll get that medicine prescribed and make some phone calls about that rape situation," Dr. Churchill said as she got up from the seat next to Desiree's bed.

16

The plainclothes female officer took a seat next to Desiree's bed and flashed her badge. "Hi, Miss Flowers. Not sure if you remember me. I'm Detective Weisberg. We spoke the other day before they moved you down here to the psych unit, about your rape case concerning your supervisor, Alex Krammer."

"Oh yes. I remember you. You were here with the other guy. I think this medicine got me messed up. I'm ready to leave this hospital, especially this stupid unit where we can only watch television in the community room," Desiree said, holding her head.

Detective Weisberg smiled. "I'm sure. You've been here for a week now."

"I don't even know anymore. I can hardly remember the days."

"Well, I'm going to need you to try very hard to remember some things," the detective said, trying to shift into more of a professional mode. "I have been investigating your case, and Mr. Krammer has produced several videos of the two of you having what appears to be consensual sex. In reviewing those videos, there was nothing about it that gave the appearance that you were doing anything against your will."

Desiree was both shocked and confused as she lifted up from her lounging position on her bed and sat up to full attention. "Videos? What videos? I don't know anything about videos. Malcolm told me if I stopped showing Alex that he was hurting me, Alex would lose interest. I told Ted Dinkins about the whole thing, but he said he knew Alex would never do such a thing and told me to pretend the conversation never happened. Alex said if I didn't do what he said, I would be fired. He even made me go to that nasty, fat man's house to get the advance I asked for and sent me a text that said, 'Make sure he is happy.' If I'm lying, why would I go see his fat friend or know where he lives? How would I know anything about him? Alex That man was like five or six hundred pounds, with one leg, and smelled like poop. Do you seriously think I would want to consensually go have sex with that under any circumstance?" She spoke a mile a minute as the tears began racing from her eyes.

Detective Weisberg got up to find some tissue for Desiree to wipe her tears as well as the snot that began escaping from her nose. "Honestly, I believe everything you have said thus far. However, if this case went to a jury and they had to watch the videos we had to watch, there is no way they would believe he made you do something against your will. Also, when we spoke with Mr. Dinkins, as expected, he denied that you came to see him about any allegations involving Mr. Krammer. When we told him that Krammer produced videos of the two of you sexually engaged, Dinkins pretty much defended Krammer by saying the company has a strict sexual harassment policy, and if employees choose to date outside of company hours or property, that's between them. My colleague pointed out a paragraph in that policy that stated supervisors are in no way allowed to date employees or they will be terminated immediately. Then Mr. Dinkins said he'd just have to counsel Mr. Krammer to remind him of that policy."

The detective's eyes shifted around the bare, Caribbean-green room that only contained a bed and the one chair. He tried to avoid Desiree's sad, attentive eyes, before dropping the next bomb on her fragile mental state. "Unfortunately, you no longer have a job. They claim it's because you haven't been with the company long and have already missed a great deal of work, and it had nothing to do with the allegations. Also, they feel with your suicide attempt, they have to make sure other employees are safe from you. So, the bottom line is, after speaking with the D.A., our investigation against Mr. Krammer will pretty much now conclude—not because we don't believe you, but because we know a jury will not, and you have no other proof beyond your word. I will say this: you may still need a lawyer. Now Krammer is making a bit of noise, trying to defend himself in the media, with an attorney talking about suing you for defamation and pressing charges for false allegations. They've created somewhat of a lynch mob against you, asserting you're making it difficult for real victims of rape. In all actuality, he's the one defaming himself, because this matter wasn't made public until *he* made it public. It was a private investigation that he's turned into a media circus. He's even gone as far as announcing that you're in a nut house right now because you are bitter and crazy and want attention because of a boyfriend dumping you."

Desiree was too stunned to speak. Her mouth was open, but she couldn't form any words.

"Miss Flowers, the reason I'm delivering this information to you is because I'm thinking it would be best for you to remain here in the hospital for a few more days. Hopefully this mess will die down soon. I can just imagine how difficult it would be for you to walk out of this door right now and get hit with the cameras and mean, heartless people desperate to write a story and twist up words and make you look like the villain instead of the victim."

Detective Weisberg took a seat on the bed next to Desiree and consoled her as she sobbed.

"Desiree—Can I call you Desiree? I just feel a bond with you."

Desiree, still unable to speak, nodded her head.

"Desiree, I'm going to tell you something I haven't told anyone before. I'm speaking woman-to-woman. I've had to deal with similar circumstances twice in my life. I was in the military before I joined the police department. I've had to deal with mess in both places. I'm telling you this because I know while you're going through it, you feel hopeless and helpless, like there's no point in going on with life. I decided to press through, and now I mainly deal with rape cases or special victims. Even now, it's hard at times when we get those cases that we can't get justice for, and we know the predator is guilty as sin.

That also makes me feel helpless. But sometimes the system works, and then it gives me a little hope and helps me to keep pushing to help as many people as I can. I know you won't see it right now, but believe me—this time will be like a blessing in disguise. One day you will be so happy that you'll feel guilty for being so happy. I know because that is where I am now in my personal life. You just have to hang in there and trust and believe that Alex Krammer will get what's coming to him. It might not be next week or next month, but karma will find him."

"Thank you," Desiree mumbled. "This is why I didn't want to say anything to anyone. I just wanted it all to end."

"I understand, but trust me, it doesn't have to all end. You don't want to throw the baby out just because the bathwater is dirty. Things will get better." Dectective Weisberg stood from the bed and continued to stroke the tangled mess on Desiree's head, "Anyhow, I have to get going. I'm going to be on the lookout for you, because I truly believe that you will find the strength to turn this tragedy into a success story, and one day, you'll be in a position to pave the way for others like yourself. Just keep your head up."

Desiree smiled as she watched the detective leave. After that, she sobbed into her pillow again.

Later that evening, while in the community room, watching the news crucify her, Desiree was shocked to see Roger Daniels being interviewed. She was even more surprised to see him in a wheelchair.

"I think it's insane how they are treating this young lady. She came to me to inform me of the abuse by Alex Krammer. I was the one who told her to go meet with Ted Dinkins about Alex, because I knew about the company's sexual harassment policy, and I knew Ted had zero tolerance for such behaviors.

"I also find it despicable that Alex has publicly declared that he had what he called a consensual relationship with a subordinate, yet he still has a job. That should let the world know that the young lady made a report to Ted which fell on deaf ears.

"On the evening of the same day Miss Flowers went to meet with Ted, I was brutally beaten and left for dead. I have been in recovery since and am still recovering. When I was attacked, I was told that I was being beaten for being a troublemaker.

"So, while the media is trying to crucify the victim, they should be asking *why* Alex is still employed with the company, despite the policy, *even if* it was consensual as he claims. No, any videos you may see would be things that Alex forced her to do. If he wanted her to look like she was enjoying it, then that's what he would force her to do in order to keep her job. He needs to show the videos of him walking her around his home on her knees with a leash around her neck while he called her his bitch or his 'N' word. Yes, these are all the things she told me about, but I made the mistake of sending her to Ted Dinkins, thinking he would be trustworthy enough to properly handle the situation. It wouldn't surprise me one bit to learn there are many other women he's done this to, who also were too afraid to speak up. I don't know who all was behind my attack, nor can I prove it, but it seems pretty damn coincidental to me, don't you think?"

That was the end of the news interview with Roger. Then other news programs started rerunning Roger's interview and later tried to get a statement from Alex's attorney and Ted Dinkins. They were all running from the media. That finally made Desiree smile. She was devastated to see Roger in a wheelchair and learn what happened to him because of him giving her advice. She tried to recall how Ted and Alex would know to go after Roger for advising her. She was also confused as to why they would hurt Roger and not her. Nonetheless, she was happy to know that Roger was still in her corner and she couldn't wait to get out of the hospital to let him know how much she appreciated him for publicly defending her honor.

17

"Mommy! Daddy!" Desiree shouted, surprised when her family came to her hospital room as she was preparing for discharge. They hugged her. "What are you doing here? How did you know where I was at?"

Her mother, Anelda, answered. "It's been all over the news and on the Facebook. How could I miss it? I heard them say something about you being in the nut house because *estupido* dumped you, so I started making some calls. Daddy was wondering where the baby was at. We called Social Services, and was able to get little Tayshon. *Es tan bonito. Mi nieto. Cuatro anos de edad.*"

Desiree couldn't stop smiling. "Where is he now?"

"They wouldn't let us bring him up here. He's with your sister," her father, Ernesto, answered. "They said he will have to go home with us until they say you can have him back. You need to just move back home anyhow. You have people in New York. You are alone here. I don't know why you wouldn't let us know where you were all this time."

"I'm sorry. I don't even know why," Desiree cried.

She was happy and sad, all rolled into one. She was thrilled to see her parents after so many years, but she was sad about not being able to have custody of her son.

"They say you go home today?" Anelda asked.

"Yes. I am waiting on my discharge papers right now."

"Daddy rented a car to pick up the baby. We can take you home to get his stuff to take with us. You should go back with us."

"I know, Mommy. It's just that I don't want to go back to live there anymore. I was so happy about being out of there, and I never wanted to have to go back there."

"You make it sound so bad there. It's beautiful there. They cleaned it up a lot since you left. All those drugs are cleaned up. They have nice gardens now."

"I just hated it there. I remember people always wanting to fight me. I wanted more for my life. I wanted to get my education and have a good life— make a lot of money and give my son the world."

"And you finish school?" Anelda asked.

"Yes. I have a bachelor's and a master's degree." Desiree proudly smiled.

"You wouldn't tell even your own *madre y popi*? *Por que no*?"

"I'm sorry, Mommy. I don't know why. I was listening to Malcolm telling me that you didn't have my best interest the way he did and you'd be using me for money."

"Desiree, no one can make you listen to that. You should know for yourself. We didn't have much, but we pull together as a family," Ernesto gently scolded.

"I said I'm sorry. I can't change what happened. I did a lot of stupid shit, and that's why I'm here in this stupid hospital," Desiree said as she began to cry again.

Her parents hugged her.

"You just remember, family comes first, from now on. You promise?" Ernesto told her.

"I promise."

The following day, Desiree's parents took Tayshon to New York with them. That night, Desiree was back home, resting in her bed and watching television. She was still having difficulty sorting out her feelings with everything, while taking the prescribed psychiatric medications from the hospital. The medicine would make her feel strange, as if living in a fog, even at times hallucinating as she'd see shadows moving in her peripheral. She also found herself having problems remembering things, but the hospital staff told her that she'd eventually adjust to the side effects.

She heard someone at the door, and it sounded like they were trying to use a key. A minute later, there was a knock. She went down to see who it was, although she was afraid. It was almost midnight. She peeped out of the window and spotted Malcolm's car. He continued to knock as she stood behind the door, fidgeting with her hands, debating whether to let him in. She finally opened the door. She felt at the very least, he owed her an explanation.

"What do you want?" she yelled as she flung the door open.

He pressed his way past her to get inside and then tried to take her into his arms. She pushed away from him.

"Baby, stop being like that. Why you trippin'?"

Desiree couldn't believe her ears. "Did you just ask me why am I tripping? No, motherfucker, *you* must be tripping to be showing up at my fucking door after all the hell I've been through."

"Why you change the locks? You know this is still my place. You can't be just locking me out and shit."

"Go tell that to the policemen who busted out the other locks when they came to take your raggedy ass to jail. Was I was supposed to just leave the door with no locks? And I want my $7,500 I had to put up to get your ass out of jail for you to run on home to your fucking wife. You are such a bitch—a fucking coward."

"Wife? What wife? If I got a wife, then how am I here now? How was I living with your ass if I have a wife?"

"You know, I tried to convince myself that the bitch was lying to me, but when I really thought about it, you were *not* home every night. And now that I really think about it, you were hardly ever home. You were always in the damn streets, or so I thought. While I was thinking you were bouncing around with all these different hoes in the streets, you were running home to your wife. Oh, and your other fucking children."

"I don't know what kind of shit you on, but I don't have any wife or other children that you didn't already know about."

"Did you tell me that Sharquita was pregnant with your baby? No! No, you didn't. There's no telling how many other children you have, and just the same way you denied our son, you have the nerve to stand in my face denying that little girl that I saw in the picture who looks just like you. I also saw the picture of the fat bitch having your baby now, and a picture of your marriage certificate. And she was sure to send me a picture of you sleeping in her bed and one of you two kissing. Now explain all that shit."

"First of all, you know damn well that baby Sharquita got is not mine. You know like I know, she's a ho, and there ain't a nigga in the hood that haven't been up inside her ass."

"But you would stick your dick up in her raw knowing she's a ho and then turn around and fuck me? You're a nasty bastard."

"You calling me all these names as if we didn't have an understanding. Have you not been fucking different motherfuckers for as long as we've been together? I had to deal with all that shit. The mother of my son—the woman that I love and asked to be my wife. And speaking of wife, if I was married, why would I ask you to be my wife? Didn't I just put a ring on your finger?"

"Actually, you didn't. You played like you were putting a ring on my finger, but then supposedly took it to get it resized. I haven't seen the shit since."

"It ain't like you didn't know I was locked the fuck up on some bullshit. You saw how them motherfuckers did me—took me out the house damn near naked just to humiliate me. And then you wonder why I didn't just pop back up at this door?"

Malcolm looked as if he wanted to cry. He went and plopped down on the sofa and buried his face in his hands. Desiree stood watching him for a few minutes and then went and sat next to him, wrapping her arm around his back.

"I'm sorry. Yeah, that was really fucked up what they did to you. I know they did that shit on purpose. They could have let you put on clothes. It wasn't like you were fighting them or anything."

Malcolm stayed silent for a while, still seeming distressed.

"Did you eat yet? You want me to fix you something to eat?" she asked.

"Yeah, fix me a sandwich."

Desiree got up to go fix him a sandwich. While she did, he made his way up the stairs and to the bed, where he began undressing. Desiree was a little put off seeing him in the bed naked under the covers. She handed him the sandwich.

"You haven't even asked about Tayshon. CPS took him from me, and now my parents have custody of him."

"That's good he's with your parents. With my situation all fucked up, there was no way I was able to go pick him up. I asked BM3 to go get him for me, but she didn't want to get involved. She said something about it being harder because she was in Pennsylvania and she's not actually related."

"I guess that makes sense," she said, accepting his explanation.

"Come here, get back in the bed. I miss you."

"I honestly don't know what to think or how to feel right now. You got me all fucked up."

"Do you love me?"

"Yes."

"Do you believe I love you?"

"Yes."

"Then that's all we need. They might try to throw shit at us, but we're going to be all right. You're my ride-or-die."

"I don't even have a job anymore, and that dumb motherfucker gets away with murder because he made videotapes of me having sex with him. The police won't even lock him up, and everybody is thinking I'm lying on him."

"Fuck them. Fuck their job. You'll get another job, and you'll be smarter about your shit the next time." After he swallowed the last of the sandwich he crammed into his mouth, he held out his arms, "Come here. Let Daddy kiss away the pain."

She playfully hit him. "You are the pain." She chuckled.

That made him laugh and then grab her, pulling her onto the bed for a kiss. Minutes later, he was making passionate love to her. She cried because of the pleasure he was giving her, and because her right mind was telling her that she had no business letting Malcolm touch her.

Afterward, they laid watching television with her wrapped in his arms. She didn't know when would be the best time to bring the subject of Carol back up, but she chose that moment.

"Malcolm, are you really married to that bitch and is she having your baby? You always say we're in this together, but you won't be honest with me. I've always told you everything."

"No, I have no wife and no baby on the way. You did some crazy shit that pissed me the fuck off and I wanted to pay you back. That's all that was."

Desiree sat up in the bed stunned. "Crazy shit that I did? What the fuck did I do? I told you about that ignorant fucker, and you knew how much I hated dealing with him."

"But you forgot to tell me about that black dude you been fucking. And you had the nerve to be having a fucking family fun day at Chuck E. Cheese with my motherfucking son. That's a big no-no, and that's why that motherfucker is lucky to be alive right now. He shouldn't even be breathing right now, but then I see his bitch ass up on TV telling everybody how he tried to help you. Why you never told me that motherfucker you were fucking was a black dude?"

Desiree could feel her heart in her throat. She wasn't sure how to answer or what to say.

"Oh, now the cat got your tongue? So, while you were telling me about this Alex dude, you've been in a relationship behind my back with that other motherfucker."

"I wasn't in a relationship with him. I went to meet with him so I would know what to do to stop Alex. He told me to go talk to the CEO, and that's what I did. I have never been with him sexually other than that one time I told you about."

"Why didn't you tell me he was black? You heard me call him a cracker time and time again, but you never corrected me. That makes me think there was more to it. And then when we beat his ass and I took his phone, I saw all kinds of pictures of my so-called woman, and I'm wondering how this motherfucker got naked photos of my woman stored up in his phone. So yeah, I wanted to pay your ass back. After I figured he wasn't a problem no more, I thought maybe we could go on with our relationship. When they had me locked up, it had me really thinking, and I realized it wasn't his fault—it was your fault. You betrayed me.

"But you know what? All that shit is behind us now. We can put all of it in the past, and you can hurry up and get back to work and make that paper so we can get our son back at home where he belongs."

"I want to go up to New York to see Tayshon. I don't even have any money anymore. I took an advance to pay your bond, and they kept my final paycheck to pay for that advance. My parents want me to move back to New York, and I'm thinking that might be best, at least until I can get back on my feet and find a new job."

"You don't belong in New York. You weren't happy there before, so why go backwards? I'll let you hold a few dollars so you can go check on Little Man, but you need to come back here to your home, with me. This is where you belong. We belong together," he said before kissing her.

Desiree was so confused, she wanted to cry. She felt like Malcolm was somehow playing her, but couldn't figure out how, since she no longer had a job. Malcolm, sensing her tension, decided to give her another round of sex to get her to relax.

18

It had been a long time since Desiree had been back in New York, and so much had changed. She still hated the long walk through the projects to get to her parents' building. The weather was pretty decent and many people were out and about, staring at her as she walked. She tried to wear something that wouldn't cause her to stand out, so she opted for a pair of sweats and sneakers. She absolutely refused to drive her car up into New York, because she was afraid of something happening to it.

"Hey, ain't you Ernesto and Anelda's girl?" an elderly lady sitting on the bench with other women asked Desiree.

"Yes, ma'am."

"Where you been? We ain't seen you in a minute. You went off to college?"

"Yes. I live in Delaware now." Desire politely smiled, wanting to get on her way, but not wanting to come off rude to the nosy bunch.

"Was that you in that sex video that was all over the internet a few weeks back?" another woman asked.

Desiree was beyond annoyed, but she kept the smile plastered on her face. "I have been asked that so many times. No, that wasn't me," she lied.

"I thought your momma told us that she got your boy because of all that scandal stuff going on with you," the woman challenged.

Desiree shook her head. "No, I travel a lot for my job. Sometimes I have to be gone for a week or two at a time. Not sure what she told you."

The women looked as if they weren't buying it, and Desiree took that moment to walk off. She was harshly reminded of her deep-seated resentment about being there.

"Mommy! Why would you tell those nosy bitches my business and you know I can't stand these people?" Desiree blasted her mother with tears in her eyes as quickly as she was through the door.

"What? What did I do?" Anelda innocently said, sitting down in the living room watching *Sesame Street* with Tayshon.

Tayshon jumped up and ran into Desiree's arms. She hugged and kissed him, but she still was unable to mask her emotions.

"Those nosy bitches just stopped me to let me know you told them that you're keeping my son because I was all caught up in that sex video scandal," she said after putting her son down.

"I don't remember saying it like that. I just said you had a lot going on, and they called me to come pick up my grandson." Anelda tried to avoid looking at Desiree as she began folding a basket of laundry.

"Who called you? No one fucking called you to pick up anyone. You and Daddy called them." Desiree quickly paced back in forth in distress. "I swear to god, this is why I can't deal with you all. I'm going to just take my fucking son and stay the hell away from you the way I have been."

Anelda spoke firmly, "Oh no! You can't take him. They gave me the papers for him. If you want to take him, you have to go to the court. You need to get yourself together. We even told you to move back here so you can be with your son, but you don't want to do that."

Tayshon just sat quietly in the midst of the argument, focused on the television, as he'd been trained to do over the years. He was never allowed to interfere in adult conversations, so he'd remain fixated on the television or any other thing to help keep him tuned out and avoid getting in trouble.

"Why do you want me to stay here? So you can take all my money like you always do? You sit on your ass all day watching television, while we go to work and give you our money?"

"You shut up talking to me like that! You took all the money you saved to go to college, so what did you give to me? I worked cleaning in the hospital until I fell down the stairs and broke my shoulder twelve years ago. I still get my own money from that. Daddy works two jobs. So, who took your money? Who needed your money? If you are grown and you live somewhere, you should be helping to pay. Do you think you should live for free? No! Your only problem is you want to run back there with that man and keep being his prostitute. You want him to take your money. You let that man control you and cut you off from your family. What man who loves you would tell you how to have sex with another man? A pimp! And if he's a pimp, then that makes you his prostitute. But you're standing there twisting an offer to help you get back on your feet as stealing your money."

Desiree was angry to the point of wanting to hit her mother, but she managed to control herself as Anelda continued to berate her.

"You took my grandson from me—from his family—for four years. Why? What have we ever done to you? You graduate college and you don't even tell us, like we did something to you. Yes, we fussed about you getting pregnant and was worried about you throwing away your future to be with a man who was someone else's boyfriend. You said that lady was your friend helping you, yet you have a baby by her children's father? Were we wrong for caring about your well-being? You didn't think we as your parents had a right to be upset about that? Instead, you just cut us off and never visit us anymore. You wouldn't even let us know our grandson was born. But you're mad at us as if we did something to you? *We* should be mad. We have every right to be mad."

Anelda got up and followed Desiree as she tried to walk away, not wanting to hear the hurtful words.

"You come in here accusing me of telling all your business. No, you made it everyone's business while you were doing all those nasty things with that man on video. I didn't put you on the internet for everyone else to see you. That's how I was able to find out what was happening with you, and that's how I knew to call about my grandson that you didn't give a damn about when you did what you did. When I got back here with him, I had to deal with everyone asking me a whole lot of questions about the video they saw you on. I have to live here with these people."

"But yet you can't understand why I don't want to live here with the nosy bitches all up in my business?" Desiree spat back.

"You don't have a job anymore. What are you going to do? How will you take care of yourself? How will you pay your rent?"

"Malcolm came back home the other day. We are working things out. He's the one who's always been taking care of me, and he even gave me the money to come up here to see my son."

"Did you just tell me that he has a wife and other children? What are you working out? He's using you! You paid $7,500 for him to get out of jail for having sex with a minor—who is pregnant by him. Did he give you that money back? Because if he gives you that, you can find you a new place away from him, so you don't have to be his prostitute anymore."

"Stop calling me his prostitute!" Desiree yelled. "I am not a prostitute. I can't believe my own mother would say that about me. You always say things to try to tear me down. What kind of mother would try to tear her daughter down? That's all you do is try to find everything wrong I do and throw it up in my face."

Anelda sat back down and covered her face as she shook her head. She was so disgusted with Desiree's lack of accountability or responsibility.

Desiree continued. "And he told me that lady was not his wife. He said he only did that because he was mad when he saw me hanging out at Chuck E. Cheese with Tayshon and talking to my former boss about the other guy that was harassing me."

Anelda looked up at Desiree, confused. "What the hell? He had to pay you back for you telling your boss that another man was being abusive to you? If he didn't know why you were there, and he's supposed to be your man, why didn't he just come and introduce himself to the boss? Why was he spying on you and your son? His son was in there, so why couldn't he just come in and spend time with his son? Was this another man you were sleeping with as well? I don't understand? Why would *estupido* have to pay you back?"

Desiree quickly turned her back to prevent her mother from seeing her guilty eyes.

"So, there was yet another man?"

Desiree swung back to face her mother. "I didn't say that."

"Forget it! I don't want to know anymore. You break my heart. You were always so smart and pretty. You had so much going for you, but this is how you want to throw your life away—chasing behind a married man with a bunch of children, and he's a pimp."

"Look! I didn't come here for all of this shit. I came here to spend time with my son. Can I do that in peace, without you nagging me about not living up to your bullshit expectations?"

"We were sitting here in peace all morning until you came busting in and being disrespectful. You shouldn't even be talking about these things in front of him. This poor boy has been exposed to way too much in his young life. Look at how he's just focused on the television, trying to act like he's not hearing your big mouth. Oh, and it was your son that told us that his daddy said he's a pimp and is going to teach him to be one as well."

Tayshon got excited when he heard Anelda repeat his very own words, making it obvious that he was very capable of hearing everything, despite his eyes being fixated on the television. "Yep, Mommy. Daddy said he's going to teach me to be a pimp too. We get free food from McDonald's."

Desiree took a seat and rested her face in her lap. She'd heard her son say those words to her plenty of times in the past, but it never seemed so bad until that moment, while he was telling her mother and probably anyone else who was willing to listen.

"Don't cry, Mommy," Tayshon said, rubbing Desiree's head.

Anelda came near Desiree and placed her hand on Desiree's back. However, Desiree jumped up and said, "Don't touch me! Don't try to act like you give a damn my life is all fucked up. I'm leaving, but believe, I will be back for my fucking son. I'll be damned if I let y'all raise him all fucked up like I had to grow up."

"Desiree! What is your problem? Spend time with your son. Don't do this to him." She was legitimately confused by Desiree's words and behavior.

"Fuck you!" Desiree yelled as she rushed out of the door.

"Mommy!" Tayshon shouted. He stood looking confused for a moment before crying.

After getting outside, Desiree was sure to rush past the women on the bench to keep from entertaining any more of their gossip.

19

Desiree felt numb the entire bus ride back to Delaware. She wanted to blame someone, but she was unsure who. She also realized that she had no business tearing into her mother the way she did, but she still felt her mother had no business calling her a prostitute. She also knew that Malcolm would often tell their son that he was a pimp, but Desiree never took the words to be literal. As far as she knew, that was just a tag guys gave themselves. She thought about the things a prostitute would do and compared her actions. She came to the conclusion that the title was not applicable to her, and she was satisfied with that. She felt Malcolm took care of her very well whenever she was down. In relationships, there's give and take, so she decided that was exactly what the dynamics were with her and Malcolm.

The smell of fried chicken smacked her in the face as she was opening the door to her home. In all the years with Malcolm, she had never known him to cook foods like that. He was more of a microwave, SpaghettiOs, TV dinner, pot pie, type of guy when he cooked.

As she came past the foyer area to enter the kitchen on her right, she saw Sharquita lounging comfortably on the sofa to her left. She was wearing one of Malcolm's wife-beater undershirts with no bra and a pair of shorts that may as well have been deemed panties, because that's how small they were on her plump bottom. Sharquita stood at four-foot-eleven, and had the face of a child, which puzzled Desiree as to how ANY grown man could have sex with her and not consider themselves a child molester. Sure, her body would be desirable to any man, but Desiree couldn't understand how men didn't see Sharquita as a child.

"What are you doing here?" Desiree asked with a confused look.

"My baby's father lives here, duh," she responded as if Desiree had no business questioning her.

"You need to get the fuck up out of my house."

Sharquita laughed. "Yeah, like that's about to happen. You should be thanking me for saving your ass instead of talking shit to me."

"Oh, I should be thanking you for fucking my man and fucking up our lives, huh? You must want him to go to prison, because you'd know not to be here."

"For your information, Malcolm said we can just move to Maryland, because it's not a crime to be with a seventeen-year-old there."

Desiree laughed. "Do you know how stupid you sound? He can't even leave the state because he's out on bond. If he leaves, he'll go back to jail until his trial. If he gets caught with you or any other minor, he'll go back to jail."

Sharquita stood up, turned her back to Desiree, patted her behind, and then said, "Minor this, bitch! Don't be trying to tell us what we can and can't do. He said you're just a hating ass he don't want anymore. Aren't you supposed to be looking for a new place to stay? When you gonna be gone? Me and *my* man don't want you here anymore. You always trying to judge some-damn-body, but you got videos of you sucking and fucking some white man. Now who's the trashy ho?"

"I'm not leaving. You're getting the fuck out of my home. This is my home and I ain't going anywhere."

"I bet you won't be trying to threaten me with any guns or knives anymore, 'cause they'll be locking your ass back up in the nut house."

Desiree turned away to walk toward the kitchen. She didn't actually know what she would do, but she didn't want Sharquita to realize that she was feeling powerless in that moment. She turned around and found Sharquita right on her heels.

"If you touch a knife, I'm calling the police."

"Don't come into my home telling me what I can and can't touch. I wish you would call the police, *minor*. Malcolm would have his yellow ass right back in lockup tonight. Is that what you want? I don't know why you won't get it through that thick skull of yours, that he doesn't want your ass."

"He don't want me? No, he don't want you! The only reason he even bothered to come back here is for me. He tried to come back here when you were in the hospital, but we didn't have the key. So now he got the key back from you, you need to just shut the fuck up thinking that he's your man. We'll be moving to Maryland soon, and you won't have shit to worry about."

"Where is Malcolm?"

"He said he's going to make some money. He should be back shortly. He told me to fix some dinner and be looking sexy for when he gets here. Why are you here? I thought you went to spend time with Little Man. Aren't you moving back to New York?"

"No one said anything about moving to New York. I went, I saw my son, and now I'm back in my home."

"Well damn! That was quick. You just left this morning. It's not even six o'clock yet."

"Sharquita, why are you doing this? I thought you and I were cool and now you be treating me as if I did something to you," Desiree said, trying to appeal to Sharquita's sense of decency.

"I never liked *you*. I liked Malcolm. I wanted Malcolm, and now I got Malcolm. Stop making everything about you. This has nothing to do with you. I'm looking out for my damn self, and if you have a problem with that then, oh well, that's your problem."

"So, you're gonna be okay with giving him all of your money and always depending on him?"

"As long as he's my man and taking care of me, why would I not want to give him my money to take care of me? That's a stupid fucking question. It was okay for you to give him your money so he could take care of you. I'm willing to do anything that my man wants me to do, because I know when he's happy, he's willing to do anything to make me happy. I know how to put his needs and whatever he wants first. If you knew how to do that, maybe he'd still want you."

"Still want me? He asked me to marry him."

"You wish." Sharquita laughed. "Can you excuse me so I can get the last of this chicken out of the fryer basket? You can help yourself to some in the microwave, since you say I treat you bad."

As Desiree was leaving out of the kitchen, she ran into Malcolm entering the home with two guys.

20

H ey baby! What you doing here? I thought you was up in the Bronx with your people."

"Well, yeah, I was there and now I'm back. What the hell is going on here? What is this bitch doing back up in my house after I spent my money getting you out of jail because of her?"

Malcolm turned to the two guys. "Yo, y'all can go in the kitchen and help yourself to some food. Might as well get this party started. Let me holler at this one a minute."

"Cool!" one of the guys said. "We running on both these bitches or just the one? I know you only mentioned the one, but I'm definitely feeling this one here," the guy said looking at Desiree's body.

She was stunned, and even more shocked when she heard Malcolm respond, "Let me have a minute. We'll see what we can work out. She ain't got a job right now, so I'm sure she'd be down for whatever."

"Bet!" the guy said, going into the kitchen with Sharquita and his friend.

"What the fuck do you mean, 'we'll see what we can work out?' What does my job situation have to do with shit?" Desiree yelled.

"First off, you better stop raising your voice, trying to embarrass me," he said, pulling Desiree's arm away from the kitchen and toward the downstairs bathroom. "Come in here so we can talk in private."

"We don't have anything to talk about, Malcolm. I want all these people out of my house."

"You keep forgetting it's my place, not yours. I don't see why you wanna act all brand new now. These motherfuckers are willing to pay for some pussy. It ain't like you ain't give up some pussy for money before. Sometimes we have to do what we have to do. They were coming here for some pregnant pussy. Sharquita's down, so you need to stop acting all stuck up. Before, you act like you would never fuck any black dude, but then I find out you're carrying on with that nigga from your job behind my back. No, you owe me just for that shit alone. I should have beat the shit out of you right then, and then gonna have his ass all around my son, playing daddy.

"All I'm saying is we need to make this money. Let's do what we have to."

"Hell no! I'm not a fucking prostitute—"

"No? Then what the fuck are you? You out here fucking and sucking dicks for whatever you can get. Then what is that? You wanted me to be cool with that shit, and I was. So now I'm asking you to be cool with this."

"You want me—the woman you say you want to marry—to be cool with letting dudes run a train on me? You tried that shit before and swore you'd never do it again." Desiree said, trying to catch her breath at the same time. She couldn't believe the conversation they were having.

"Okay, but I wasn't trying to involve you, and I set the shit up while you were going to be gone for a few days, but now you're here and nigga wanna hit that. You think I'm gonna fuck everything up and tell him no because you wanna act like a fucking virgin all of a sudden?"

"I'm not doing that shit, and you can't make me."

"You're going to do it. I'm trying to be nice about this shit."

"You can't make me. I guess you forgot I can simply call the police. I'm tired of you making me do things I don't want to do. Look at the shit I have to deal with because of that damn video, from doing what you told me to do."

Malcolm laughed. "You really think someone would believe your lying ass about anything ever again? They all said you were a liar, remember?"

Desiree tried to push to get past Malcolm and out of the bathroom. He grabbed her by the throat.

"Where you think you're going?"

"Let me go," she whispered through his grasp.

"Are we on the same page about what will happen once I open this door, or will you insist on embarrassing me?"

Tears poured from her eyes, and he loosened his grip and kissed her lips.

"Baby, we're in this together. You are my Bonnie and I'm your Clyde. I've done so much for you for all these years and all I ask is this one thing. Can you do this for us? We still need to be able to support our son until you find a job. Sharquita ain't even my Bonnie, and she's acting more like it."

"She said y'all are supposed to be moving to Maryland so y'all can be together. So you can legally fuck her."

"Is that what you're all upset about? You know I just told her that shit. She's the one telling me that mess about it's legal in Maryland. Ain't nobody doing all of that and she'll be eighteen in a few months. Stop sweating Sharquita. She gets us paper. She will never replace you. I keep telling you, don't be dumb like BM3 and give me away to the next bitch."

Malcolm kissed Desiree again. That time he kissed her as if he were in love with her. "Come on, let's go upstairs."

They left the bathroom and he led Desiree to the steps, but stopped in the kitchen to quickly say something before following her up.

When they arrived in the master bedroom, Desiree fought her tears as Malcolm caressed her face and gently kissed her. She even thought that maybe if she could make Malcolm remember how much he loved her that he wouldn't dare want the others to touch her. She tried to muster up all the passion she could to kiss him. She even whispered, "I love you so much."

"And that's why you are the lady that I love. We're going to be all right, you hear me. I know you're feeling down about the whole job thing, but you and me—we're going to rise above it all and will be together forever. You are my princess."

That made Desiree smile. It seemed so long since he called her his princess. She would have preferred being called his queen, but he had long ago told her that one of his exes used to always want him to call her that, so he didn't want to be thinking about her each time he'd say it to Desiree.

Malcolm tenderly kissed down Desiree's neck while unzipping the jacket to her sweat suit. When that was off, he gently bit her breasts through her top as he squeezed them. As he was doing that, through a narrow crack in the door, Desiree spied the two guys going into the second bedroom with Sharquita. She tried to block them out of her mind. As long as she had Malcolm alone with her, she didn't care what the others did.

Malcolm eventually peeled off all of Desiree's clothes, laid her on the bed, and gently nibbled between her thighs, working his way up to her cookie jar. She was raised up on her elbows as she watched in anticipation. When his mouth savagely made contact with its intended target, she allowed her head to fall backwards on the bed as she gripped his head to pull him into her. While that was going on, Desiree could hear moans and screams coming from the other bedroom. Malcolm inserted a couple of fingers inside of her honey-filled cave, bringing her attention back to what he was doing to her.

"Ahhh," she quietly yelled out. "Damn baby, that feels so fucking good."

Occasionally, she'd raise her head back up to make eye contact with him. She let her orgasm be known to him as her nails dug deeper into his scalp and her thighs tensed. Her head once again fell backwards as Malcolm continued to suck up her spill. She played with her own breasts as he kissed his way up. She was sure to stop him, causing him to pay them some attention before his lips met hers. He brought her hips toward the edge of the bed and tickled her wetness before inserting his money-making rod inside of her.

"Ahhh!" she said much louder that time as he penetrated her.

She wrapped her arms around his neck to hold on as she slowly rotated her hips, causing Malcolm to let out a few moans of his own. One of the biggest things she took pride in with regards to her Puerto Rican and Caribbean heritage was that she learned how to wine her hips since she was young, because that was much of the music she grew up on. She'd practice for hours to be able to wine like her mother and other elder women of her family. And as an adult, she was sure to put that wining to work in the bedroom, which was one of the things she knew that Malcolm loved the most when having sex with her. Sometimes she'd hold back just so he could beg her to "Wine that pussy for me."

As they were fully on the bed, with her lying on her back when she reached yet another orgasm, Malcolm quickly pulled out of her and brought his wet volcano up to her opened mouth, to erupt into her throat. However, while he was fully immersed deep in her throat, she felt her thighs being pushed apart, her hips raised, and felt yet another penetration between her legs. She tried to jerk up, but was unable to with Malcolm's dick in her mouth and his weight bearing down on her upper body. She was having difficulty breathing and kept trying to pull her head away. Malcolm stuck with her until he was emptied out, and then climbed off of her, kissing her as another guy desperately pounded between her legs. As he was kissing her, she felt her breasts being sucked on. Before she could figure out how the other guy was doing that, Malcolm got up from the bed, and she was able to see it was the second guy. Malcolm disappeared from the room as the guy took over Malcolm's last position and inserted his dick into Desiree's mouth.

The tears were already in her eyes, but when the guy roughly grabbed her by the hair and said, "Suck this, bitch!" she really cried. The pair didn't have an ounce of sympathy for her tears or her grief. They turned her in various positions and would swap off for what seemed like an eternity. While that was going on, she could hear Sharquita screaming out Malcolm's name, repeatedly telling him to fuck her ass real good. One of the guys took that as his cue to go for Desiree's asshole. That was one of Alex's favorite things to do to her when treating her like a dog and definitely one of Desiree's least favorites.

At one point Sharquita and the three men decided to take a break to go eat more food. Afterward, they returned for what seemed like an endless rotation, with Malcolm seemingly treating her like a common whore instead of someone he actually cared about.

She was unsure of when or even how she fell asleep, but when she awoke, one of the guys was lying asleep next to her. She eased off the bed and rushed to the bathroom to relieve herself and allow mounds of multiple men's cum to drop out of her. As she sat on the toilet, she realized she didn't hear anyone else in the house and wondered if they were all asleep. After quickly washing herself and then leaving the bathroom, she picked up her clothes and and tiptoed across the hall to Tayshon's empty bedroom to ease her clothes back on. She was hoping to make a mad dash out of the house, since she realized no one else was in the home. She went downstairs to grab her purse, but before she could make it out the door, she saw two cars pull up. She quietly rushed back up the stairs to go hide in the closet in Tayshon's room, since it had a lot of junk down at the bottom and was large enough for her to fit in without being seen.

She heard Malcolm, Sharquita, and yet two other men laughing and talking. Malcolm called out for Desiree. That woke the guy in the bed up.

Malcolm asked, "Yo, where's my girl?"

"Damn, my ass was knocked the fuck out. I didn't even realize she wasn't on the bed."

"What the fuck! I told you to keep an eye on my girl until we got back. Now I got these niggas down here wanting some pussy, and what am I supposed to tell them?"

"What happened to that other little ho?"

"Sharquita's downstairs with them now, but they wanted to tag both bitches."

Desiree was appalled to hear how Malcolm spoke of her when he thought she wasn't around.

"I'll make a quick run and go bring another ho."

"I promised them a freaky, sexy, black Puerto Rican bitch. Where you gonna go find me one of those in the next ten minutes?" Malcolm asked.

"Malcolm, what's up? We ready to get started," Sharquita came up the stairs saying.

"This clown let that bitch slip out of here."

"You sure she's gone? Her car's still outside," Sharquita told him.

Then Malcolm started going through the house opening up closets, but Desiree was able to remain hidden when he opened the closet in Tayshon's room. "I don't know where the fuck she's at, but she's not in this house. You see her pocketbook? It was down on the coffee table?"

"Nah, it's gone," Sharquita answered.

"Are we going to get to fucking or what?" one guy from downstairs shouted with a Jamaican accent. "Where da pussy?"

"Yo, I don't know where the other bitch got to. She probably went to the store, but this one will definitely make you happy."

"She's a little girl. I thought you said you had a taller one with good hair and nice titties," another guy said. "That's the one I want. This bitch here looks like jailbait."

"I ain't no damn jailbait," Sharquita protested. "And trust me, my titties are way better, my ass is fatter and my pussy is wetter. Oh, and I damn sure give better head."

"She damn sure do," the sleeping guy said to convince the others. "That other bitch's head game was whack."

"Show me!" the Jamaican said.

While the two men were sexing Sharquita in the master bedroom, Malcolm and the sleeping guy stepped in Tayshon's room to talk in private.

"I'm gonna fuck that bitch up when I find her. She's fucking with my money now. I need you to run and see if you can hurry up and find a couple more hoes to deal with these niggas. I promised them hours of entertainment. I don't know how long Sharquita's gonna be able to hold them, though, because dude don't even wanna fuck with her. That's why I promised them Desiree. Stupid bitch!"

"Cool."

"And try to find some pretty ones, not just bitches who like to fuck."

"Sure thing. I already got a few in mind. It's the least I can do since I fucked up and let the other bitch out of my sight."

"You damn right!"

Both men left Tayshon's room, with Malcolm returning to the master bedroom and the other guy leaving the house. Not long after, Desiree heard the other guy return with two other girls, and the four men and three ladies were spread between the two bedrooms, filling the house up with the heavy smell of marijuana. Desiree sat listening for hours until she silently cried herself to sleep.

When she awoke just before daybreak and heard all quiet, she attempted to peep out of the closet and saw that the coast was clear. Before tiptoeing out of Tayshon's room, she was a bit startled when she peeped over toward her bedroom and saw Sharquita sleeping alone. With her purse in tow, she stayed low as she passed the open room door. She was able to quietly ease down the stairs and eventually out of the house, escaping the den of iniquity. She drove until she crossed the state line into Maryland, still afraid of Malcolm catching her. She parked at one of the rest stops along the highway until she could figure out her next move.

21

When she woke up, parked at the rest stop, Desiree's body was aching from the previous day's activities. She didn't know where she'd go or what to do. She used her phone internet to go into her email account to find Roger's number that she hid there long ago, just in case of an emergency. She had never wanted to keep his number programmed in her phone, since she knew Malcolm often went through it. She dialed the number she had for Roger, hoping that he'd answer.

"Hello."

"Oh thank god! Roger, this is Desiree," she said, recognizing his voice.

"Oh, hey Desiree. How are you? I haven't heard from you and wasn't sure what's been happening with you. I tried to contact you at the hospital, but they wouldn't let me speak to you. Are you all right?"

Desiree sobbed into the phone. She wanted to talk, but the more she tried, the harder she cried.

"Desiree, please, tell me what's going on."

"My ex-boyfriend. My son's father. I have to get away. I don't know what to do or where to go. He moved his pregnant girlfriend into my house and brought in a bunch of guys to do what they wanted to us. He told me I couldn't call the police and say they raped me because no one would believe me after the Alex situation," she blabbed when she was coherent enough to speak.

"Oh my goodness, Desiree. I'm so sorry this is happening to you. Where's your son? Is he with you?"

"No, he's in New York with my parents. I tried to go see them yesterday morning before all the other mess, and that was a disaster. She kept calling me a prostitute."

"Who called you that?"

"My mother. She said it over and over, and I had to get out of there. Child Protective Services gave my son to my mother, and I can't get him back until I get myself together and go to court."

"This is horrible. You have no other family to stay with or to call?"

"No, especially now that everyone knows about those videos. Before I could make it to my mother's door, all of her nosy neighbors were questioning me about the sex videos. I swear to you, I didn't know anything about them, and I was only trying to play nice with Alex, hoping he'd back off. I thought that would make him lose interest and leave me alone. I hadn't heard from you after Chuck E. Cheese, and I didn't know what happened. I went to Ted Dinkins, and he told me he'd pretend I never came to his office about Alex, because that's his good friend. But then I saw you on the news. Are you really in a wheelchair?"

"I've been getting better with therapy. Unfortunately, that beating forced me to go back to living with my wife. She's been helping me get through this. I just wish I had a way to prove that Ted and Alex was somehow behind this. Those animals belong underneath a jail."

Desiree got quiet. She debated on letting him know that it was Malcolm who hurt him. She was also hurt to hear he was back with his wife.

"I hear you're very quiet over there now. I know this must be hurtful to hear about me being back with my wife. I really did want you and me to be together and perhaps start our own company. Still, I'm going to find a way to help you. Where are you right now?"

"I've been at this rest stop in Maryland, right outside of Delaware. I was worried about my ex following me."

"Okay, stay put. I'm going to call one of my aunts in Jersey. She lives in Cherry Hill, so she's not that far. Do you have money for the tolls to get there if she says it's all right to come?"

"Yes. I have a little over a hundred dollars."

"Okay, great. I'll call you right back."

When it was arranged, he called her back and provided her with the address and his aunt's name.

As Desiree crossed back into Delaware to head to New Jersey, she realized she didn't have any clothes other than the two sporty outfits she had in the gym bag that she had taken with her when she went to New York, expecting to stay a couple of days. She cautiously entered her neighborhood, looking to see if she saw Malcolm or his car anywhere. There were no cars in front of her house. She parked away from her home and snuck back to her house. She could hear her heart beating the entire time. She quietly entered, unsure if maybe Sharquita was in the house. She didn't hear anything. She rushed up the stairs and grabbed an envelope with her and Tayshon's important papers and as many clothes and shoes she could get into a large duffel bag. She also went up in the closet to look for the shoebox that she knew Malcolm would keep money in. There was three-hundred dollars inside. She took one, afraid to take it all.

Desiree had accomplished everything in under five minutes, and didn't want to push her luck. She could feel her heartbeat almost out of her chest as she reached the bottom of the steps, and in walked Sharquita. Thankfully she was alone.

"Where you been? Malcolm's looking for you. He's pissed."

"Just get the hell out of my way. Fuck you and Malcolm."

"What you all uptight about? After all that good dick, you should be floating on a cloud right now. I know I am."

"You fuck whoever you want. I don't care anymore."

"Funny, I used to think you were all uppity and what not. You're just a common ho." Sharquita laughed. "I know I better not ever hear you talking shit about what I do again. You're a big ho, and you be doing sex videos with white men. At least I only fuck black dicks. You nasty."

Desiree dropped the duffel bag and was about to hit Sharquita, but she stopped herself.

"I know you didn't think you was going to lay a finger on me. That's why Malcolm's going to whip your ass as soon as he catches you. You done fucked up his money, and you should know better than that."

Those words were enough to remind Desiree to get the hell out of there before Malcolm came back from wherever he was at. She grabbed the duffel bag, pushed Sharquita, who was blocking her path, and bolted out the door.

"Ho!" Sharquita yelled out the door behind her. "I'm calling Malcolm right now, bitch!"

Desire sprinted all the way back to her car with the heavy bag, refusing to stop to catch her breath. She threw the bag into the backseat and took off as quickly as she could, and not a moment too soon. She spotted Malcolm driving some other youthful looking girl, although he didn't see her. As she watched him drive past in his pimped out Cadillac, she couldn't understand why she never took him at his word when he'd refer to himself as a pimp. Looking at his car in that moment, he definitely seemed to be playing the part of a pimp. She guessed she never paid it any attention because he'd have her son, and she hadn't known of pimps riding around with their young child.

"Hi, Mrs. Arnolds. I'm Desiree. Your nephew, Roger Daniels, told me you'd be expecting me."

"Please, call me Sharon." The woman smiled, looking Desiree up and down as she stepped back to allow her into her home.

"How about I call you Miss Sharon? I'm only twenty-three years old. It just seems disrespectful for me to call my elders by their first name. I grew up in the projects, but even there, we had manners." Desiree smiled, happy as can be that she actually had a place to go.

The woman didn't look that old, so it was hard for Desiree to envision Sharon as Roger's aunt. She was expecting an old, old woman. However, the home furnishings looked a bit old fashioned according to Desiree's taste.

"Come in and have a seat. Get comfortable."

Desiree felt like Sharon was somehow studying her. She didn't take a seat until Desiree was seated.

"Thank you so much. By the way, your home is very lovely, and I appreciate you allowing me to be here."

"My pleasure. It's not often my nephew calls me for a favor, so I figured it must have been a really dire situation."

"I'm sorry for staring, but you look way too young to be Mr. Daniels's aunt. I was expecting to see someone way older."

"Why thank you. I try to do my best to stay in shape and youthful looking. I'm sixty-four. My brother is Roger's father. He was out making babies while our mother was still making babies." She laughed. "Our family has always been pretty close. Most of them are out west, which is where we are from. Roger and I are the only ones left here on the east coast. I had another sister out here, but she passed a few years back."

"Oh my goodness, I'm so sorry to hear."

"Thank you. I appreciate it. Have you eaten? I don't know what you normally look like, but you look as though you may have had a really rough night. If you have a bag to grab, I can show you to your room so you can get relaxed. If you're hungry, there's plenty of food in the refrigerator."

"Oh, great! Thank you. I've pretty much been camped out at a rest stop in Maryland. Crazy ex-boyfriend drama. Well, actually, he's my son's father." Desiree's eyes quickly shifted to the floor.

"It's okay. You don't have to talk about it right now. Just know, I am a psychologist. I have an office here in the house where I do some video sessions on the computer with patients, and some days I actually go into my other office to see patients. I've been trying to cut back a little lately. I don't mean to embarrass you, but I can see that you look as though you've been broken. You've been through quite a bit in your young life."

Desiree nodded her head as the tears formed. She didn't want to cry yet again, and she tried to look elsewhere to keep from crying.

"I have to say this, and it's no disrespect to you, but I have a very frisky husband. He's seventy-eight years old, but he still thinks he got it going on. He's a deacon over at the church, but that doesn't mean a thing in his mind. He always thinks all the young ladies want him." Sharon laughed. "Just try not to be around the house alone with him. I don't want him to say or do anything to make you feel uncomfortable. He's typically at the church every other morning, every Sunday, and most Saturdays if they're having something going on. Most of the times, we have breakfast and dinner together, so you're welcome to join us if you'd like. Don't ever feel like you're intruding. We've been married over forty years. Trust me; there ain't much he talks about that I haven't heard already." She laughed again.

"Forty years? Wow! That's wonderful. Are your children grown?"

"Wouldn't you know it, the old buzzard shoots blanks. No children."

"Oh wow! I'm sorry to hear that."

"It's okay. I have plenty of nieces, nephews, great-nieces and great-nephews to make me glad I never had any kids of my own. I kind of enjoy our freedom. We used to travel a lot. Ben— oh, that's my husband's name, Benjamin—he had a heart attack when he was about sixty-one. Too much weight. That's what slowed us down a bit. We still travel, but not as often, and as old as he is, he still needs to lose some of that weight. I try to cook healthy for him, but he eats out in the street or in the church, knowing it violates his diet. But at seventy-eight, other than his cholesterol issues, he's pretty healthy for his age. The sister I mentioned that passed, she died from a heart attack, and she was almost as thin as you. She was into all that fitness stuff, and a heart attack took her out when she was only sixty-three. So Ben would always use that as an excuse to be able to live life on his terms. I don't even try to fight it anymore. However, that being said, he has been known to say some inappropriate things to women he finds attractive. He claims he's just talking, but I just wanted to give you a heads up."

Desiree's eyes widened and she forced a smile. "Okay . . . I'm not sure how I should take that."

"I'm home every evening, except when we go to bible study on Wednesdays. Only thing I'd suggest is try not to be in the house on his off days. I'm here some of the time, but not all the time. I try to have a recreational life when I'm not working. Helps keep me sane. I'll be sure to keep you informed of his work schedule. He doesn't have to work, but he insists he'll work until the day he dies. I take it you're job hunting? Do you have a laptop? I can't let you use my office computer, since it has confidential information. I would suggest Ben's computer, but there's no telling what kind of inappropriate materials you'll find on it." Sharon laughed, shaking her head. "Like I said, some things

I stopped fighting long ago. But if you don't have a laptop, there's a library not too far away, and I'm sure you could use the computers there."

"I do have a laptop inside my car. I think I might need a Wi-Fi code, if you have one."

"Yes, I can give you that. Anyhow, I won't hold you up. I'm sure you're probably dying for a nice hot shower and some good rest, since you said you were sleeping in a rest stop."

"Oh my god, yes! That sounds so perfect right now."

"Well, go ahead and get your bags, and I'll show you to your room and the rest of the house. I'll fix you a salad with grilled salmon while you take your shower. That should be lite enough to eat before getting some rest."

Desiree stood to head to the car for her belongings. "I can't begin to tell you how much I appreciate everything you're doing for me right now. Honestly, just a few hours ago, I felt like all hope was lost. Now . . . Now, I feel like I am getting my strength back to press on."

"Well Amen! I'm so glad to help. Also, you don't have to feel obligated, but we go to church every Sunday morning and Wednesday evenings. I also have to do that to help keep my sanity." Sharon smiled.

23

THREE WEEKS LATER

While the hospitality Sharon had shown Desiree was beyond wonderful, the post-traumatic stress still had her teetering with thoughts of suicide. During one of her forbidden conversations with Roger, he advised her to cast her net out farther than just the northeast corridor of the United States, so she had been sending out resumes all over the country. She was missing her son, and somehow, she was still missing Malcolm—or what she thought they used to have.

She hated the guilt she felt each time she spoke with Roger and he blamed Ted and Alex for his brutal beating. She desperately wanted to tell him the truth, but she was afraid of the consequences. More specifically, she was terrified of his aunt putting her out, leaving her with no place to go.

She'd get discouraged during her job pursuits; every posting asked for experience or references. Roger had already offered to provide her with a reference, but that was all she had, aside from a couple of her college professors. She was hesitant about even listing Roger as a reference, since she couldn't even mention the job on her resume.

Each day was like a rollercoaster. In the three weeks Desiree had been staying there, Sharon treated her to a movie once each week. She got to go out to dinner with Sharon and Ben at a fancy steakhouse and attended a paint-and-sip class with Sharon and a couple of her friends, who all seemed to adore Desiree. And being able to go to church was a definite help. The large non-denominational church was like none she'd ever been to, because she had only gone to Catholic churches in her early life. However, on the flip side of it all, not only did she battle with those other issues, but she was becoming fearful of the boat being rocked.

Like clockwork, Ben always seemed to be in the upstairs hall each night Desiree was coming from taking her bath or shower. It didn't matter if he had already gone to bed or he was previously downstairs watching television, there he'd be, making awkward small talk and blocking her path to her room.

He hadn't said or done anything overtly inappropriate, so Desiree wasn't sure exactly how she should read into the situation. He seemed to stare below her neck while talking. Desiree would never wear a bra to bed, but she started wearing one when leaving the bathroom after her baths so Ben would have one less reason to get excited. Once inside her room, she'd remove the bra. However, on two occasions, she got up in the middle of the night to use the bathroom without wearing a bra, and on both occasions, there was Ben in the hallway, seeming to be coming out of his room or just going back into it. He'd actually stand there and try to hold a conversation while she was dead-to-the-world tired.

One day she finally asked Sharon about always seeing him in the hallway, even in the middle of the night.

"I guess I should have warned you about that. He has this thing where he roams the house through the night. He's been doing it for the past three or four years. I asked the doctor about it, but they said sometimes when people get up in age, that's what they do. I just make sure he's locked in the house at night and let him roam. Sometimes he'll get up and go on his computer and look at smut, and other times he'll get up and be up in the refrigerator or cabinets, stuffing his face. That's why he's so fat. He probably doesn't look as big, because he's so tall. He used to be six-foot-seven. He's shrunk over the years. I think he's down to six-four or six-five. His last doctor appointment, he weighed in at 293."

Desiree looked especially surprised. Ben definitely didn't look that heavy.

Sharon continued with an apologetic smile. "I'm sorry if he's making you feel uncomfortable in any way. I really wish I could say I could talk to him—which I will—but it'll probably do no good. That roaming-the-house thing is like a tic of his. I always said, if he dies in here, I could most definitely count on his haunting spirit still roaming the house."

Desiree laughed with Sharon and then shrugged. "I guess it's not a problem. I just didn't know what to make of it. It did kind of scare me at first, but now that you tell me he does that all the time, I'll just make sure to stay in my room and out of his way at night."

"You shouldn't have to feel confined to your room, especially since I have yet to go get a TV for that room. I keep meaning to order one. Maybe we can go pick you out one later this week."

"Wow! You don't have to do that. That is so kind of you. But honestly, I don't watch television that often. There's like one or two shows I might watch. That's it. I used to love to read, but when I was working on the two degrees at once, it caused me to hate books." Desiree laughed. "I used to say I couldn't wait to graduate, just to be able to read some gritty, fictional books. I haven't done that yet, because I'm still so traumatized from all those school books."

"I think that is very impressive; you obtained both your bachelor's and your master's together and had a baby. If you could pull something like that off, there's no limit to what you'll accomplish with your mind set on the desires of your heart. I know things might seem a bit rough right now, but everything in this life might give an occasional bump or bruise. You just have to be stronger than those situations. A friendly, helping hand definitely helps."

"I definitely agree, because I don't know where I'd be right now without your helping hand."

"It's my pleasure, dear. You've been great company. As a matter of fact, you better go figure out what movie we're going to see next week."

Desiree smiled. "That's been the highlight of my week—especially stopping off at the dollar store to pick up snacks to smuggle in."

Sharon put her finger to her lips. "Shhh, someone might hear." She laughed, because they were in her house alone having the conversation. "I guess I better get this dinner started. I have a video appointment with a patient this evening. This patient is one of my ninety-minute sessions. If you think you have problems . . ." She laughed again.

"What's the difference between the video patients and the patients you have in your office?" Desiree asked.

"I started doing the video appointments about a year or two ago. I saw this medical doctor app one day, where you can talk with a doctor online about your conditions and never step foot in their office. I thought that was insane, but then I started thinking, I could do something like that with my profession, much easier. I did a little bit more research, and found there was an online program for psychologists. We get to say what days or nights we'll be available, and we get to schedule appointments. Sometimes, if you don't have appointments, you could still be available for someone who may be bordering on crisis mode. The system will send us a notification that there's an emergency patient. A lot of times, they become regular patients. Other first-timers will schedule an appointment. They get to read our bios and pick the psychologist that they feel most comfortable with. We have special software that the patient can download to access a one-on-one video-chat session."

"Wow! That sounds really cool. I might have to try that out myself sometime. How do people pay for it, or is it only for people with insurance?"

"Patients pay for the sessions out of their own pockets with a credit card, but then they can submit it to their insurance for a reimbursement."

"That is great! This is good to know. I've been sending resumes out all over the country, so I'm not sure where I might end up. At least now I know about this service and can use it no matter where I go."

"Absolutely. Sometimes it's hard for a patient to get connected with a psychologist and then they lose their insurance, or their insurance changes, leaving the patient in a bind. This service is not that expensive, making it more accessible to more people in need. I personally think it is a wonderful program, and I am glad I found it. It's also helpful to some of us older doctors who don't want to rush to an office every day anymore, or the doctors who might be physically disabled."

"Yes, I definitely agree."

"Okay, I'm heading to the kitchen for real this time."

"Would you like me to help with dinner?"

"I appreciate it, but Ben is funny about stuff like that. He can eat in the street or at church, but no one else can cook for him in our house. I know you probably can't understand. Heck, I've been with that man for forty-three years now, and I still don't understand him at times."

They both laughed. Sharon went into the kitchen, while Desiree got back on her computer to search for jobs and potential cities she'd want to live in.

There weren't too many programs on television that Desiree would watch, but *Black-ish* was one that she hated to miss, even when it was a rerun. Later that evening, she sat in the family room alone while Sharon was on her video call. Ben had gone up to get his bath for the night. The episode of *Black-ish* had her laughing, reflecting on life, as well as thinking of all the possibilities that life had yet to offer her. It made her smile. She was starting to feel positive and optimistic about life again. That is, until a commercial came on and she looked up at the figure propped up in the doorway. It was Ben. He stood wearing a silk robe, opened, with nothing underneath and a hand on his hip to keep the robe open. He stood with an erection. When Desiree made eye contact, she tried to quickly look away and cover her eyes. She could feel him getting closer.

"You wanna touch it? It's big, right?" he whispered, sure to keep his voice down so his wife couldn't hear him, as he stood about two feet from Desiree.

He wasn't kidding. His dick was huge, but there was no way that she would tell him.

"Go on and touch it," he said, standing with both hands on his hips, holding his robe open.

"Please don't do this, Mister Ben. I don't want to touch it or see it. You're making me very uncomfortable right now," Desiree said, still trying to look away from him.

"Oh, I'm sorry. I didn't mean to make you uncomfortable."

He quickly closed up his robe and disappeared.

Desiree wanted to quickly jump up and run to her room, but she wasn't sure where he had gotten to and didn't want to chance running into him on the way up. She was determined to stay put until she knew Sharon was done with her video patients. Sharon didn't get done until midnight, and Desiree was still a fixture in front of that television until then.

"Oh, you're still up," she said when seeing Desiree. "I'm so exhausted. Some of these patients are on the west coast, so it's not as late over there. That's the only drawback to this. I have to be up early tomorrow to go into the office, so I'm going to go get my bath and I'll see you in the morning." She yawned.

Desiree forced a smile. "Yeah, I guess I better get some rest myself."

She followed Sharon up the stairs and still had yet to see where Ben was at. She assumed he must have gone to his room to go to sleep.

Two nights later, on a Friday night, Desiree sat watching another of her favorite shows, which was *Shark Tank*. Before then, she had sat at breakfast and dinner with Sharon and Ben, and everything was like normal. Desiree decided to chalk the robe incident up to Ben just being an old—possibly senile—man and figured he probably had no knowledge or recollection of what he had done. She didn't recall Sharon mentioning that she had video appointments that night, but she hadn't seen either of them after dinner. She even thought that they may be in their room having sex. However, as she sat watching *Shark Tank*, Ben startled Desiree when he came and sat next to her on the sofa, again wearing his robe with nothing underneath, and exposed his erection.

"You wanna touch it?" he asked. "Ain't it big?"

"Mister Ben, please cover yourself up. You're making me nervous and uncomfortable," she said, hoping that strategy would work for her again and he would go away.

"You want me to touch your pussy? I wanna lick it. Let me touch it. You can touch me."

"Please don't say that to me. You're making me uncomfortable," she repeated.

"I was licking your titties while you were sleeping last night. Next time I'll lick your pussy for you." Desiree was absolutely horrified at that point. She stood up to leave, and he grabbed her hand. "Here, touch it."

She snatched her hand and ran off to her room. She had to go to the bathroom, but was scared to come out of the room. She checked the lock on the door to see if there was any way he could have really been in her room the night before. The lock was fine.

Although Desiree was afraid, she couldn't help but laugh. She even laughed at the thought of Sharon having stayed with Ben for so long because he had such a huge dick. Something was going to have to give, because the old man was definitely going crazy. For safe measure, she propped a chair at the door, just in case there was some way he was able to bypass the lock.

24

Desiree had been with the Arnolds for a total of six weeks. Aside from the couple of uncomfortable incidents, things still were going well in the household. She had decided to stay away from the television unless she knew Sharon would also be sitting there watching. That eliminated problems with Ben. She was still struggling to find a job, which was discouraging. The two interviews she did get called for, she wore professional attire, but based on how the men interviewing her looked at her, she felt she would have definitely had either job had she dressed as Malcolm had taught her.

She had spent the evening watching television with Sharon, while her phone remained in her room. When she made it to her phone, she saw there were several missed calls from Malcolm. It was the very first time he had called since she had escaped that night. He had been calling for hours.

She thought she'd have a heart attack when she heard one of his messages say, "Babe, you need to come get Little Man. He's been crying for his mommy." The words made it sound as if he had possession of her son, but she couldn't understand how that could be. In yet another message, Malcolm actually had Tayshon speak in the phone to tell his mommy to come home because they missed her.

Desiree quickly called her parents, who confirmed that Malcolm came to pick up his son, and told them that he had more rights because he was the boy's father. Desiree screamed at them for doing something so stupid. After getting off of the phone, she sobbed loudly, causing Sharon to come knock on her door to see what the problem was.

Desiree explained that Malcolm took her son from her parents and was using him to bait her back, and she was terrified of what would happen.

"Oh my lord, Desiree. You need to go to the police right away. That man sounds crazy."

"They won't do anything or help me because he's the father, and I had custody taken away when I attempted suicide. They gave Tayshon to my parents, and he was there all the time. Malcolm is not even supposed to leave the state because he's out on bail, so I'm not sure how he made the trip to my parents'. I'm not even sure how he got their phone number or address to get my son."

Desiree covered her face and sobbed again. Sharon tried to console her.

"I still think you should try getting a police officer to at least go with you. I'm afraid of what he'll do to you if you don't. From what you have told me about that last night there, this sounds like a trap. And you said the other girl told you he would beat you up when he sees you. Please call the police."

As suspected, when Sharon sat with Desiree to call the police, they informed her that they couldn't interfere in custodial matters, especially if Desiree had already lost custody. They told her to contact the bond company regarding the violation of him leaving the state, but they also let her know that it was possible that he had been granted special permission to go pick up his son, because he would have the right to possession. Sharon continually apologized to Desiree, as she felt helpless and didn't know what else to do for her.

Desiree finally called Malcolm back, and he warned her that she better come alone if she wanted to see her son. Feeling like she had no other choice, she made the trip back to Delaware, in hopes of collecting her son.

Desiree arrived to the house first thing that morning, but no one was there. She waited for over two hours, constantly trying to reach Malcolm, but he didn't answer. Finally, he arrived alone and she was terrified that he was going to beat her up. Actually, it was quite the contrary.

"Where's my son?" she immediately asked.

"Relax. I wanted us to talk. We need to get our shit worked out and fix this relationship. Our son needs his mommy and daddy. I don't know how things got so fucked up. I went up there and saw that rat hole your people trying to raise my son in—that shit ain't about to happen like that. They wanna fuck up your life, and now they think they're gonna fuck up my son's life. Not happening!"

"How did you know where to find him? You're not even supposed to leave the state."

"Please! Ain't nobody worried about those cornball motherfuckers. I have every right to go get my son if I want. I didn't lose custody of him. No one said I couldn't have him. So, I went to get what's mine."

"How'd you know where to go?"

"I know a bitch down at the CPS office. She gave me the address. I told her I wanted my fucking son."

Desiree was fuming. She wished she had a way of finding out who the woman was, so she could report her. "Well, where is he? I want to see my son."

"I told you we need to talk first. We need to figure out when we're getting married and stop playing all these damn games."

"How you wanna talk about getting married and you treat me like a fucking hooker?"

She tried to stay strong when she spoke, but the recurring memories from that night caused her to break down. Malcolm took her in his arms and held her like she was the most precious thing in the world to him. She felt herself melting in his arms. He kissed her, and she whole-heartedly received the passion in his kiss. He took her by the hand and started heading for the stairs. She stopped briefly, because in that moment, she wanted to put up resistance, especially not knowing where her child was, but then he got behind her and started gently coaxing her up the stairs.

The smell in the room was enough to make her vomit. It was obvious that no one attempted to change a sheet, clean the room after all the sexual activities. Although it was her bed, she didn't even want to sit on it, let alone lie on it. Feeling like she had no choice, she went along with whatever he wanted to do, keeping in mind that she'd flee the moment she got hold of her son.

While in the midst of their sex act, Sharquita barged into the room. "Malcolm! What the fuck! I thought you said you was done with this bitch?"

Desiree wanted to get up and beat the hell out of Sharquita. As much as she didn't even want Malcolm touching her, it irked the hell out of her that Sharquita was trying to dictate their relationship and they had a child together. At first, Desiree wasn't really into the sex, but then she decided to put on a performance for Sharquita.

"This is some bullshit, Malcolm! You got me watching that bitch's son, and then you up in here fucking her. What happen to you beating her ass? Remember that?"

"Yo, shut the fuck up!" Malcolm told Sharquita, causing Desiree to smile. "Go get my little man situated and you can come join us."

"Bet!" she said, suddenly switching to happy as she ran back downstairs to get Tayshon situated, as she was told.

"Wait! What?" Desiree said, also suddenly switching her tune.

"Just this once, baby. This means so much to me. I promise, I'll bounce that ho tomorrow if you give me this one thing."

"I don't want that nasty bitch near me, Malcolm."

Desiree was on top of Malcolm in that moment, but he quickly flipped her onto her back so he'd be in control. He ignored Desiree's protest and continued to stroke her. While he had Desiree's legs pushed back and bent deep up inside of her, Sharquita decided to join in by putting her face down to Malcolm's ass and licking it, also using a finger to play with Desiree's asshole. That sensation, which actually angered Desiree, caused her body to jerk, giving Malcolm the impression that Desiree was really enjoying what he and Sharquita were doing to her.

As many times as she had been violated in her life, Desiree felt the worst violation came when Malcolm pulled out of her and held her thighs apart while Sharquita buried her face in Desiree's pussy. The entire time they took turns violating Desiree. Sharquita grinded her pussy on Desiree's face as Malcolm pinned her down, Malcolm butt-fucked Desiree while Sharquita climbed underneath to eat Desiree's pussy, then he flipped Desiree on her back and shoved his dick into her mouth, while Sharquita attempted to grind pussies with Desiree. With each vile sex act, Desiree was visualizing the gun she had once hidden up in the ceiling of the hallway linen closet.

The minute Malcolm and Sharquita passed out from exhaustion, Desiree was slipping off the bed, grabbing her clothes, and making her way to that closet. After she got her clothes on and got the gun out, she snuck back in the room for Malcolm's pants. She checked his pockets and took his phone, his keys, and the twelve hundred-dollar bills he had in it. She wanted to wash the grossness from her face and body, but in that moment, she was most focused on grabbing her son and getting out of Dodge. Tayshon was lying on the sofa sleeping. She gently picked him up, with the gun tucked behind her. She saw Sharquita's purse and key ring, set next to her own. She collected everything and was able to make it out the door, spitefully leaving the front door open.

When she was in the car and on the road, she called Sharon to see if it was okay for her to return with her son. Sharon allowed her to return with Tayshon.

25

Wanna touch it?"

Desiree had just gotten Tayshon to sleep and was looking forward to indulging in the bowl of ice cream she had scooped for herself. She happily sat at the table, dug her spoon in, and opened her mouth for the decadent treat. However, before the spoon could reach her mouth, she heard those familiar words. She turned just in time to see Ben approaching the table in his favorite robe, wearing nothing. He sat down at the table in a chair adjacent to hers, literally, just letting it all hang out.

Desiree put the spoon back in the bowl and covered her face as if she had a headache. But that time, instead of being offended, she just broke out laughing.

"Mr. Ben, would you please? This is hilarious. You need to stop this mess before I tell your wife."

"I won't be upset if you touch it. I know you want to touch it. I can see your nipples getting hard. You want me to lick on them for you?"

She looked down and was stunned to see her nipples betraying her like that. Although she wore a robe over her pajamas, her nipples were protruding. By the time she looked back from her nipples, Ben had a full hard on held within his grip. She didn't want to look at it, but it was both huge and attractive. It was actually causing her nipples to throb. She tried to fold her arms across her bosom to hide her nipples.

She had been back for a week with her son, and things couldn't have been better. Both Ben and Sharon were loving Tayshon, and Tayshon was seemingly loving them. Sharon had gone out to buy a television for Tayshon to be able to watch his favorite programs, in addition to a Fisher Price computer. They went shopping to get him new clothes and shoes for church, as well as items for every day. Ben would try to teach Tayshon to play their piano and even allowed him to play with his collection of model cars he had been collecting for over sixty years. Sharon got him enrolled at the church's daycare center to allow Desiree time to herself to do whatever she had to do. He was put on a bedtime schedule, with him getting a bath, reading a book, prayer and to sleep by 8:30 each night, and he had a morning routine of praying, brushing his teeth, washing his face, and a hot breakfast by 7:30. Desiree loved the structure that her son was receiving for the first time in his four years of life.

Yet, in that moment, Ben was disrupting the joy that Desiree was just thankful for finally finding.

"Your ice cream is melting. Aren't you going to eat it?" he asked.

"Well, it's kind of hard to eat with you sitting there like that. Could you cover yourself up, please? It's making me uncomfortable."

"If you let that ice cream melt, I can do all kinds of things with it. I can put it on those hard nipples and suck it off."

"Oh my lord, Mr. Ben, please!" She laughed again. She didn't want to laugh, and she tried to tell herself that it wasn't a laughing moment, but when she felt that jolt between her legs, she wasn't sure what else to do or say.

"You wanna put some of that ice cream up on here and taste it?" he said, masturbating at the table.

Desiree didn't want to see it, because she had already found herself thinking about what he'd feel like from the previous occasions when he had exposed himself.

"Go on, touch it. I can see you want to. It's okay."

"Ben! Where you at?" Sharon called out.

He quickly covered himself, tightly closing up his robe.

"We here in the kitchen talking. The girl eating her ice cream."

By that point, Sharon was in the doorway of the kitchen. "Well come on out of here and let her eat her ice cream in peace." She chuckled, and then redirected her attention to Desiree. "Isn't that ice cream delicious? I know the people who make that ice cream from scratch. I try not to buy it too often, or else I'd get fat like this one here, and he'd get fatter."

Desiree laughed. Although she had yet to taste it, she lied and said, "This is really, really good. I couldn't wait to get the little one down just to get a bowl." She tried to quickly take a spoonful so it wouldn't be a complete lie.

Ben got up from the table after sitting long enough for his erection to go back down for when he stood. "Well, young lady, we'll see you both in the morning. Keep doing a good job with that little boy. He's super smart."

Sharon nodded and smiled. "Yes, he is. I just love him to pieces already. You know by the time you leave here, he'll be spoiled rotten."

"Thank you so much." Desiree smiled. "Sometimes I think he's too smart. And again, thank you both for everything you are doing for him. I can tell he's already in love with you as well."

"Well, goodnight. See you in the morning," Sharon said, leaving the kitchen with Ben on her heels.

When they were gone, Desiree couldn't help but laugh again as she thought about that old man having way more dick than most guys half his age. She figured he was at least twelve or thirteen inches, and because of the extra skin, it made her wonder if it may have been even longer in his earlier days. She thought, if she had one of those, she'd stay married to it for over forty years as well. Especially if it still worked.

The next two nights, he'd find a way to expose himself to her and she was becoming less and less offended or uncomfortable. With Tayshon sharing a bed with her, it wasn't as easy staying confined to the room, since he went to sleep at 8:30. Not only was she becoming less offended, she began thinking of ways to return the favor, by subtly flashing something of her own. One night after Tayshon was down for the night and Sharon was in her office for her late-night video sessions, Desiree sat watching television in pajamas that had a camisole-type top, covered with a robe. She had no idea where Ben was at, but she figured she'd be prepared for him whenever he did surface. She was leaned back with her robe opened and the camisole top, exposing ample viewing.

When he appeared in her peripheral view, she tried to pretend she didn't see him standing there watching her as he massaged himself in the doorway. After a while, he finally grunted, causing her to look in his direction. He continued to masturbate where he stood. Then she covered herself up.

He came and sat on the sofa next to her, still rubbing himself. "Let me see that again."

"See what? What are you talking about? You need to stop doing that in front of me."

"Let me see that tittie again."

"I see I'm going to have to stay confined to the room again," she said, acting bothered by his behavior.

"I'm being nice to let y'all stay in my house, and the only thing I ask is to just let me see that tittie again."

Desiree wasn't sure how to take his words. That almost sounded as a threat. That caused her to get up and go to her room, where she stayed for the remainder of the night.

That next day, she got a call from Roger.

"Hey, dear. I thought I'd check up on you and see how everything's going for you, and to see if you have any job leads yet."

"Hey Roger," she responded, sounding down.

"What's wrong? You getting depressed about not finding a job yet?"

"That too. Things here had been going really great, but now I don't know."

"Why? What happened?"

Desiree took a deep breath and then blew it out. "Your uncle."

"My uncle? Uncle Ben? He's giving you a hard way to go?"

"He's been exposing himself to me and I keep trying to avoid him. Your aunt told me from day one that he was frisky and to not be in the house alone with him, so I always make sure to do that. However, since my son has been here, it's kind of hard to avoid him, or else I have to stay in my bedroom with the lights off so my son can sleep. If I leave the room, there he is, exposing himself."

"Wow! That's crazy. I take it that Aunt Sharon doesn't know?"

"No, but I've been thinking about telling her. I was worried about what might happen if I told her. I think she'd probably want us to leave. I most certainly wouldn't expect her to get rid of her husband on my account."

"Oh Desiree, I'm so sorry to hear that. And no, no you don't want to tell her that, because that would definitely upset her. She has another bedroom. Why don't you stay in that room to maybe watch television or whatever? You think that would help?"

"She uses that room for storage. It is really packed up. She mentioned about trying to get it cleaned up for us one day, but it's a lot of stuff in there. It would take weeks to clear that room out."

"Yeah, I guess I could imagine. They've been in that house for a really long time. I'm sure it's accumulated a bunch of junk over the years."

"Yes, it has." Desiree chuckled.

"How are your job prospects coming along?"

"Not so great. I get a bunch of responses letting me know they are impressed with my credentials, but everyone seems to want a lot of experience. At this pace, I keep feeling like I'll be here forever."

"Hmm, understood. I know it's not easy, but something'll work out for you soon enough. I'm wondering if maybe I wire you some money for a hotel or an efficiency, could that help?"

"I don't know. She has my son in the daycare at the church, so I'd have to find someplace near there to be able to take him each day."

"Okay, let me see what I can do, and then I'll text you the wire info and a decent place that's near the church."

"Oh my goodness, Roger. Thank you. You are truly a godsend."

"Trust me, I have my devilish moments. That's how I became so smitten with you, remember?" He laughed.

"How's your therapy coming along? Are you going to be walking soon?" she asked, still feeling guilt about what Malcolm did to him.

"Oh, I haven't updated you. I'm out of the wheelchair, finally, but I still need the walker to help get around. I'm hoping to be able to drive on my own again soon. Right now, I have to wait on others to get me where I need to go, or I have to do everything online."

"Well, I don't know if I should say I'm sorry to hear, or I'm happy to hear—about your progress, that is."

"I appreciate it. I'll be back on my feet as normal eventually. I'm just thankful to at least be alive."

"Yes, indeed. Lord knows I don't know what I'd do without you or where I'd be."

"Well, try not to focus on that. Let's just focus on the positive, and hopefully soon, you'll be back to letting some lucky employer know how very, super smart you are."

Desiree couldn't stop smiling.

"Anyhow, let me get off of here and try to see what I can get worked out. I might need a little something for inspiration, you know."

"I'll see what I can come up with. You sure it's safe? Remember what happened before."

"I'm stuck in the house pretty much every day that I'm not in therapy. What's to check for? Besides, you can crop out the face and I'll save it to my phone and delete the message."

"If you think that'll work. Whatever."

"And be sure to send me a close up shot of that wetness. I want you to think of us together and then snap the picture."

"Okay, you better stop talking like that, making me horny as hell." She laughed.

"Good, I want you horny. My dick is hard right now just thinking about you. Hopefully, I can find you a nice efficiency and come visit you one day. Would you like that?"

"Hell yeah! I would love that," she said to placate his feelings. The truth was, she didn't want to see him because she didn't want to have to face him and tell him the truth about what happened to him. Sure, she wanted to feel his touch and his kisses, particularly down there, but she just didn't want to have to look him in the eye and continue to lie to him. Just as she was becoming more and more uncomfortable looking Sharon in the eye, knowing she had been wondering what Ben would feel like if she touched it.

"I'll text you the information as soon as I have everything together. Hopefully, it'll be by the end of the day. If not, definitely by tomorrow afternoon. I don't want to just find you any kind of junk in an unsafe area."

"Okay. I'll be on the lookout."

That next day, after receiving the text that he promised, Desiree went to try to retrieve the Western Union that he sent. There was nothing there. She waited a few hours and tried again, but still, nothing. She didn't want to have to call him because she didn't know when his wife might have been around, but she did send a text letting him know the wire hadn't gone through. She had gone to see the cute studio that he let her know about, but due to the lack of funds, she couldn't get it.

26

That Sunday evening, Sharon provided Desiree with a full schedule for both her and Ben. Typically, Sharon only went to work in the office three days during the week, but she had a five-day work schedule for that week. Although Ben didn't really need to be at the church each day, he went each morning, and typically didn't return until after three in the afternoon. Because Desiree didn't trust him to drive her son, she had been dropping him off at daycare herself, rather than letting Ben take him. It also helped her feel like having a purpose each morning she woke up, since she had no job to go to.

She was still disappointed about not hearing back from Roger. She was feeling a bit regretful of the text she sent to him, reminding him about Ben's behavior. She wasn't sure if Roger's wife would see it, but she needed Roger to get that money to her. Her hormones were raging and she was hoping to get into her own place for Roger to come see her.

Tuesday morning, she had just returned from dropping Tayshon off at daycare and was taking her shower, since she skipped it the night before to avoid Ben. He was getting bolder by standing in the hall outside of the bathroom to expose himself to her, even with his wife on the other side of the door in their bedroom. She was all set to figure out some employment options, even if it was outside of her profession. However, it hadn't occurred to her to lock the bathroom door, since she knew no one was home and she had already seen Ben at the church when she dropped Tayshon off.

"What the hell?" she shouted after turning the water off and opening up the shower curtain.

Ben stood with his same bathrobe on and nothing under it.

She reached for the towel to cover her nudity.

"Move that towel. I wanna see."

"I can't do that. Plus, I'm cold. It's getting cold in here with the door open and the water off."

She stepped out of the tub onto the bathmat. She tried to take mental measurements of how she'd successfully be able to squeeze past Ben without touching him. It was looking pretty much impossible, given the bathroom space was not large. She was also annoyed with herself for leaving her clothes on her bed, so she could comfortably lotion up before dressing.

"Could you excuse me, Mr. Ben? I need to get to my room."

She didn't like the look he was giving her. He had a much more aggressive look, and not just a simple, horny-old-man look.

"Touch it!"

She noted how he told her to touch it, instead of asking if she wanted to touch it, as he normally would.

"I want you to touch it."

"I thought you were at the church. Aren't you supposed to be at the church? I'm not trying to be disrespectful to your wife. I'm not touching you, and I'd appreciate if you'd excuse me, so I could get out of the bathroom and into my room."

Ben stepped out of the bathroom to let Desiree out. She quickly headed to her bedroom, covered with just the towel. Before she could close the door, Ben was blocking it.

"Excuse me. I need to close the door so I could get dressed. You're scaring me right now. You're making me very uncomfortable."

"You show me your tittie and now you want to play like you don't want me to lick it. Remember you showed me your tittie? I want you to move the towel. Now I want to lick it, and I want you to touch this."

For a brief moment, Desiree thought of trying to make a mad dash out to her car and grabbing the gun she had stashed underneath the seat, but then her entire life flashed before her eyes in just nanoseconds, of all the consequences she'd have. She tried to conjure up Malcolm's twisted wisdom, thinking of what he'd tell her to do in this situation.

"Mr. Ben, could you please close the door so I can get dressed?"

He then nudged his way inside the room and closed the door. "Now the door is closed. I want you to touch it."

She was ready to cry. She was kicking herself for even having thoughts of what he'd feel like.

He wasn't rough, but he pulled one of her hands holding her towel, and guided it to his semi-erect penis. She tried to keep her hand in a fist to avoid gripping it.

"Open your hand and touch it."

Although she hadn't opened her fist yet, he still rubbed her hand along his shaft. As her eyes focused in a different direction, she missed his other hand coming up to snatch her towel off. The towel fell, and his large hand cupped one of her breasts. Without realizing it, her fist opened and he was able to get her hand gripped around his growing rod. She didn't want to be turned on, but she was in the process of battling the feelings that had her body tingling. She hadn't even realized the point when she began massaging his dick on her own, but it became apparent when his other hand cupped her other breast. One hand left her breast and travelled downwards to play in between her lower lips. The contact sent a jolt throughout her entire body, and caused her to grip him tighter. It was in that moment, she decided she was going to stop playing games, acting like she didn't want him to fuck the hell out of her.

Since the room wasn't that big, she didn't have to step back too far to make it to the bed. He was sure to keep up with her baby steps, backwards. When she made it to the bed, she lifted onto the bed, sure to keep her thighs spread so he could play in her forming wetness. He bent to lick her breasts as he had been begging to do for some time. His fingers would rotate from rubbing her clit to going inside her cave, causing her hips to find a rhythm. She released her grip on him and pushed herself farther onto the bed so he could have his way with her youthful body.

She fully separated her thighs in anticipation of him tasting her sweet nectar, and when he did, she was very pleased. When she was satisfied, she stopped him and decided to go down on him. At first he was standing, but then he decided to lie on his back to receive her treat. The more she sucked, the longer he became. She then figured he had to be about fourteen inches long, and she couldn't wait to mount up on it. When she finally did, she realized she was unable to take all of him inside of her without it causing her great pain. Instead, he turned her over, brought her to the edge of the bed, raised her hips up to meet his, and that's the position he gave her pleasure in. When he was ready, he flipped her onto her stomach and entered her from the back while gripping a tit as if trying to squeeze milk from it.

The fucking he was putting on her, she would have never thought it was a man over thirty-five. She didn't know what kind of pills he was taking, but he had plenty of stamina. For a hot second, she was actually jealous of what Sharon had. It suddenly made her think of how she ended up with Malcolm, in a very similar manner. Stolen from the woman trying to help her. She felt guilt, but not enough to stop that massive climax she was on the verge of. When her body began convulsing, he pumped her a few more times and abruptly pulled out of her and left. She stayed in position, anticipating that he'd return for his own release. Instead, he was fully dressed and leaving. He didn't even say goodbye. That made her feel offended, because she was under the impression that she failed to satisfy him.

Over the next two weeks, they had sex daily. They'd find ways. He had a hobby room in the basement. She'd meet him there in the middle of the night for quickies. The days when Sharon was out at her office, he'd sneak from the church to rendezvous with Desiree while Tayshon was in daycare. When Sharon would be on her video appointments, Ben would suck her breasts and finger-fuck Desiree in the family room with the television on. They even got so bold that he'd be in the hallway waiting for when she got out the shower at night, and he'd briefly play in her pussy before she went into her room, and he back into his, or wherever he'd disappear to.

Things had been so perfect for her that she was actually disappointed when she got called for a job that would interfere with her time spent with Ben. She was getting so addicted to him, that she was the one to beg him for an opportunity to touch it.

27

Desiree had just gotten Tayshon down for the night and was eager to meet Ben in the basement, once Sharon went to bed. Very rarely did the couple have visitors, and definitely, never at that late hour of the evening. Desiree was still up in her room choosing what she'd wear for her late night rendezvous when she heard the doorbell. Whoever it was, it seemed Sharon was happy for the visit. Desiree tried to listen from the top of the stairs, but she was pretty certain she heard Roger's name, and she thought the voice sounded very much like his wife's. In that moment, she made up her mind to stay away. However, she heard her name being called.

She tried to go downstairs cheery where she found Roger's wife, Sharon, and Ben all sitting in the living room.

"Hey Desiree, this is my nephew's wife, Evelyn. She said you two met a while back when you worked with Roger," Sharon innocently said, as Evelyn wore a broad smile.

"Oh yeah, yes, we did meet I believe just once."

"I was just explaining to Sharon that Roger couldn't make it. He's been working so hard with his physical therapy, since he's anxious to hurry up and get back on his feet and get back to work. And with my hectic work schedule, it's kind of difficult to get where I want or need at times, and this was the soonest I could make it here. I really should have been here weeks ago."

Desiree gave a phony smile to be polite, because she figured Evelyn to be up to no good.

"Sharon, did you know this young lady used to be my husband's mistress?"

Both Desiree and Sharon's eyes widened.

"Mistress? I haven't seen the man since I started my new position with the company, after leaving my position as his admin assistant. What kind of mistress is that?" Desiree tried to quickly defend herself, and Sharon seemed to be on her side.

"Evelyn, I hope you didn't take me from the things I need to do to come over here starting some mess. I've spoke with my nephew and he told me the nature of their relationship, and mistress was not what he told me. He doesn't have to lie to me. And for the record, he did indeed let me know that he in fact seduced this young lady in his office one time, which led to her having all the grief that followed, which is why he wanted to help her. Last I checked, your home in Philadelphia is not that far from my house in Cherry Hill, and Roger has not been here once to see this woman. He'll occasionally call either of us to check up on her progress. Now, I'm thinking, if he was trying to be with her, he would simply come here to see her, wouldn't he?"

"Oh, Sharon, I don't believe you've ever cared much for me, have you?" Evelyn asked with a phony laugh.

"I don't like some of the things my nephew has told me, so no. I've always pegged you to be the messy type. With that out of the way, it's almost 9:30. What brings you by? Because it's obvious you came to be messy, since you never call to see how we're doing."

"Sharon, Sharon, Sharon. Tsk! I came to warn you about this home-wrecker and help save your marriage, and you have such unkind words for me."

"Home-wrecker? Save my marriage? We've been married over forty years. Who's supposed to wreck my marriage?"

"Well, according to the information I've gathered, my husband was attempting to send this hussy some money to move into a studio with her son, so she could get away from your husband trying to have sex with her, and my simple-minded husband had every intention on visiting her for sex in that studio. I have a recording of the entire conversation for your listening pleasure, along with the text messages, the wire info, and the filthy, naked photo she sent to him just a few of weeks ago."

Desiree's mouth opened from the shock, while Sharon's head ping ponged from looking at both Ben and Desiree.

Evelyn continued. "I will say, in the hussy's defense, she did say that she wanted to tell you, but my horny husband told her not to say anything because he'd find her a place for them to be together instead. Still, I wouldn't trust her up under my roof, and I'm pretty certain, if you would have seen how she went to work dressed, I could just imagine how she's the one actually trying to seduce your husband, the way she did mine. She likes to play the victim. Just like she tried to cry rape, but then there are sex videos of her voluntarily going to see that person she accused of rape."

"Desiree, is this true? And if so, why wouldn't you immediately let me know?" Sharon asked with tears in her eyes.

Before Desiree could answer, Ben volunteered, "It ain't none of her business who I sleep with. Whatever go on in this household is not any of her business."

Sharon looked at him as if he were crazy. "Sleep with?"

"Ain't that why she's under my roof?" he senselessly asked.

"Wait! Are you two sleeping together? Are you having sex with one another?" Sharon asked, rising from her seat.

While Desiree quickly denied the accusation, Ben acknowledged it.

He repeated, "Ain't that what you brought the girl here to stay for? Why wouldn't I want something pretty and young?"

"Desiree, you could stand in my face and lie to me? Him making a pass at you is one thing, but having sex with my husband is a big difference, and I'm not sure why you didn't feel you could tell me when he first made a pass at you. Why would you tell my nephew instead of me? I treated you like a daughter. I loved you and your son. I let you stay in my home and never asked for a dime, so why would you betray me in such an ugly manner?"

Desiree wanted to still deny it, but couldn't see any way of doing it, since Ben had already fessed up. "I'm sorry. I didn't know what to do. I wanted to tell you."

"So, you wanted to tell me that you were having sex with my husband? When were you planning to do that?"

"I didn't want to have sex with him. I just didn't know what else to do," Desiree cried.

Sharon closed her eyes and laughed. "You didn't know what else to do? But you couldn't just tell me? That wasn't something else for you to do?"

"When I spoke with Roger about it, he told me that you'd put me out the minute I told you, because you would never get rid of your husband. That's why he was supposed to have been helping me get out of here before things went any further."

"You told my nephew before you had sex with my husband? Then you decide to have sex with him after that? How long did you plan on continuing this affair right under my nose?"

"I start my new job in a couple of days. I planned to leave when I got paid."

"And you planned on having sex with my husband for a few more weeks, at least until you got paid?"

"I swear, I didn't know what else to do after I didn't hear back from Roger. I would never have set out to hurt you."

"You're telling me that my husband forced you to do something you didn't want to do?"

"I repeatedly told him he was making me uncomfortable and I was offended," Desiree defended.

"I didn't make her. I thought she wanted to. She came down in the basement to see me, and she asked me if she could come in my basement later tonight," Ben said, seeming unfazed.

Sharon had to take a seat and covered her face. Evelyn sat looking quite pleased with herself. Sharon took a deep breath before turning to Desiree.

"If you would have come to me and told me, no, I would not have put my husband out. However, I would have given you the money to get another place—even this studio someone mentioned, but you said nothing. Instead, you want to crush me as if I have done something to hurt you. Now I see how you end up in the predicaments that you do. And now I'm inclined to agree with this one here," she said pointing to Evelyn, "You do like to play the victim and fail to take any accountability for your own actions. I can't believe you'd think I would have somehow punished you for my husband's actions. I was the one who told you to avoid being alone with him from day one, because I knew he was frisky, which is why I always supplied you with both our schedules. Despite all that, you still found a way to be alone with him. You are truly a tramp, and you need to get your son and get out of my home right now. I'll be damned if I'm going to let you stay another night so you could meet my husband in the basement to do what you claim he made you do. Get out!"

"Oh, and if you're wondering what ever happened to that money my husband tried to wire you, I intercepted it. I wasn't going to let you have a dime after what you've done to our lives, causing my husband to quit his job and take a beating for your slutty butt. You're a whore! Also, you better not attempt to contact my husband again for any reason. The fact that you knew that I monitor his communications, and chose to turn around and send him a nude photo of yourself, that's like a slap in the face to me. Like you wanted me to see how you're trying to take my husband away. You know he's a married man. We've met before, and I told you then to back off, only to learn that you slept with him afterward, in his office. You were already going to go work for the other guy, so you had no business being in the office with my husband late at night, leaving your son wherever. Simply put, you're a home-wrecking whore. I can't wait for you to one day get married and someone takes your husband."

After Evelyn was done, Sharon spoke again. "I owe you an apology, Evelyn. Thanks for letting me know about the wolf wearing sheep's clothing I had living right underneath my nose." Sharon turned to a crying Desiree. "Please get your belongings and get out of my home. Now."

"I have no place to go," Desiree pleaded.

"That is no longer my problem. If you weren't planning on whatever, with my husband tonight, I would have at least given you until the morning for the little boy's sake, but no—there's no way I can let you stay, knowing I'd have to stay awake all night long just to prevent it. This is my husband's home, so it's not like I will put him out. You're the one who must go."

Defeated, Desiree turned to go back up the stairs to pack up all of their belongings, not having a clue where she'd go from there.

28

With no place else to go, Desiree ended up back at her parents' home. At one point, she considered returning to Malcolm, but then she thought about how he would more than likely physically batter her and subject her to other brutal forms of punishment. That thought made her realize that going back there wasn't an option. She even desperately called Roger and left him a voice message letting him know that his wife was the reason she never received his wire and was forced to stay and be subjected to Ben's advances. At that point, she had nothing left to lose and didn't give a damn about Evelyn also hearing her message. Despite her own actions, she still felt like everything was Evelyn's fault.

She didn't dare let on to her parents why she became homeless in the middle of the night. As a matter of fact, she parked in a rest stop along the turnpike to sleep until early in the morning before she called her father and acted like she and Tayshon were just coming up for a while to visit.

Desiree was at such a low point in her life, she began making plans to end it. She figured once her son was safe, she could carry out her plan to go out to her car, take an overdose of pills, and then use the gun to shoot herself in the head. She felt like despite all of her degrees, nothing would ever go her way.

Her parents were taking Tayshon on a boat ride, and Desiree opted to not attend so she could carry out her plan. That morning, she went around town trying to round up as many pills as she could from corner drug dealers. She got in her car to drive to a remote location where she could go through with ending her life. Before she could make it to her destination, her phone rang. It was a California number. Curiosity made her wonder why the number looked familiar but wasn't programmed in her phone, so she pulled over to answer the call.

"Hello," she said, trying to mask the fact that she was crying.

"Good morning, I'm trying to reach Desiree Flowers."

Desiree looked at her car clock and saw it was already after one, but then realized the person hadn't considered the time difference.

"This is she."

"Hi Desiree, this is Micah, and I was calling to follow up with a Skype interview you had about a week ago for the brand manager position with our company, Edge 4000. The managers would like to fly you out to San Francisco to meet with you in person."

Desiree's hand covered her mouth to keep from screaming. She couldn't believe the sudden stroke of luck right at the moment she was about to end it all. She wondered if that was God's way of stopping her from ending her life.

"Oh, that would be great. When would they like me to fly out?" she asked when she got it together.

"If you're able to fly out tomorrow, that would be perfect. They're hoping to get you started within the next three weeks, so I'm not sure what all you'd have to wrap up on your end."

"Yes, tomorrow will be fine."

"Great! I'll shoot you over an email with your flight and hotel info."

"Wonderful, I'll be on the lookout."

Desiree was beyond amazed, especially because she hadn't even applied for the position. She received a phone call saying they were told she was in the market and happened to have a copy of her resume. She even remembered that day being a good day, because she received the call the same afternoon as her first day of having great sex with Ben. The Skype interview was a few days later, but then she hadn't heard anything else. She had only got a callback for an office clerk position, which she was scheduled to start but couldn't because she had to leave New Jersey.

After checking her email and finding the flight and hotel confirmation, she went to toss her collection of pills in the river.

It didn't surprise Desiree that her family was not at all supportive of her moving across the country or even going to California to see about a job she hadn't even applied for. They even suggested it was some type of sex-trafficking trap. Nonetheless, they kept her son while she trotted off to the west coast.

The meeting was more of a formality, because the job was pretty much already hers. Unlike her previous interviews when she was with Malcolm, she went in full professional mode, and didn't even reveal any cleavage from her blouse. She wore a conservative heel, as Sharon had recommended while she was living there. She completely allowed her mind to be the focus of her interview, and for the first time in her life, she felt a level of pride in herself that was beyond what she'd imagined.

Not only were her new employers giving her a generous sign-on bonus, but they were also providing relocation assistance. The company wasn't a large one, but it definitely had plenty of room for growth. It was one she'd hope to grow with for many years to come.

In the back of her mind, Desiree felt as if she owed gratitude to Sharon for helping to transform her way of thinking of herself as a respectable, professional person instead of a sexy, pretty face. Although she wanted to call, she opted for an email, since she figured the wounds were still raw.

Hi Miss Sharon. First, I want to truly, truly apologize to you for betraying your trust and faith in me. There hasn't been a day that has gone by that that thought alone causes me to cry—the thought of hurting you so deeply. I am so sorry. I know words can never repair the damage I have caused, but hopefully you'll find it in you to forgive me one day.

I am now in California and was offered that job that I did the Skype interview for a few weeks back. As happy as that makes me, I still hurt because I realize that without your guidance and your help, none of this would be happening for me. I remember how you worked tirelessly to prepare me for that interview and told me how to dress and conduct myself for any professional interview. As long as I live, I will owe this honor to you. Thank you.

They say you never miss the water until the well goes dry. I didn't know what that meant before, but since losing your love, now I know, and it hurts like hell. I know you told me to strive for success for myself and no one else, but I will always keep you in mind along my pursuit of success, because one day, I would like for you to see me on a television or a newspaper and feel a sense of pride in knowing that you had a hand in helping groom me into a better person. I just wish I could have been that better person before I burned that bridge with you, but nonetheless, I will continue to work to make you proud.

Again, I thank you and I am so very sorry. I definitely don't blame you for anything, and you had every right to be angry and react the way you did. I surely deserved it. You told me I had a problem taking accountability for my actions. Hopefully, this is a start. Believe it or not, I really did love you. You were like the mom I wished I had while growing up. I even smile at the thought of how great my life would have been growing up with you as my mother. As such, you are the first person I'm telling about my new job offer, which was just made official an hour ago. I couldn't wait to get out of there and to my computer just so I could let you know.

Please be well. I want nothing but the best for you. Take care.

Less than an hour later, Desiree's phone was ringing, and it was Sharon. She was afraid to answer, because she didn't know if Sharon was calling to tell her never to contact her again, and she didn't want to receive the crushing words. Instead, she let the call go to voicemail, and decided to listen to the message first.

"Hi, Desiree. This is Miss Sharon. I got your email, and am happy to hear things are going well for you. I've been worried since you left and wished I had handled things better than what I did. It still hurts, but I definitely can find it in my heart to forgive you. Perhaps from time to time, you can check in just to let me know how you're getting along. That would mean a lot to me. And that little boy of yours. You know I love him to pieces." She chuckled.

"I've spoken with my nephew, and he said he feels partly to blame for telling you not to say anything to me, and based on everything you had already gone through in your life, I can now understand how you may have felt a sense of desperation to keep a roof over you and lil Tayshon's head, and for that, I apologize for my husband's actions.

"And yes, I am so very proud of you on your new job. I knew you had it in you all along. You just needed to believe in yourself. Okay, I'm just an old lady rambling now, but do call me when you get all situated and let me know how the job is going and how you're enjoying California. Who knows? I might move back west one of these days and leave this old fool behind, so don't be surprised." She laughed.

"Take care, and I do love you and Tayshon. All right, bye for now."

Desiree sat and emptied her soul. The tears would not stop. Instead of calling back at that moment, she decided to wait until she started her new job and had something to really tell.

Although Desiree went back to New York to get her belongings, she held off on bringing her son until she was able to get herself situated in a home of her own and find a school for him. For the time being, she stayed in an efficiency hotel across the bridge from San Francisco until she had an opportunity to really explore the Bay Area and decide where she wanted to settle in.

29

Three weeks after her interview, Desiree was reporting for her first day of work and was excitedly sitting in her new office, reading some of the company manuals. Her first day pretty much consisted of filling out personnel forms and reading up in more detail about the company. Some of the stuff seemed a bit overwhelming, and she wondered if she'd be able to live up to their professional expectations, since she was really lacking in experience. The people were very different from the people on the east coast, and everyone seemed so kind, which she couldn't remember ever experiencing on any job.

After the wonderful catered lunch in her honor, she went back in her office reading manuals when she felt a quiet presence standing in her doorway. She looked up and was shocked. It was Roger standing propped against the doorframe with a smile. She wanted to scream and run into his arms, but she had to remember where she was. She covered her mouth as the tears formed. She stood to go receive the hug he was offering.

"Oh my god! What are you doing here? I can't believe you are standing here. How did you know where to find me?"

"Ah, so many questions to answer. Let me see if I can answer them all." He laughed. "First, I am standing here because I stopped in to see you. Second, I'm here because I, too, will be working here. I left my wife and actually filed for divorce. Once that is done, I will become part owner of this company. I just didn't want to do it before my divorce was finalized and end up dragging the company through my personal mud. And third, I knew where to find you because it was me who made some phone calls and was shopping out your resume—let's just say, being your own private headhunter. I knew the people here and we discussed me coming on board as one of the owners, and of course, I let them know about you. Do know you are here on your own merit, and not as a favor to me. Not only that, I spoke with my aunt Sharon, and she told me about the heartfelt email you sent to her saying you got a job in California. When I let her know I was heading this way, she asked that I give you this—" He hugged her again. "Yeah, apparently you've made an impression on her, so she wanted you to have a great big hug."

Desiree couldn't stop smiling. She was happier about the hug sent from Sharon than seeing Roger. "Wow! This day keeps getting better by the minute. The people here are so wonderful. This office is amazing. San Francisco is amazing. California is amazing. And now here you are. This is so wonderful, and you're looking great."

"All right now. Now I know you're just trying to be kind. I know I don't look as great as when you saw me last. I feel like I look ten years older."

"No, really, you look great. You're walking on your own. I remember you said you had to use a walker or cane or something."

Roger laughed. "This is the look of sheer determination. I was determined to get out of that hell I was in with Evelyn. I told you before, I had left her. I felt cursed having to be back with her. And it was even crazier when my aunt told me about her having some recording of the conversation you and I had. That's just insane. I'm not sure if you knew, but my family is from out here on the west coast. They're spread from San Diego to Washington state and all points in between. There are a few living in Las Vegas and Phoenix as well. It kind of feels good to be home. Well, not technically home. My home was in Oregon—Portland area. Perhaps one day we can take a trip up that way. You haven't been on the west coast before now, correct?"

"No, I haven't. It's amazing out here. Even the air is so different. This kind of feels like being in New York, but with kinder people." She laughed. "It's a big melting pot."

"That is true. You know San Francisco is notorious for its gay population. That's a very big thing here. Just keep that in mind for when you decide to venture out to any clubs." He laughed.

"Oh my god, I don't know the last time I've been to a club. I think I went for my twenty-first birthday, and that was it. Everything has been work, school, and being a mother. Maybe a club is just what I need to cut loose and let my hair down."

"Speaking of hair, I see you cut your hair off. It looks great. Very sharp and professional."

"You like?"

"I do. It is really nice on you."

"I figured it was time to start making some changes in my life, and the hair was the first thing to go. I had it chopped off and straightened out right before I flew out here for my interview. I was also kind of tired of people questioning my nationality. Right now, all they see is a professional looking black woman."

Roger laughed. "Uhm, I don't know if you know this, but you still have an accent that's indicative of a Hispanic background. And I definitely hear the New York when you speak."

"Really? I thought I sound normal—whatever that is. Oh well, I tried." She laughed.

"Are you bilingual?"

"Please!" she laughed. "My parents speak half-ass Spanish. I'd try speaking to other Spanish people and they'd look at me like I was stupid. I'd be so embarrassed. I can understand pretty well, but I don't dare try to speak it anymore."

"You said your parents are from Puerto Rico, right?"

"My mother is from Puerto Rico and my father's family is from the Dominican, but somehow found their way living in Puerto Rico before they came to the U.S. Both of my parents spent their lives in New York from the time they were their teens, and we were born in New York, so both of them were speaking mostly English by the time we came along."

"Interesting. I'm looking forward to getting to know much more about you. Not sure if you're interested, but I have a nice apartment not too far from here. Well, it's here on this side of the bridge. I don't know if you and your little one are situated in your own place as yet, but you're more than welcome to stay with me."

"Oh wow! That is so nice. My son is still in New York with my parents. I wanted to get situated and find a home and school for him before I brought him out here."

"That's understandable. Well, in that case, perhaps you'll join me for dinner then. It's just about quitting time for the day."

Desiree smiled uncomfortably. "Will they allow that here? I don't know how that works, about dating coworkers or bosses. I don't want to lose my job before I can get started. I'm trying to read through all the manuals, but I haven't reached that part just yet."

"You're such a sweetheart." Roger chuckled. "We'll be fine. It's not like we're in here carrying on. I don't think you've met Sabrina yet. She and Dave are the ones who started this company. Sabrina is now Dave's wife, and she's home expecting a baby any day now."

"Aww, that's sweet. No, I haven't met her, but he did mention that he and his wife started the company five years ago. I didn't know they weren't married back then."

"Nope. I knew Dave before he started this company. He tried to get me to come on board back then, but I couldn't see walking away from the money I was making. Looking back now, I feel like I sold my soul to those devils."

Desiree couldn't take the torture any longer. "Roger, please have a seat. I have something to tell you."

Roger looked at her oddly but did as she requested, and she closed her door for privacy.

She cringed trying to find the best way to say what she had to say. "Roger, I really, really do care for you deeply, and I really would like to come and stay with you, but there's something I have to confess to you before I can go any further."

Roger looked confused. "I'm listening. You kind of have me worried."

"I'm sorry. I truly wish I would have told you the truth long ago, but I was in this desperate state and all I could do was think about myself or how something would hurt me or inconvenience me. You had a chance to get the justice you deserved, and I stole that from you."

"Huh?"

Desiree had tears in her eyes. "Your beating—it was not Ted or Alex. It was Malcolm."

"What?" Roger asked, still not fully processing her words.

"I know you thought somehow Ted was responsible for your brutal beating. It wasn't him. I didn't know it until much later, but Malcolm confessed to me that he was responsible for it. He saw you and me together at Chuck E. Cheese with our son. Malcolm is my son's father. We were together—living together, supposedly engaged to be married, all the way up until the time I ran away. He knew about you and me, and he was okay about it until he learned that you were a black man, then he had a problem with it. He felt as if I was in love with you, which is why I hid the fact that you were black."

Roger was still confused. "I'm not quite following here. You're saying he knew that you and I were together, but he was okay with it as long as it wasn't a black man? Were you a prostitute or something? Was he your pimp? I mean, that kind of sounds crazy."

The tears poured from her eyes from seeing the hurt that Roger was obviously feeling. She kept trying to wipe them. "I don't know what to call myself. Looking back on it now, it would seem that way. I just didn't know or realize it then. When I met you, what I felt with you was real. That's the reason I hid it. I believe I was in love with you. I didn't know what I was feeling. Nonetheless, I knew he'd go ballistic if he knew you were black. He didn't care about me sleeping with white men. As a matter of fact, he'd always be the one pushing me to sleep with whoever just because it was supposed to help elevate us in his grand scheme of things. When he brought some little young girl to come live with us—some girl he actually got locked up for getting pregnant, which was the reason I went to Alex for the pay advance to bail him out—I think that was the point when I began to realize he was like a pimp. This girl was having sex with different guys that he'd arrange, and she'd give him the money. When he brought her into our home, I guess that's when I learned what he thought of me. He kept calling me his fiancée, telling me we were in this together, when all along, I was the game he was playing."

"I don't even know what to say right now. I don't know which part I'm the most pissed about. You call me, begging me to help you, all while you were protecting the animal who tried to kill me? Wait, and did I hear you say something about you loved me? What is his name?"

"Malcolm. Malcolm Waters. I wasn't trying to protect him. Not at all. I was just afraid to tell you because I was worried about you being angry at me for bringing this mess into your life, and then you'd turn your back on me when I needed you."

"Do you know how stupid that sounds, Desiree? Why would I have been mad at you for bringing mess in my life? I was under the impression that your mess caused the beating when I thought it was Ted and Alex," he said, on the verge of raising his voice. "You know what? I'm glad this came out now, because it really would not have been good for me to learn this while we were living together. Yeah, you can forget about that. I don't even know who or what you are. A glorified prostitute. What was I—the john? The trick?"

"No! Oh course not!" she cried.

He got up from his seat, went and flung the door open, and left without saying another word to her. She wanted to chase after him, but she didn't want others to know anything about her and Roger being together, especially not on her first day on the job. Her greatest fear in that moment was losing her job and being forced to return to her parents' home in New York.

30

Desiree had been reporting to work for two months, and things had been going exceptionally well. She didn't have to do anything unethical, and she was learning quite a bit about her occupation, and none of it entailed sex. For a reason unknown to her, Roger hadn't shown up for work. Still, she was afraid to get too comfortable, not knowing how Roger would retaliate against her for withholding that piece of information. She wanted to call Sharon to get an idea of what Roger may have been up to, but she didn't want her call to be a probing call. She wanted all conversations to be a genuine and without motive.

The day before, she actually met what she felt might have been a suitable man. He was tall, dark, and handsome, stylish and very professional looking. They met in the Starbucks near her job. She wasn't a coffee drinker, but she decided to try it out since it appeared to be the trendy thing to do. She stood in line trying to figure out the differences between the flavors of coffee while everyone seemed to be in a rush.

Out of nowhere she heard a sexy voice say, "Oh, you must be a virgin, huh?"

Desiree turned to the voice, offended and embarrassed. "What!"

"Yikes! Please don't beat me up. I was just talking about the coffee. Anytime anyone comes in, they know what they want and are in and out the door in minutes."

Desiree laughed. "Oh—Oh yeah. I don't know. It just looked like the popular thing to do. I'm just trying to fit in."

"Why try to fit in when you can be fabulous? I've been checking you out while you've been holding up the line, and I must say, you look fabulous from head to toe. Hair, shoes, makeup, skin, outfit—fabulous!"

"Thank you. You have definitely made my day." She gave him a broad grin.

"And, might I add, don't start any ugly coffee habits, if you don't already have one. This stuff gets to be addicting. I would suggest a disgusting smoothie habit." He laughed. "There's a place right across the street, and if you're going to get hooked on something, at least let it be something healthy."

"Uh-oh. I already ordered a coffee."

He dug into his pocket. "Here's ten dollars. Walk away from the coffee. Go get the smoothie."

"Wow! This is very generous of you."

"No, not really. I plan to take your cup once you walk away." He laughed again. "Brian Mitchel," he said extending a hand to shake hers.

"Desiree Flowers."

"I hear an accent. I'm trying to figure out if you're from the islands or from New York. Maybe a combination, huh?"

"Wow! Very impressive. I'm from New York, and my parents are from the islands."

Both coffee orders came up to the counter. Brian grabbed both cups. "Come on, I'll walk with you to the smoothie shop and let you know which are the best ones to get."

"Sure."

The more she saw how handsome he was, she couldn't stop smiling. When they got to the smoothie shop, they chatted some more, and he let her know the best smoothie choices and the benefits of each. She told him she was new to town and was still trying to figure out places to go and things to do outside of work. He then invited to take her out to dinner at the Fisherman's Wharf the following night. That whole day, she felt as though she was walking on clouds.

While in her hotel room preparing for her date, she was surprised by the knock on the door. She hadn't given Brian her suite number, as she planned to come down to meet him when he called from downstairs. She opened the door.

"Roger? What are you doing here? How did you know where to find me?"

He looked so defeated. "We need to talk. I've just been dealing with so much and—" He looked her up and down. "Are you preparing for a date?" he asked, sounding offended.

"Roger, you show up at my door a whole two months after you walked out of my office, and I haven't heard a word from you. What was I to think? You told me you no longer wanted me to come and stay with you. I don't understand, what's the problem? Why are you here questioning what I'm doing?"

"After everything I have done for you, you have the nerve to be preparing to go out with another man? Why would you do this to me?"

"What am I doing to you? Oh my god, Roger! You're confusing the hell out of me. I have never been out on a real date in my life. Malcolm never even took me on a real date. Now, I actually have a real date with someone I want to go on a date with."

"You need to cancel this date, Desiree. You and I will have plenty of time to go on dates."

"No!"

"No? What do you mean, no?"

"Just what I said. I'm not canceling my date. If you plan on sticking around, then you and I still will have plenty of time to go on dates, but I'm not canceling my date this evening."

"You plan on sleeping with this guy too?"

"What do you mean, too? Who else am I sleeping with? I haven't been with you in almost a year. I thought we were going to be together until you walked out on me and never contacted me again. I'm done waiting for other people to decide the direction of my life. I want to make decisions for myself, and tonight, I've decided I'm going on this date. And no, I have no plans to sleep with anyone, but if I do, that would be my business and my decision."

"So, you don't give a damn about not having a job to return to, huh?"

"What? What does my job have to do with this?"

"You wouldn't even have this job if it weren't for me."

"I got this job on my own merit, remember?"

"You do know I could have you prosecuted right along with that other motherfucker for the beating I had to suffer—the one where you protected that rotten bastard." Roger then got close up behind Desiree and tried to kiss her neck. "Please cancel that date. I need you. I want to be with you right now."

Desiree stepped away from his hold and laughed despite the tears streaming. "So, you want to threaten me, and then you want to make love to me? Man, you have no idea how badly broken I am, thanks to Malcolm. You can't break me anymore. All those threats and then talking about how you want to be with me, that's exactly what he used to do to me. The more you talk, the more you're making yourself sound just like him. I had nothing but respect and adoration for you, but now you want to come at me like this? Why? As for my job, I really love it and appreciate it, but if I lose it—I'm now strong enough to realize, if I lose it, it just wasn't meant for me, and there'll be something even better up the road. You know something else I've never had before? Friends. I am finally making some, and now you come along and want me to stop my life so you can control me and try to break me. So no, again, you cannot break me any further."

Desiree stood looking at Roger who stared in disbelief.

Roger wasn't thrilled with the new and improved Desiree. "Fuck it! This is some bullshit! Here I leave my fucking wife to be with your ass, and all you want to do is play games," he yelled before once again storming out the door.

Desiree really wanted to cry because she was confused. She had just professed her independence and her inability to be further broken. Therefore, she knew she had to pull herself together. She hated dismissing Roger the way that she had, but she felt Brian was more age appropriate, and more of what she wanted. Also, she certainly didn't want to be in another controlling relationship, and Roger was seeming to suggest that was how it would be.

31

Desiree was amazed by the spectacular waterfront views from the restaurant. The food was equally fabulous, as was the company. However, she wasn't making for good company, since she was still troubled by the interaction with Roger.

"You know, I've been trying to figure out if I said or did something, but then I realized you haven't quite been yourself since I picked you up. It's not like I know you all that well, but still, it seems like something might be bothering you. I saw the views take your breath away, but then in the next second, you were looking down again. Would you like to talk about it? I consider myself a good listener," Brian said.

"I probably should have canceled, but I don't know . . . No, you haven't said or done anything wrong. All of this is wonderful. And because I don't really know you, I don't want to burden you with my issues, 'cause lord knows I have more than my fair share of them." She lightly chuckled.

"How about we make a deal: today, you get to unleash all of your burdens on me, and then I'll owe you one." He laughed. "Shoot, you think you have problems . . . Surprisingly, you've caught me during my only drama-free moments in my life. I own stock in the Lifetime channel now, because that's how much drama I keep."

Although Brian spoke with a straight face about the Lifetime channel stock, she knew he had to be joking, and that made her laugh.

"Yeah, I hear you, but I don't want to run you away. You might say it's just too much and never want to see me again."

"Please, you must think I scare easy. Besides, at the very least, you would be able to get junk off of your chest. As many cars that I have, sometimes I take a bus or train just so I can unload on a stranger. Yep, I'll sit there and tell that stranger all of my problems and then feel so much better. Almost like a therapy."

"But what if you try to hold my mess against me?" she asked, still testing the waters.

"Are you wanted?"

Desiree looked at him as if he were crazy. "No! Why would you ask that?"

"Because I can't imagine anything else being held over your head."

"Okay, and you promise you won't give me the boot after I tell you?"

"If it's good and juicy, I'll be back just to get more tea." He laughed. "Now quit with the fifty questions and spill it!"

She went on to give him a little back-story about her and Roger, and how she learned that he was instrumental in helping her get her current job but was now holding it over her head and trying to use it as leverage. She admitted that she wanted to be with him, but since he stormed out on her a couple of months ago, she felt differently and preferred to be with someone closer to her own age with less drama, and perhaps someone who might one day would want to marry her.

"Okay, I heard everything you've had to say, but I'm trying to understand why you are so troubled by this. Why can't you start your own company and be in control of your own path?"

Desiree laughed. "Uh, and I guess you forget, it takes money to make money. I'm in a brand new town, where I hardly know anyone. Most of the people I do know are from my job, and then there's you. I wouldn't know the first thing about getting clients and setting up shop here."

"Well, then I guess you're lucky that you do know me. That's pretty much all you need."

Desiree didn't know what to make of his arrogance.

"That probably sounded conceited as hell, didn't it?" he asked before she could say anything. "In case you didn't know, I am a venture capitalist. I make my money by providing funds for people like you to start or grow their businesses. As for knowing people—*trust*, I know many people. I often try to connect people together, because in the end, I always seem to benefit from those arrangements. I can help you with anything you want to do, but you have to first want it bad enough, because if you don't then you'd just be wasting my money, and that doesn't make me too happy. So, do you want it?"

Desiree's mouth was wide open. She couldn't believe the pot of gold she had stumbled upon. "Oh wow! I really don't know what to say. That is so generous of you to offer."

"It's not all that generous. Like I said, that's how I make my money." He laughed. "I'm being a little bit selfish."

She laughed as well. "Honestly, I really don't feel all that confident in myself. I'm really just starting out and actually learning my trade."

"I remember you had all these bright ideas when we were chatting the other day . You just said that you were even planning on going out on your own with that Roger guy."

"Yeah, but he's been in the business for a long time. Working with him, I would have been able to learn the industry better."

"So build the team that possesses the experience you think it would take for your company to run smoothly. I think before you shoot the idea down, you should at least take some time to think about it and try to put some ideas together on paper. I'm sure when you were in college you had to put together companies—the financials and everything, right?"

"Oh yeah!" She laughed.

"Well, didn't that make you want it?"

She thought back to those days when she fantasized that one day she would be running the company she had put together on paper for her class projects. "Yes. Yes, I really did want it."

"Do you not still want it?"

She shrugged her shoulders. "I don't know. I guess. I haven't thought too much more about it since then. And with everything I had to go through in my previous job, I wasn't even sure I wanted to be in the profession anymore. If I didn't to see how different things could be with the job I have now, I may have been ready to throw in the towel."

"So, will you take some time to think on it? Don't take too long, because just like that ship you see sailing on by—" he pointed out the window to a boat sailing past "—this ship might sail as well."

"Ahggg! The pressure!" She smiled. "I will think on it."

"By the way, your beautiful smile is back. I told you that sometimes it helps to unload."

"Yeah, but now you've put new pressure on me," she clowned.

"I'd rather have get-paid-big-time pressures on me than some damn old-man-with-a-crazy-wife pressure." He laughed.

"True! So true."

"Oh, and I know I said I make my money by other people's businesses, but I want you to be clear—I'm willing to help you with no strings attached. I will still be your friend and I don't expect you to do anything crazy like you had to do in the past. That's not me. It's not that often that I take time out for friends, but I actually like you. You have that New York, keep-it-real type of real." He laughed. "I look forward to building our friendship."

"Me too." She smiled warmly.

She noticed his use of the word, *friendship* and not *relationship*, but figured that might be a good thing, since she'd never experienced a real relationship that started off as a friendship. Whatever the case, she was definitely looking forward to it.

32

Desiree cringed the moment she stepped into the office and spotted Roger in one of the conference rooms, seemingly working. She hadn't seen or heard from him since his visit to her hotel room a few nights before. She was even more on edge when she was summoned to that conference room to sit in on their meeting. She was worried that it was about her, but it turned out it was regarding an account. They wanted her input. When she gave it, everyone but Roger was impressed. Instead, Roger decided to give her a hard way to go and criticized her thought process. He ended up dismissing her from the meeting and sending her back to her office.

The next several weeks were pretty much more of the same, with him nitpicking her performance, which had otherwise been exceptional prior to his arrival. She wasn't sure what she would do, because the tension was getting thicker and thicker to the point that other employees were beginning to question why he was being such an ass toward her. Nonetheless, she channeled that negative energy to figure out what she'd want for her own company, building on some of her ideas from when she was in college and combining them with ideas she was picking up from being in the real business world.

Desiree hadn't seen Brian since their one date, and she was a bit discouraged that he wasn't interested in her after telling him about her Roger drama. She did speak with him twice since then, and he texted her almost every day, saying,

"Hey Gorgeous! Hope your day is a great one! Think success today!" That would make her smile and encourage her to stay positive and focused. Even without seeing him, she was catching feelings for him. She liked the positive attention he gave her without making a single sexual reference, and he always let her know he was thinking about her.

She floated on air from the moment he called her to ask her to meet him at a restaurant. He even offered to reimburse her for her gas and tolls, which she would have gladly paid for just to be in his company.

Her heart sank as the hostess led her to the table Brian was already seated at with five other men. She wanted to cry, thinking he was no different from the others and probably expected her to do something sexual for them. Before she could make a U-turn and bolt out the door, he spotted her and got up to greet her. She tried to put on her game face, but she had already made up her mind that she wouldn't do anything with any of the men, and if Brian so much as suggested it, she'd never speak with him again.

The conversations seemed to be all business. There weren't any personal questions asked about her life. They'd throw out different scenarios and look to her for her input. Whenever she was challenged on her positions, she was sharp with her comebacks, yet remained professional the entire time. Collectively, the men decided to leave, telling Brian that they'd be in touch. That thoroughly confused Desiree.

"So, have you given any further thought to my suggestion of you venturing out on your own?" Brian asked when the men were gone and it was just him and Desiree.

Desiree dug into her large pocketbook and pulled out a folder. She handed it to Brian. "These are my ideas I've put on paper. I incorporated my ideas from school with things I've picked up along the way. I've even considered what it would take financially to make it happen. So, to answer your question, yes, I've given it quite a bit of thought." She winked.

"Wow! I'm impressed," he said, flipping through the pages in the folder. "I see a couple of items missing, which will alter your numbers, but that's an easy fix. Overall, this is a great start. I see you were a bit stingy with the number of employees. Why is that?"

"I figured I needed to keep the costs down starting off."

"Okay, but if you got, let's say, five new accounts tomorrow, how would you manage them and give the clients the attention their accounts need if you have a staff of just five employees, with only two being marketing managers?"

"I don't know." She laughed. "This was just a thought. I know it's not perfect. I figure it would take months before I got to five clients. I'm sure at that point I could consider increasing my staff."

"But the problem with that is you would have failed to factor in that cost, and you wouldn't be able to price correctly to you clients. You would have lowballed your numbers and would end up losing money because all of your costs were not factored in."

Desiree was getting frustrated and frowned. "And this is just why I said I didn't feel I was ready to venture out on my own just yet."

"So, how is life, working with Mr. Rogers?"

"His name is Roger—Roger Daniels. Not Mr. Rogers."

"I know. I was just messing. There used to be a show with some old man talking to the kids on the PBS channel called *Mister Rogers' Neighborhood*. You've never heard of it?"

She tried to think. "No, never heard of it. I'm not that old. I'm only twenty-three."

"Don't you have a birthday coming up?"

"Wow! You remembered?"

"How could I forget? It's written on my desk calendar at home, big as day—'Desiree's 24th birthday'."

"Awww, how sweet. I don't even know yours. As a matter fact, I don't think I've ever asked how old you are. I just figured you're close to my age. And since you have my birthday written big as day on your calendar, I take it there's no wife there."

Brian tightly closed his eyes and then opened them as if offended. "Wife?" He laughed. "No, no wife. I am thirty-three, and my birthday is January 2nd."

"Wow! You're almost ten years older than me. I figured you were around twenty-seven-ish. Definitely didn't think you were thirty yet."

"I moisturize day and night. Everyone don't have that natural good skin like you." He laughed again. "Anyhow, getting back to my question—what's going on with Mr. Rogers?"

Desiree rolled her eyes. "Ugh! I was trying to forget. He's been such an asshole. The entire time I've been on this job, things have been great, and everyone has had only wonderful things to say about my performance. Now this idiot comes up in there, challenging everything I say or do."

"Has he talked about trying to get back with you?"

"No, and I'm glad he hasn't. I did notice he came in one day wearing his wedding ring. I could tell he wanted me to take notice or say something. I didn't say shit. If he wants to get back with his wife, that's his problem. I didn't ask him to leave her in the first place. But ironically, he only wore the ring that one day and never again." She laughed.

Brian also laughed. "Damn, you must have really turned his ass out. Got old dude playing childish games."

"I look at him now and I'm actually embarrassed. Regardless, I'm still thankful for the opportunity he helped me to have. If he would stop acting like an ass, I'd tell him that. I just wanted to keep him as a friend going forward, but I see that won't be possible."

"Then that means it's time for you to leave there and start your own."

"Even you said it yourself—I'm not ready for all of that. I just know every time Roger acts like an ass, I go straight back to my hotel and try to iron out the details of starting my own company. I surf that net, trying to do as much research as possible. Despite all the research, I still really don't know how to go about getting clients, especially because I don't have a portfolio of clients to even reference. At least when I work on getting clients in my current position,

I can tell them about the company's track record. Everyone is about experience and who you know."

"Well, who do you know?"

"In California? Aside from you, Roger, and some of my coworkers, I don't know anyone."

"But who do you *need* to know?"

Desiree thought of the right answer to his question. "I don't know. I guess people who could help me get in front of the right people to help open up some doors for opportunities for me."

"Such as the five guys you just met?"

"Yeah, that would be great."

Brian sat silent with a smirk on his face, waiting for Desiree to put two and two together. When she observed his reaction and his silence, she started processing it all.

"Wait, did I miss something here? Who were those men? They didn't seem like they even knew each other. Hell, at first when I saw them, I thought you were trying to pimp me out."

Brian laughed. "Oh yeah, I'm trying to pimp you out all right. I'm trying to get you to get us that money. Those were five potential clients for your new company that you have yet to form. I let them know that you were looking to branch out on your own and would be in need of clients, so since they each have a need, I had them each come here tonight to meet and speak with you to see if you're a good fit. And I must say you handled yourself exceptionally well. At one point I saw you got a little frustrated from the line of questions, but still, you were on point. Totally unprepared and off-guard, you handled them as if you knew you were walking into the lion's den. Each of those men run multimillion-dollar companies. That Asian guy, Tao—he has the largest number of assets, and he has multiple companies."

Desiree was stunned. When she broke out of her shock, she stood up to go hug and kiss Brian. Although she was going for his lips, he turned his head and just hugged her back. She was unsure what to make of the rejection but was then kicking herself for being so forward with someone who obviously wanted just a business relationship with her.

"Okay, before you get all up in your feelings, because I can see it in your face, I am gay. I don't get down with women like that. It's not that I wouldn't kiss you on the lips, but not in a girlfriend-boyfriend manner. I kiss women on the lips like women kiss other women on the lips."

Desiree covered her face in embarrassment. He stood from his seat, pulled her hands from in front of her face, and kissed her on the lips. Then he took his seat with a big smile.

"Wait! Are you fucking playing with me or what?" she asked.

"No, I'm really gay. Never been with a woman in my life. I love women, but not for bedding them. I think women are beautiful, gorgeous, and sexy, but I'm gay."

"But how can you think women are beautiful, gorgeous, and sexy but be gay?"

"You're a woman. Have you ever looked at a woman and said, 'Damn, she's gorgeous'?"

Desiree twisted her lips, following where he was going. "Wow! Damn!" She laughed. "You are so damn fine. You're killing me. Shoot, I thought I finally found me a good one."

"You did find you a good one. Hell, I'll be all the man you need me to be—just not in bed." He laughed. "Girl, I'll take care of you like it's nobody's business—have the world envious of your ass. But I'll say this one thing, when you do get you a man, he better damn sure be treating you better than I."

"So what am I supposed to do when I get horny—which I might add is already the case?" She playfully pouted.

"Girlfriend, you better get you some stock in Duracell, Energizer or both of them to hold you over in the meantime."

Desiree cracked up laughing.

"You have a little boy who is way on the other side of the country, and he needs you to be on top of your game. You need to be able to set a good example for him, and you don't need to be focusing on a bunch of men and how to get your freak on. You like being wined and dined? I'll do that for you and for him, but all that other shit you think you have to do, toss that mess out the window."

Desiree got teary eyed, took a deep breath, and then decided to tell him about her past and all the hell that she'd endured and the turning point when Sharon helped her to get her act together, all while she betrayed the woman.

He sat wide-eyed while she spoke of one thing more shocking than the next. When she finished, he tried to ease the tension by joking, "Okay, so now that means you owe me two dumpings. I get to unload my drama on you twice in the future." He laughed. "And do know, you would do good investing in that Lifetime channel stock too."

That made her also laugh as she wiped away her tears, that he then helped her wipe before giving her a big hug. In that moment, everything felt right in the world.

"I know the things you have told me might seem hurtful to you, but I want you to hold onto them so you can be able to compare the difference of how far your mind has taken you, compared to giving away your body. You are a superstar and you will go so far in life once you put your mind to it. You say that other fool was able to take advantage of you because you always wanted to be like *The Jeffersons*. Well, damn it, get focused and you'll get your deluxe apartment in the sky. Hell, say the word, and I'll help you get it financed so you can hurry up and get your son here where he belongs. If you become your own boss, you can have a 'take your child to work day' whenever you feel like it." He laughed.

"I think back on all the jacked up things I've done and I'm trying to figure out what I did so right to meet such an amazing man like you."

"I am amazing, aren't I?" he joked. "No, but really, you need to stop shortchanging yourself and know you are a brilliant, phenomenal mind. You don't need me or anyone else to think for you. In all reality, everyone needs a little help along the way. Hell, I grew up in the hood myself, but just like you,

I used those things to help propel me to where I am today. I ain't trying to have you counting what's in my wallet, but I could be sitting on the panel with those cats on *Shark Tank*. I make people's dreams come true, and I get to live the life that I've always wanted. Eventually, you will too. And when you finish living those dreams, you'll create new dreams to strive for."

"I was just sitting here thinking about the day I attempted to start a Starbucks habit. That will go down as the best day of my life." She smiled.

"Girl, you better hush that talk before you have me in tears out here in public."

They hugged again.

<h1 style="text-align:center">33</h1>

Brian helped Desiree get her condo and the perfect location for her business. It was close to her home and the private school they picked out for Tayshon. Since all five clients opted to take a chance by giving their business to Desiree, Brian worked with her to pull the perfect team of employees together so they could hit the ground running.

Things couldn't have been going better in Desiree's life. However, one day, out of the blue, Tayshon asked her if his daddy would be coming to live with them. Desiree felt like she got a punch in the gut. She had to explain that he would not be coming, and that he probably wouldn't be seeing him for a long, long time. She wanted to say, 'never again,' but she knew that would be too harsh for her son to have to deal with.

After Tayshon was in bed for the night, Desiree decided to surf the web to see if she could find out any information about what was going on in Malcolm's life. She still loved him, despite knowing she'd never be with him again. She couldn't believe her eyes when she saw multiple articles talking about him being charged on several counts of child molestation and statutory rape. According to one of the articles, there were three other young girls aside from Sharquita, ranging in the ages of thirteen to sixteen, and each was pregnant. He was also charged with sex trafficking, accused of having a huge prostitution ring running in Maryland, Pennsylvania, Delaware, and New Jersey. Although the arrest was a month prior, she saw that the media seemed to be hunting down all of his children's mothers and trying to figure out how long Malcolm had been preying on young girls. But what disturbed her most was when she stumbled on the video of a woman leaving the court with an attorney, swearing her husband was innocent of all the charges and that people were just making up stories about him. She said they had a little girl that he'd been a perfect father to, and just had a son, which was why people were jealous of their relationship and making up all the lies. Desiree recognized the voice to be Carol, whom she had previously spoken to, and she remembered from the photo of them kissing. It was obvious that the woman had money, based on her attire and the chauffeured SUV she climbed into as the media tried to stay hot on her trail. They were asking her about all of his other children, and she swore that any bitch claiming to have his child was lying.

Desiree started worrying about the media circus finding its way to her and causing her new business bad publicity. She called Brian to share her discovery. The following day, he had her meet him for lunch to introduce her to a friend of his, who owned a public relations firm. Desiree knew she was supposed to be focused on the situation at hand and not men, but the friend that Brian introduced her to was beyond gorgeous. She figured she wouldn't dare set herself up the way she did when she was hoping to date Brian. His name was Edward Hairston. He was twenty-nine, six-foot-three, muscles bulging despite his business suit, and he was her favorite shade of chocolate—dark chocolate.

After the meeting when it was just her and Brian sitting in the elegant lobby of the office building, he asked, "Ain't he fine as hell?"

"Huh?" she asked, put off by Brian's question.

"Ed—he's too fine. Shoot, I know a whole bunch of PR's, but I only called his fine ass just so I could have a reason to see him again."

"See him again? I thought he was your friend."

"He is, but he doesn't like coming around me. He said I make him feel violated." Brian laughed.

"Why is that?"

"Because people have complimented the two of us on how handsome a couple we are."

"Why is that a problem?" she asked, still confused.

"Duh! Because he's straight. He gets mad when people think he's gay just because they know I'm gay and think that when they see us together."

"Ohhh! . . . Oh," she said, first excited that she understood what he was saying, but then the second 'oh' because he let her know that Edward was heterosexual. She wanted to ask a million questions about Edward's love life and his availability, but she knew Brian would scold her, because he always reminded her to stay focused on her business and her child.

"Go ahead and ask."

"Ask what?"

"Girl, there were a few times I thought I was going to have to wipe the drool falling from your mouth." He laughed.

Desiree instinctively wiped the imaginary drool, embarrassed that it might have really been there. That made Brian laugh harder.

"He's sexy and single. He has a five-year-old son that he has full custody of. He owns his firm, and I think he has like seventy employees. Now, if you're gonna have your eyes set on someone, *that* is who you need to be setting your sights on. I wouldn't even be mad at you. Hell, I might be jealous of you if you snag him."

"Really?" Desiree asked. She couldn't believe Brian was giving her his blessing.

"Now, before you get your hopes all up high, I'm not sure how he is about getting involved with clients. That might be your only problem. But on the bright side, you don't have to be a client forever, right?"

Desiree hugged Brian. "Oh my god! Thank you! I won't lie, when I first met you, I was like, 'Whew! It got hot in here.' But I'm telling you, that dude right there—Yeah. You gonna have me going home fantasizing all night."

"Damn! All night?"

"All night!"

The next two months were rough, because that was how long it took before the media found their way to Desiree and brought her sex video from Alex along with them. However, Edward had her fully prepared. He helped her create a nonprofit organization for young girls who were on that dark path to help them turn their lives around. That was able to garner positive attention and accolades for her accomplishments and it helped her advertising company grow and brought in tons of donations to her nonprofit.

In less than a year, Desiree managed to start her own successful business and an organization she hadn't planned on, which was the most fulfilling ever. She was even more thrilled when the invitation she extended Sharon to come to California to work for the nonprofit was accepted. Desiree couldn't think of anyone better to run the organization, because she accredited Sharon with all of her current success and felt she would also impact all the young ladies coming through the doors.

With time and Sharon's presence, Desiree was finally able to get back on speaking terms with Roger. He was actually happy for her success, and he apologized for all the grief he had caused her. After Brian let Edward know that Roger was probably going to try to slide his way back into Desiree's life, Edward did the unthinkable.

34

Desiree, I had a conversation with Tayshon and I asked him if it was okay for me to ask his mother to be my wife. I know we haven't been on any official dates, and that was because we had to rush to set up the new nonprofit and you've been swamped with a ton of new clients and all. Despite it all, I've observed enough to know you are the woman I want to spend the rest of my life with. You are as real as real gets. There's nothing fake about you. You have battle scars and you wear them with pride. I've watched you with your little boy, and I see the love and how you'd lay down your life for him. Honestly, before I met you, I wasn't too sure what I wanted in a woman or a wife. Having been involved in your life for all these months, I'll be damned if I'm going to keep dragging my feet and possibly allow some joker to come in and sweep you off yours. You are a queen and you deserve a king. I think I can be that king for you.

"Now, I know this seems really unorthodox and out of order, because we haven't ever actually been on a real date-date, but I've seen and experienced enough to know that I would like for you to be my wife and a mother to my son as well—and who knows, maybe others down the road."

Edward got down on one knee as Desiree covered her mouth from the shock. Even Brian was in shock as Edward pulled a diamond ring from his pocket.

"Desiree Flowers, would you do me the honor of being my wife? We don't have to rush to the altar, and we'll take as much time as you'd like, but just know, I want to spend my life with you."

The tears poured from her eyes as she continually nodded her head over and over. She was going to throw all caution to the wind, because she knew she wasn't going to be someone's "forever, ring-less fiancée" ever again. She had loved everything about Edward just the same, despite not having any official dates. They had gotten together plenty of times for lunches, dinners, ballgames, and other activities that included bunches of people, such as the black-tie charity event they were currently at for his jaw-dropping proposal.

"Yes! Yes! Yess! Yessss!" Desiree shouted, and everyone cheered. And for the first time ever, she got to kiss Edward, and it was so wonderful that they both forgot there was a crowd watching. The crowd continued to cheer for as long as the kiss lasted. Brian kept trying to break them apart, but Edward kept playfully swatting Brian away, as he continued to kiss Desiree.

One year to the date of the magical proposal, Desiree walked down the aisle of her fairytale wedding. Her parents and sisters flew into town for the event. Sharon was her maid of honor, and her bridesmaids were her two sisters and two close friends she had made when she first arrived in California. Although Roger was invited, he opted not to attend. Brian was the best man. It was a large wedding, and it even made the papers. They honeymooned for one week in Europe, and then the second week on a Disney cruise with the kids.

Using their previous residences as rental properties, Edward brought them together in a beautiful penthouse apartment with sweeping views of the Bay Area, which he purchased just to help fulfill Desiree's dream of moving on up.

THE END

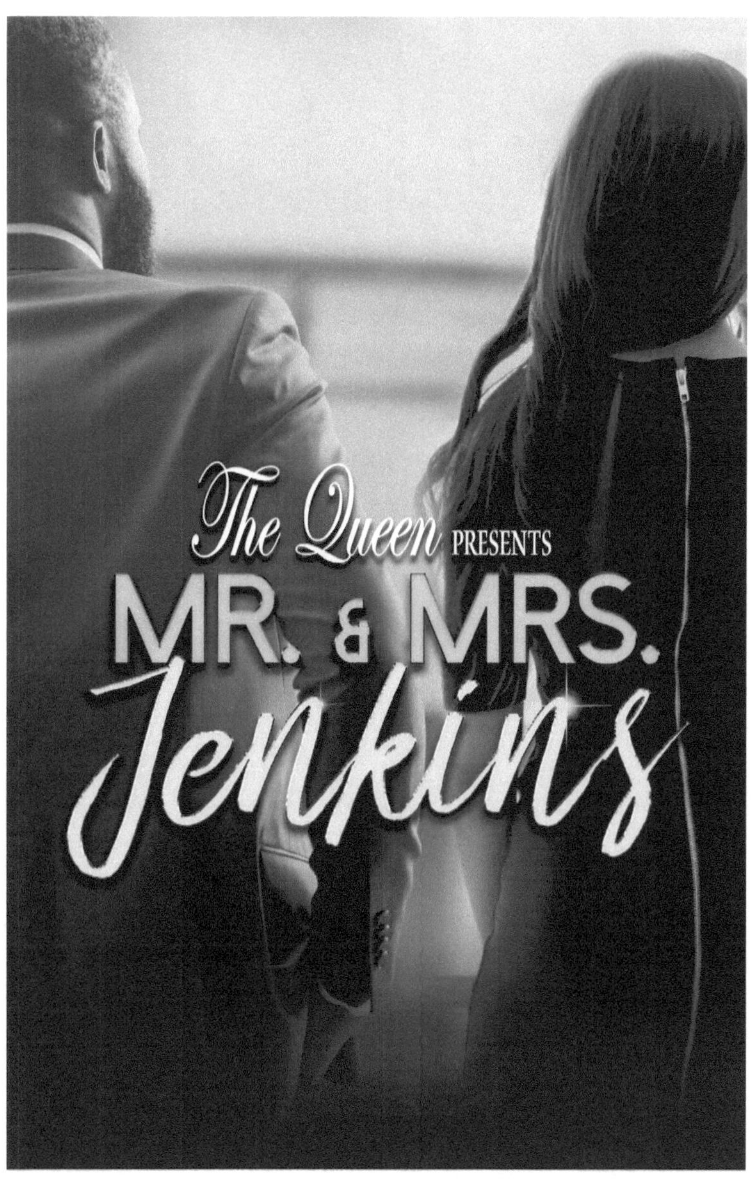
The Queen PRESENTS
MR. & MRS.
Jenkins

1

JENKINS & JENKINS

In a huff, Monica walked into the spacious white office she shared with her brother-in-law, Anthony, and slammed her bags down on her desk as he looked up from his computer and watched as some of the items fell from her desk.

"FUCK!" she yelled, as she stooped down to collect some of the files that had scattered.

"Well, good morning to you," Anthony said, trying to lighten the moment.

"It's anything but," she snapped as she continued trying to gather the fallen items.

"Not sure if this will help, but I stopped by and picked up some of your favorite pastries this morning," he said, nodding his head in the direction of where a box of pastries sat on their meeting table.

That caused Monica to soften up, and tears formed in her eyes. "Aww Anthony, that was so sweet of you. I really needed it. This entire morning has been a mess."

"You want to talk about it before we get to work?"

"It looks like you've already been hard at work." She pointed to his cluttered desk.

He chuckled. "Yeah, I've been here since six-thirty this morning, but I could use a little break. Besides, I have some ideas I want to bounce off of you for this new campaign, and I need your mind cleared of all the junk first."

After collecting everything from the floor, Monica stood from her squatting position and stared at him for a moment without speaking.

"I bet your ass is cold," he said, catching her off-guard. "That's probably why you're so angry."

"Ha ha. I see we got jokes." She chortled after snapping out of her trance.

"Monica, it's like twelve degrees outside. You have that skimpy leather jacket on, and that skirt is made of what—nylon?" Anthony scolded, pointing toward the wall-to-wall windows.

After putting the files back on her desk, Monica went for the hand sanitizer on the wall. As she rubbed her hands together, she took her daily inventory of the collection of successful ad campaigns on the wall before going to open the box of fresh pastries.

"For your information, my coat is in the car, but I was just too angry to realize I left it. And, if you must know, there is about forty percent nylon in this skirt. It's a cashmere blend that my well-paid stylist selected for me."

"About that. When are you going to get rid of the dude and go do your own clothes shopping? I know how much you make, and we're not banking the big bucks like that."

"How many hours a day do we spend stuck in this office or in someone else's office? When am I supposed to go shopping for myself? Hell, you *need* to hire my stylist to shop for your wife, because that is one sad looking chick. The way my sister dresses makes *you* look bad. If I didn't know any better, I would think your business was struggling to make ends meet, and she was getting paid minimum wage on her job. Hell, I'm the one with a barely working husband that doesn't contribute to the fucking household," Monica said, getting angry all over again. "Do you know, every dime he gets paid from the church, he's always giving right back to pay the ten different offerings that corrupt-ass church collects, or he's using it to travel with that crooked-ass pastor of his?"

"Hey! That used to be my pastor, once upon a time. We grew up in that church. Well, sort of. There were only about five hundred or so members back then. Now, they went and got all mega."

"Tell me Pastor Wade ain't shady as shit," Monica said before swallowing a bite of bear claw pastry. "Oh my god! This is so fucking good. Thank you. This just made my day—but that motherfucker is still shady as hell."

Anthony laughed as he got up from his desk to get a pastry for himself and took a seat across from Monica at the round meeting table. "How do you take the Lord's name in vain and cuss all in the same sentence?"

"First of all, I didn't take the Lord's name in vain, because when I said, 'god,' I was speaking in the lowercase 'g' sense, and not the capital 'g.' Big difference."

Anthony laughed so hard, he almost choked on his cruller. "You can't be serious, right? I guess that 'g' makes all the difference in the world."

"It does. It really does. The same as when we say 'Lord' and 'lord.' One has a lowercase 'l' and the other has an uppercase. When we use the uppercase, that's the same as talking about the uppercase 'g' God."

Anthony covered his face and shook his head. "Okay, you win. I'm sure the man upstairs knows your heart." He laughed again.

"Whatever!" she said, rolling her eyes while a laugh escaped her. "And getting back to your brother—my dear husband—don't they teach you that the man is supposed to be the provider in the house? Could you imagine if we had kids? We'd be homeless, because I wouldn't be able to work as much *and* care for a baby. Speaking of babies, is my sister still trying to get pregnant and doing all that extra fertility stuff?"

"Pfft!" Anthony turned his focus to the windows to keep Monica from seeing his deep-seated frustration. "You have to have sex in order to get pregnant. Now she's talking about going to a fertility clinic to see if something might be wrong with me because she hasn't gotten pregnant."

"I always tell you, she should have married Aaron. They would be perfect for each other. No matter what I do, he's always too tired or too busy or gone."

"I know. I'm sorry," Anthony said, placing a hand over her hand resting on the table.

"What are you sorry about? Hell, I'm sorry for you. I hate what Mya does to you. She's always trying to give everyone advice on how to fix their lives, but she doesn't have sense enough to know that a man has needs that should be taken care of."

Just then, Monica and Anthony's eyes locked, and they both became uncomfortable.

"Yeah, I guess we better get back to work now," Anthony said as he quickly shuffled back over to his desk with the rest of his pastry.

At times, Monica got a kick out of making Anthony uncomfortable, especially when her hormones were raging and she was being neglected by her own husband. That was the reason she had their office set up with their desks facing each other from across the large space. She'd often catch Anthony staring at her when he didn't think she knew, and when she'd look up at him, he'd quickly turn away. Sure, it was cold outside, and the wind quickly whipped through her flimsy fabric, but her hormones wanted Anthony to take notice of her panty-less derriere. Monica had curves for days compared to her sister, who barely had hips or breasts. She couldn't understand what Anthony could have found attractive about Mya.

Monica thought she was getting a good deal by getting with Anthony's identical twin, although their facial hair and weight made them easy to tell apart. Anthony stayed well-groomed and had a lush, neatly trimmed beard that made Monica moist between her legs at the mere thought of it, along with his perfect white teeth and thick lips.

Despite also having the same perfect teeth and thick lips, Aaron, on the other hand, wore no facial hair, and his barber was any student at the beauty school on $5.00 Haircut Day, diminishing her attraction to him. He had facial hair and was better groomed when they were in college, but without having a full-time job over the years and Monica's weariness of providing for his grooming needs, he resorted to the beauty school.

While Anthony sported dapper suits or name-brand dress shirts, Aaron got many of his items from the second-hand store or hand-me-downs from other men in the church. The only time he'd ever have something new was at Christmas or his birthday. Anthony took pride in his body and made an effort to stay fit, while Aaron never passed up a meal offered by the church parishioners, adding to his continually growing waistline. Monica dressed in mostly name-brand items, while her sister bought her clothes off a rack in Walmart, Kmart, TJ Maxx, or Burlington's clearance section.

Monica and Anthony Jenkins started their successful ad agency almost five years ago after graduating from Howard University, which they attended with each of their twin siblings. Anthony's brother, Aaron, was working to answer the ministry calling that he received several months before their graduation. Monica's fraternal twin sister, Mya, opted to further her education to pursue her dream job of being a social worker. Monica spent many years fighting the undeniable chemistry between she and Anthony, because of her marriage to his brother.

When Monica and Aaron married straight out of college, she had no idea that he would forego having a real job as he pursued a ministry career. She had no idea that he'd be leaving her home alone most nights while he followed the pastor of his church on his travels, in hopes of one day filling those shoes. However, being married to her business partner's brother wasn't the only reason Monica had to fight her desires to be with him; her business partner was also married to her sister, Mya.

Anthony met Mya in their sophomore year of college when they shared a sociology class and had to work on a group project together. They often bumped heads on the project, but somehow, Anthony found Mya's "know-it-all" logic both annoying and attractive. Although the pair began dating that semester, it wasn't until the following semester that Anthony found himself sharing just about every class with Monica. The two had a great number of things in common, but Anthony didn't feel comfortable pursuing anything with Mya's twin sister. Instead, he introduced her to his twin brother, who was an accounting major before he switched to theology in his last year.

Aaron proposed marriage to Monica at the time he received his ministry calling, because he felt that was the right thing to do. In the back of her mind, she knew she was most compatible with Anthony, but since her sister was dating him, she went on to accept Aaron's marriage proposal. Not to be outdone, Mya pressed Anthony to get married as well. She wanted to have a double wedding, which consisted of a quick trip to Las Vegas.

Despite being twins, Anthony hated the fact that he found Monica to be so much more attractive that his wife. Actually, had they not told anyone they were twins, no one would have ever guessed it. Monica took her father's mellow yet humorous attitude; height; full, heart-shaped lips; and cocoa complexion along with her mother's sensual curves. Mya inherited her mother's fiery personality, short height, thin lips, and pale complexion, along with her father's thin frame. Even though they were twins, Mya always behaved much older than Monica.

While most twins typically have close relationships, Monica now despised her sister because she had the man Monica wanted. She and Mya weren't all that close by the time they made it to high school, because Monica resented Mya's authoritative demeanor.

Their mother was a biracial woman with a British mother and a Senegalese father who was absent during her upbringing. She'd often tell Monica that Mya meant well and only had her best interest at heart. Mya was their mother's pet, while Monica was their father's pet. Although their father cheated on their mother more times than a few, he could still do no wrong in Monica's eyes. She adored the ground he walked on. Mya, on the other hand, would team up with their mother on holding grudges or finding ways to punish him for his infidelities. Despite the numerous infidelities, their mother was determined to hold onto him and not allow some other woman the benefit of saying she took him. Although their mother possessed a beautiful light-golden complexion, somehow Mya took on a pale complexion. Monica would often joke and tell Mya to stay out of the sun or that she needed a blood transfusion to get some color and would often ask Mya if she needed to borrow some ass or tits. However, when Mya managed to snag Anthony, knowing Monica was wishing she had him, there were no insults that Monica could hurl to cause Mya any insecurities.

"So, what's new? Tell me about this new campaign you have," Monica said once she got situated at her desk and turned her computer on.

"It's for a political fundraiser. I received this email asking if we could handle the ads."

"Wow! Really? That's great. We're gonna finally get to add some political campaign ads to our wall now. A senator?" she asked, pointing to the wall filled with their photos and posters.

"Not quite." Anthony laughed. "Just city council, but it's a start. If we do well on this, it could open up the gates for many other political ad campaigns."

"True, but what type of budget are they talking about? I don't want to waste our time handling charity cases—I already have one at home," she said, rolling her eyes at the disgusting thought of her freeloading husband. "We make our best coins dealing with corporations, and Momma needs a new pair of shoes."

"Momma or you?" Anthony laughed. "You have a different pair of shoes for every day of the year."

"That's not true. I don't even have fifty pairs of shoes."

"Fifty! I only have a total of fifteen, and that includes my sneakers."

"That's because of who your wife is. You make all the money, and she's always ragging on you when you buy something nice for yourself. She'd rather have you live like poor people while she saves a college fund for a baby that hasn't even been conceived. That's just ridiculous."

"I can't even argue with you on that," he responded, looking off into the distance.

Monica shook her head. "That's crazy; you two have been living in that cramped up apartment since you've been married. With her little salary and her trying to bank every one of your dimes for a baby, y'all will never move. What I don't understand is, why won't you just get a backbone and tell her how it's going to be? Why do you let her control everything?"

"I tried that, and it didn't work. You know how your sister is. I told her I was going to start searching for a house for us, and she told me I couldn't buy a house without her signature, and she didn't feel we needed to begin a house search until she becomes pregnant."

"It's five damn years later!"

"I guess that's why she's now insisting that I go see what's wrong with me. We only have sex when she thinks she's ovulating, and she thinks I'm the problem. Even then, there's no romance or anything. It's just, 'I think I'm ovulating. Come on and let's do it'."

"Why don't you just take the initiative? You're the man. Stop letting my sister treat you like a punk."

"Stop acting like you don't know your sister. You do remember that time when she went crying to you, talking about she felt like she was raped by her own husband that time when I decided to be the man and take initiative? She told your mom, and your mom told my mom, and it was all kinds of disasters. So now, I just wait."

"You don't think about just getting yours outside of the marriage? I mean, it doesn't seem like you'll ever be fulfilled in that marriage."

"Of course the thought has crossed my mind, but I am a married man. If I'm going to stay married, then it is what it is. I just try to focus on this business and how we can make it grow. We have seventeen employees right now. Eventually, I'd like us to have our names on the building in lights and have several layers to our management team. The last thing we need is my marriage problems creating waves for our business."

"Yeah, I guess. It just seems so tragic for you to have to work so hard to make everyone else happy, but you have no life of your own. You don't even have any real friends."

"I still have friends from Howard that I keep in touch with."

Monica waved her hand. "Keep in touch with is all you do. You don't get to go hang out with them. When is the last time you just went out and it wasn't job-related or networking? I mean, just went and hung out with your boys and talked shit while ogling over some hot-ass women?"

Anthony took a moment to think about it. Monica was right. Although he maintained phone conversations with his friends from college, he never spent any time with them, because Mya would always accuse him of wanting to go out and open up the doors for problems in their marriage. To keep the peace, he'd decline the offers from his friends. "Again, I can't even argue."

"You know what really makes me sad when I think about you two? The only time you two spend a night on the town is when it's her birthday, and you would plan some beautiful surprise that she'd always manage to jack up with her fucked-up attitude. When it's your birthday, what do you get? She'll invite the family over to your little-ass apartment for a dinner she sucks at cooking."

Anthony laughed so hard. "Stop ragging on my wife like that. Her cooking ain't that bad."

"Oh, it's that bad and then some. You ain't fooling anyone with that smoothie diet bullshit. I know you do the smoothies because you can't get a good meal at home. We've been at your mom's house, my mom's house, and my house for dinner, and trust me—I see the difference when it's time for you to sit down to eat. That bitch can't cook worth a damn, and since she's my sister, I can say anything I want about the stuck-up bitch. Not sure if you know this or not, salmon is NOT supposed to be dehydrated when cooked. I'm not sure why she bothers steaming broccoli. She might as well serve it raw since hers is so hard and flavorless."

By this time, Anthony had tears in his eyes from laughing so hard.

"Look at how you're laughing. You know I'm right. Tell me I'm lying." Monica laughed.

Anthony held his hands up while still laughing. "I'm not saying a thing."

"I thought so. Anyhow, let's get back to this new campaign. Are we going to assign it to one of the others or is it something you're going to work on personally?"

"Uh . . . Well . . . I think it's something *we* are going to be working on. They are under the impression that we are a husband-and-wife team, and they said that was something that helped influence their decision to choose us for this campaign."

"Huh? Why would they think we're husband and wife? What does that have to do with anything?"

"I guess it might have something to do with our business name, Jenkins & Jenkins, as well as our picture together on our website. Honestly, even Mya had a problem with our photos and wanted me to have the website changed."

"Oh, really?" Monica twisted her lips and rolled her eyes. "We were just having fun during our photo shoot, and that was the image we wanted to portray—that we are a fun and creative bunch. She's so stupid. Don't tell me anything else about her today. She gets on my damn nerves." Her eyes narrowed. "You know, I do remember a while back, Momma had something to say about why you and I were so close up on each other in photos. I asked her if she had a problem with the photos we took with the rest of our core team as well, because we were just as close. Now that you're telling me this, it must have been Mya that went to Momma to get her to say something to me, because that bitch knows better than to come to me with the bullshit."

"Okay, I see you're getting yourself all worked up again, and we did a good job of calming the storm that blew in here this morning. Speaking of which, what had you in a huff this morning?"

"Your brother. What else?"

"What happened?"

"Same shit as always. Last night he's too tired, and this morning he needs to save his energy to work on the church's Valentine's Day music festival."

Anthony looked confused. "That's like three weeks away. He wants you to wait until that's over?"

"I don't know, but I do know I'm getting sick and tired of begging his fat ass for a piece of dick. He ought to be glad I'm willing to fuck his fat ass. I'm trying to figure out how the sexy, 185-pound man that I married is 330 pounds now. I know all them bitches in the church keep feeding him, and he don't know how to say 'no' to food. Even your momma keeps telling him he needs to cut back and go on a diet before he has a heart attack like your father did. Y'all are supposed to be identical twins. How could this be?"

"I keep telling him as well. I told him to do the smoothie diet with me. Dad hasn't been the same since he had that heart attack, and that was four years ago. He just sits around like he's waiting to die."

"I know. That's sad. My dad always goes to see him and swears he's not going anymore but ends up there the following week." Monica chuckled.

"Yeah, I like your dad. One of the perks to being married to your sister."

Monica laughed. "Hang around my dad enough, he'll help you find all kinds of side pieces. And you see, in all these years, my mom ain't letting him go. Teeth falling out, and starting to look like a pregnant pencil, and she ain't letting none of them bitches get to keep him."

Anthony burst out laughing. "A pregnant pencil? Damn! He don't look that bad. He got a little pot belly, but that's it. He's sixty, sixty-one, right?"

"No, he's going to be sixty-five in May. He did so much drinking all those years that his liver's all fucked up now, got him looking like a pregnant pencil."

"Your mom still looks good for her age."

"I guess she would. She's only forty-three. You know my dad was a dirty ol' man all of his life." Monica laughed again. "He only married our mother because he didn't want us growing up without a father, like she did."

"You ever wonder if he might have some other seeds out there?"

"I doubt it. He might be a dog, but he's big on family unity. If he had other kids, he'd want them to be a part of our lives. I don't think he'd hide it from us. Not only that, I remember Daddy telling me a long time ago that after us, he knew never to mess with anyone without some birth control, because he couldn't afford any more twins."

"Well, I guess we can't be mad at him if your mother isn't."

"Please, my mother harasses every young girl he messes with. Even about a month ago, she was talking about going and fighting some nineteen-year-old girl he messed with."

"Damn! A nineteen-year-old? I could see what he'd see in them, but what do they want with him? No disrespect to you. He's old, married, his wife takes all his money, and like you said, he's missing a few teeth. I don't get it."

"Probably some young, dumb ho with 'daddy syndrome.'"

"So, what was so special about this girl? Why not try to fight the others?"

"My mother tries to fight all of them, but the nineteen-year-old happens to be the latest one."

"You ever ask your dad why he does what he does, with the cheating?"

"Yeah. You know he and I are very close, so he tells me just about everything. My mother is always putting him on sexual punishment and making him sleep on the sofa for one thing or another. She always wants to try to control him, and sometimes he just wants to be somewhere where he could have peace . . . and sex. I tried talking to Momma about her controlling ways, but then she'll clap back, saying that's why she still has her man and not some other bitch. She feels if she doesn't control him, he would have *been* left."

"Hey, I guess I can't knock it. He's still there after all these years."

"Funny, I see you following down the same path when I look at you with my sister."

"Please! It ain't even like that with us."

"Oh? And why haven't you been able to buy that new house that you've been wanting? That condo you're in used to be nice when y'all first bought it a few years back, but now that thing is a hiccup away from being called the ghetto."

"Ha ha, I see we back with the jokes again."

"You know it's true. You better man up and take what you want out of life before you become my father. Oh, and in case you didn't know, he lost his first tooth when my mother smashed him in the mouth with an aluminum foil box after one of his cheating escapades that kept him out for two or three nights. I think we were like fifteen at the time. I loved my daddy, and he could do no wrong in my eyes. I remember hating my mother for doing that. I felt like she didn't want him to be attractive to other women anymore. I also remember that next time he stayed out, I was glad, because I felt my mother deserved it based on what she did to him."

"You still feel the same?" Anthony asked.

"No. I mean, she didn't have to do that to him, but I see that he was wrong for what he did. I remember I used to ask Daddy to leave Momma and take me with him, but to leave miserable Mya to be miserable with Momma." Monica laughed. "Daddy would always say that he'd never split his babies up like that, and he would never leave us. Guess he kept his word, at all costs."

"Yeah, that he did do," Anthony responded, staring off into space, thinking of his own marriage.

"Well, we need to get back to working on this new campaign. So, are we going to let these people believe that you and I are married?"

"We are married."

Monica punched Anthony in the shoulder. "You know what I mean."

Anthony laughed and played like he was afraid. "Oh, violent like your mother."

"No, that's my sister. She's the violent one."

"Yeah, I've seen that temper." He chuckled. "Anyhow, I say we let them believe whatever they want to believe. I doubt if they'll ever ask if we're married to each other. And if the truth ever comes up and they think we lied, we can honestly say we didn't."

"Hey, it works for me. They just better have a decent budget, or else they'll only be getting just you on this campaign. I've never heard of any city council members having a whole lot of money. As a matter of fact, they're usually broke and live in public housing, or close to it."

"Girl, you are too much." Anthony laughed heartily and shook his head. "I think we can just work on this fundraiser and see where it goes from there.

I'm sure it'll open up plenty of other doors to people who are well connected. Broke people don't typically attend fundraisers."

"You have a point there. Okay. I'll follow your lead on this one."

"See, that's why you and I make such a dynamic team."

As quickly as the words left his mouth, Anthony was filled with regret for saying it. He could see that look in Monica's eyes that said she wanted to be more than a dynamic business team.

After Monica snapped out of the momentary trance induced by Anthony's words, she made her way to the office door. "I'm going to go check on the others and see where everyone's at."

"Good deal," Anthony responded.

2

ANTHONY

Anthony sat in the parking lot of the apartment complex for a good fifteen minutes after turning off the ignition. The thought of going home was becoming more and more unbearable. He'd leave extra early in the mornings and tried to return as late as possible to avoid the daily drama he received each time he stepped inside of his home.

Earlier that morning, he left before six in the morning, because his attempt to get sex from his wife escalated into an argument of sex being pointless since he couldn't seem to make the baby that she so desperately wanted. That turned into Mya demanding he find time in his busy schedule to go see a doctor about his possible infertility. So many times he thought about going out and finding another woman to impregnate just to prove that he wasn't the problem. He was already medically checked when his wife first made the accusation that he must have a problem. His tests came back fine, but three years later, she was questioning the validity of the previous results.

Another big problem he was struggling with was his growing feelings for his sister-in-law. Monica was everything he could possibly want. She had a sensational sense of humor. She was compassionate. She was super sexy and beautiful. She was talented and smart. She was creative at the drop of a hat. She wore her blackness regally. She was stylish, yet financially savvy and business-oriented. She always smelled good. She was a homeowner. She could cook. She knew good food and wines. She loved the arts. But, she was his brother's wife and his wife's sister, and that meant she was off-limits.

There were many times when Anthony considered cheating on his wife, but he was not as concerned that Mya would find out as he was about Monica finding out. He didn't know what would become of their friendship and their working relationship. Although Monica suggested he go out and find him some action on the side, he didn't believe she really meant it, and he thought she'd be crushed if he did. Basically, he found himself being faithful to his wife more for his sister-in-law than for his wife.

In the back of his mind, Anthony didn't want to have any children with Mya, because he wasn't sure how much longer he'd be able to tolerate her. On the other hand, the thought of having a daughter or son to come home to each day would bring a smile to his face. The other thing that would make him smile was each night before going to bed, he'd pull up the company's website just to look at the photos. He could remember the jolt of lightening that shot through his entire body while he and Monica played around on the set, and the photographer captured most of those moments. Only a person with their head in the sand would deny that there was chemistry between the two. He'd sleep peacefully each night with Monica's smile etched in his mind. Unfortunately, that same smile caused him to wake up horny and wanting sex from his wife.

Oftentimes, when he'd look at Mya compared to her twin sister, he couldn't understand how she looked so undernourished while Monica had every curve, perfectly set where it needed to be. Although Mya wasn't albino, she was very sun-sensitive and would never be caught wearing a sexy bikini at a beach or pool, as her cocoa-colored sister would.

Frostbite started nipping away at his toes as he sat in the car, letting him know it was time for him to go in the house to face whatever drama awaited him. He got out of the car and made his way up the walkway to enter his building. There were a bunch of kids sitting out there smoking weed, and he was reminded of Monica's words about them living in a ghetto. He acknowledged the teenage boys as he did each night when he got home. However, this night one of them had something extra to say.

"Yo, Mr. Anthony, I sure hope you ate before you got home. Your wife had the whole hallway lit the hell up with whatever she was burning. That was hours ago, and the hallway still stinks. My moms was about to call the fire department, but we decided to go check first. She burned your dinner." The boy laughed, and the others joined in. Even Anthony laughed.

"Thanks for the heads-up. I usually make my smoothie at night, so I can stay in shape," Anthony said, patting his flat abs.

"You gonna stay in shape just from missing meals," another boy added, and again they all laughed.

Anthony went into the building and made his way to the elevator. Although their apartment was on the fourth floor, he could already smell the burnt smell from the ground floor. The fourth floor smelled even worse. But that was the least of his problems.

"What the hell are you doing ordering another credit card?" Mya yelled as quickly as he turned the doorknob and opened the door. She had been sitting there waiting for him. "And what the hell were you doing sitting in that car for all that time? You didn't think I saw you pull up almost twenty minutes ago? Were you on your phone talking to some bitch?"

"I'm doing well. My day was just fine. Thanks for asking," Anthony responded.

"I didn't ask you all of that. I want to know why you would apply for another credit card, knowing we are trying to save money for this baby."

"What baby, Mya? We don't have any baby. We don't even have sex to have a baby, and I figured it would be good if we took a nice vacation or something, just to get away for a few days. I wanted to do something romantic with my wife, and I ordered that credit card for that purpose."

"And I cut the shit up for the purpose of our child, when we do have one. We don't need to be racking up debt and wasting any money on any stupid trips. You saw one beach, you saw them all. I don't drink alcohol, so I don't need any of those fruity drinks, and I can't stand when you drink, because then you want to get all freaky and do stupid shit."

"Me wanting to make love to my wife is stupid shit? Really? Stupid shit is you almost burning the house down and having the neighbors ready to call the fire department."

"They need to mind their business. They only knocked on the door to see what I was doing, just to have something to talk about."

"Mya, I could smell the shit down on the first floor before I reached the elevator. But getting back to this credit card thing, what do you mean, you cut it up? Did I hear you right?"

"Yes, I cut it up. We don't need any extra debt."

"What debt? This condo is paid in full. My student loans are paid in full. You only have a small balance left on your loans, which should be finished by the end of this year. My car is paid for. Your car is paid for. So what extra debt are you talking about?"

"Well, we need to stay debt-free. I don't want our child struggling through college and having to take out loans. What if he wants to become a lawyer or doctor? That's over $100,000 right there for his education."

"And what if he or she decides they don't want to go to college? Are you going to tell him or her that they can't enjoy life today because they might need some money tomorrow?"

"You know, you sound just like my stupid father. That sounds like some stupid shit he'd say."

"Are you calling me stupid? Because you certainly are not sounding like any social worker I've ever known of—belittling people instead of trying to build them up."

"That's because your arrogant ass needs to be brought down a notch or two sometimes."

"*I'm* arrogant?" Anthony asked in disbelief. Every fiber of his being was telling him to just walk away from her because things would get worse.

"Yes, you are arrogant. You have the nerve to park right outside of our window, not giving a damn if I could see you on the phone with some bitch."

"Okay, so now you saw me on the phone, huh?" Anthony laughed. "I give up with you. You're a piece of work."

"So now you're saying I'm lying and I don't know what my eyes saw? I saw your ass on the phone while you were sitting in your car."

"You're right. I was sitting there trying to line up some ass for tomorrow night, since I can't get any from my wife."

Mya stood and stared at Anthony for the longest. "Let me tell you something, I am NOT my mother, and I would cut your dick off while you sleep if you think I'm going to just let you cheat on me and get away with it."

That time Anthony stood and stared at Mya before responding. "So now you're threatening to mutilate me in my sleep over your foolish insecurities? You know what, Mya? I should have done this a long time ago. I think it's time for us to go our separate ways. This marriage ain't working. I've tried to be everything you needed me to be, so much to the point that I don't even know who I am anymore."

"Divorce? A divorce? You can't divorce me. I won't let you."

"You won't let me? And how do you plan on stopping me? The only way you can stop me, is to try being the wife that I want and need. Other than that, I can't do this with you anymore. I should have left your ass that time you went around telling people I raped you."

"You did. I told you I didn't want to have sex, and you just took it."

"Okay, it is what it is. I'll be moving out this weekend," he said, walking toward the bedroom.

She ran to get in front of him. "So where are you going this weekend? You going to stay at some bitch's house? That's the only reason you're suddenly talking this divorce shit. How do you go one minute from talking about 'let's have a baby' to 'I want a divorce'?"

"First of all, it's only been you obsessed with this whole baby thing. I'm not in any rush for kids, truth be known. I want a house to have friends and family over for barbeques and hang out. I want to travel the world before I have kids."

"You're so full of shit. You wanted kids just as much as I wanted them."

"Mya, you don't want any damn kids. We'd have to have sex in order to have kids. You and I don't have sex unless you think you're ovulating—once a fucking month. You keep buying all those stupid test kits to tell you when you might be ovulating, and that's the only time you want to give me some pussy."

"Well, if you didn't want a baby, why go along with it? Why run to have sex when you think I'm ovulating?"

"Has it ever occurred to you that I was just simply horny as fuck? You keep me waiting and waiting, and that's the only time you throw me a bone." Anthony threw his hands up in the air in disgust. "Damn, the more I think of it, I can't believe I hung around this long. I should have *been* left your manipulative ass. I'm done. There's nothing left to talk about."

"We have lots to talk about. I don't want a divorce. My parents didn't divorce, and I'm not divorcing. We made a vow to one another, or did you forget that?"

"No, I didn't forget that, but you obviously did."

"Anthony, we can't divorce. I'm sorry. I won't do it."

"Goodnight, Mya."

"That's all you have to say? No! We need to talk about this shit. You're not going to have me out here looking all stupid to my coworkers, wondering what happened to my husband."

Anthony shook his head and laughed. "Your coworkers? You're worried about what your coworkers might think? What a fucking joke. Tell your nosy-ass coworkers to mind their fucking business. How about that? And on that note, we have nothing else to discuss. It is what it is."

"Then if you're going, go! Get the fuck out of here right now. There's no need to wait for the weekend. Go see your bitch now. I know that's what this is all about. This has nothing to do with me. This is all about you wanting your dick greased."

"I want my dick greased by my wife, but she decides when or if it will be greased, because she wants to control every fucking thing. As for leaving now, I'm tired. It's late. It's cold as hell outside, and I'm not going anywhere until I leave for work in the morning."

"Close your eyes up in here if you want to. I guarantee you won't have a peaceful moment of rest in here tonight. You're not going to just fuck me over and toss me to the side and think I'm going to just take it laying down. You try to make me look bad, I'll make you look bad to all of your business clients."

"You have a problem with me—whatever that is—but you'd try to destroy a business that has provided well for you, a business that your own sister helped build, and you'd try to destroy the livelihood of our clients who depend on what we do for them because you're feeling jilted? That's some sick shit. The more you speak, the more I see I need to get out of here."

Anthony went into the closet to pull out a suitcase and went into the second bedroom, where he kept his clothes, along with his home office, and began packing.

"So you're really doing this? You really want to declare a war with me?" Mya asked when she saw him quickly packing to leave.

He remained silent. She snatched the frame off the wall that held his college diploma, and smashed it against his glass desk, startling him.

"Mya, if you don't stop this shit, I will call the police, and you will be carried out of here in handcuffs, and your job will find out, causing you to lose your license. Now, I'm trying to get out tonight like you told me to, but I will not stand by while you destroy my property and think that's going to be okay."

"Oh, you're going to call the police on me? How about I call the police on you? They'll believe me before they believe you, and they'll carry you off to jail after they tase your ass, and you won't get to skip over to your bitch's house after all."

"Go ahead, call them if that'll make you feel better. And all the neighbors will look at you and laugh at you every time you go in and out of the building. You want them in your business, call the police."

"Fuck you!"

Anthony continued to stuff as much as he could in his suitcase and another duffle bag. He took the stuff out to his car and came back in for his home computer and files, which he was pretty certain that Mya would sabotage the minute he left. He also went into the master bedroom to collect his toiletries.

By this point, Mya was sitting on the sofa sobbing. She begged him not to leave and promised she'd do whatever she had to do to fix their marriage. He almost fell for it until she said, "Do you know how embarrassing it will be for me when the neighbors realize that you haven't been home? How am I supposed to explain that?"

"I don't know, Mya. Tell them whatever suits you. I don't give a shit anymore. I can't live my life according to what others might have to say about it. Let people believe what they want to."

"You know what? You're such a bitch. I can't believe you'd just walk out on your marriage rather than be a man and deal with the issues. Every marriage has problems. I don't believe for a minute that Monica's marriage is all perfect like she tries to pretend. You don't see them running away. They deal with their issues and move forward."

Anthony wanted to laugh at Mya's perception of Monica trying to portray a perfect marriage, but this wasn't a time for laughing.

"Well, if you're done now, I'm going to take my *bitchness* on out the door now, so you can reflect on where things went wrong with our marriage. I'll be by in a day or two to get the rest of my belongings."

"They'll be destroyed if you walk out of this door tonight."

"You told me I had to leave tonight, now you're telling me I can't, which is why I really have to get the fuck up out of here. If it makes you feel better to destroy my belongings, then you do that. I don't give a shit anymore. Bye!" he said, rushing out the door with the items he collected on his second trip.

He could hear Mya screaming as if someone was killing her by the time he made it to the elevator. Some of the neighbors opened their doors to see what was happening.

He rode around to find a decent hotel he could crash in for a few days until he figured out where he would go. He thought about calling his brother to see if he could crash there, but he didn't feel like answering a bunch of questions that night. However, by midnight, Aaron was calling him. Mya had called her mother and her mother called Monica to tell her about Anthony walking out to be with some other woman and how things got so heated that the neighbors called the police, but he was already gone when they arrived.

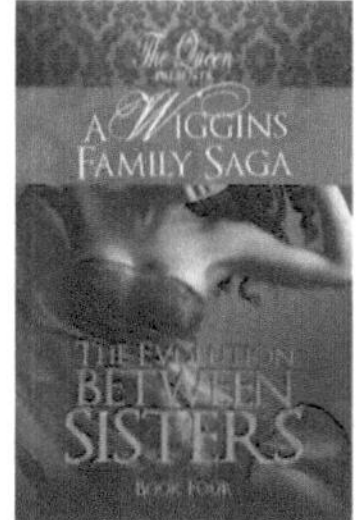

Queendom Dreams

NOTE FROM THE AUTHOR

Thank you for reading *Movin' On Up*. When you're all done, be sure to leave a review and let others know how much you've enjoyed the story. No spoilers! If you enjoyed this book, be sure to check out:

9ine of Fools
Tapioca Pudding Next Door
Trapped in the Closet
Superwoman
A Scorned Woman

Between Sisters
Between More Sisters
Caught Up Between Sisters
The Evolution Between Sisters
Revenge Between Sisters
Sister's Daughter
Never Again Between Sisters

NOTE: Tapioca Pudding's sequel is in ***Never Again Between Sisters (of the Between Sisters series).***

To find out what other books Queendom Dreams will be releasing and other authors with Queendom Dreams Publishing, please visit us online at www.queendomdreamspublishing.com.

ABOUT THE QUEEN

The Queen has been writing for many years, ranging in short stories, poetry, plays, professional and other writings. She is a native of (Queensbridge) Long Island City, New York. Her debut novel was *Between Sisters* (of the Between Sisters series). Her education includes Business and International Business Administration, as well as Travel & Tourism. When she's not writing, she loves to travel to sunny climates with clear and turquoise waters or near mountains for inspiration.